The boy had flowing silvery hair, a teasing smile on his face, and a long scarf around his neck. He looked startlingly similar to Ende... Maybe a little too similar.

n Another World With My Smartphone 22

ALL DRESSED UP FOR A

GRAND MASQUERADE!

"...HEHE!"

"WELL, MOTHER? WHAT DO YOU THINK?"

"I THINK IT'S INCREDIBLE. IT TOOK ME TWO HUNDRED YEARS TO DEVELOP PAULA... IT MAY BE A GOLLEM, BUT IT'S CERTAINLY IMPRESSIVE."

Quun chuckled and smiled from ear to ear after hearing Leen's words of praise. Her smiling face was as cute as her mother's too. Leen smiled right back and gently stroked her daughter's hair. It was a heartwarming sight to be sure.

In Another World With My Smartphone

22

Patora Fuyuhara
illustration・Eiji Usatsuka

Luli
The fourth of Touya's summoned Heavenly Beasts. She is the Azure Monarch, the ruler of dragons. She often clashes with Kohaku due to her condescending personality.

Kougyoku
The third of Touya's summoned Heavenly Beasts. She is the Flame Monarch, ruler of feathered things. Though her appearance is flashy and extravagant, she's actually quite cool and collected.

Sango and Kokuyou
The second of Touya's summoned Heavenly Beasts. They are the Black Monarch, two in one. The rulers of scaled beasts. They can freely manipulate water. Sango is a tortoise, and Kokuyou is a snake. Sango is a female, and Kokuyou is a male (but he's very much a female at heart).

Kohaku
The first of Touya's summoned Heavenly Beasts. She's the White Monarch, the ruler of beasts, the guardian of the west and a beautiful White Tiger. She can create devastating shockwaves, and also change size at will.

High Rosetta
Terminal Gynoid in charge of the Workshop, one of the Babylon relics. She's called Rosetta for short. Her Airframe Serial Number is #27. For whatever reason, she's the most reliable of the bunch.

Francesca
Terminal Gynoid in charge of the Hanging Garden, one of the Babylon relics. She's called Cesca for short. Her Airframe Serial Number is #23. She likes to tell very inappropriate jokes.

Mochizuki Moroha
The God of Swords. Claims to be Touya's older sister. She trains the and advises the knights of Brunhild. She's gallant and brave, but also a bit of an airhead at times.

Mochizuki Karen
The God of Love. Claims to be Touya's older sister. She stays in Brunhild because she says she needs to catch a servile god, but doesn't really do all that much in the way of hunting him. She's a total pain in the butt.

Pamela Noël
Terminal Gynoid in charge of the Tower, one of the Babylon relics. She's called Noël for short and wears a jersey. Her Airframe Serial Number is #25. She sleeps all the time, and eats laying down. Her tremendous laziness means she doesn't do all that much.

Preliora
Terminal Gynoid in charge of the Rampart, one of the Babylon relics. She's called Liora for short and wears a blazer. Her Airframe Serial Number is #20. She's the oldest of the Babylon Gynoids, and would attend to the... Personal night-time needs of Doctor Babylon herself. She has no experience with men.

Fredmonica
Terminal Gynoid in charge of the Hangar, one of the Babylon relics. She's called Monica for short. Her Airframe Serial Number is #28. She's a funny little hard worker who has a bit of a casual streak. She's a good friend of Rosetta, and is the Gynoid with the most knowledge of the Frame Gears.

Bell Flora
Terminal Gynoid in charge of the Alchemy Lab, one of the Babylon relics. She's called Flora for short and wears a nurse outfit. Her Airframe Serial Number is #21. A nurse with dangerously big boobs and even more dangerous medicines.

Doctor Regina Babylon
An ancient genius from a lost civilization, reborn into an artificial body that resembles a small girl. She is the "Babylon" that created the many artifacts and forgotten technologies scattered around the world today. Her Airframe serial number is #29. She remained in stasis for five-thousand years before finally being awakened.

Atlantica
Terminal Gynoid in charge of the Research Lab, one of the Babylon relics. She's called Tica for short. Her Airframe serial number is #22. Of the Babylon Numbers, she is the one who best embodies Doctor Babylon's inappropriately perverse side.

Lileleparshe
Terminal Gynoid in charge of the Storehouse, one of the Babylon relics. She's called Parshe for short and wears a shrine maiden outfit. Her Airframe Serial Number is #26. She's tremendously clumsy, even if she's just trying to help. The amount of stuff she ruins is troublingly high.

Irisfam
Terminal Gynoid in charge of the Library, one of the Babylon relics. She's called Fam for short and wears a school uniform. Her Airframe Serial Number is #24. She's a total book fanatic and hates being interrupted when she's reading.

Character Profiles

Elze Silhoueska
One of Touya's wives.
The elder of the twin sisters saved by Touya some time ago. A ferocious melee fighter, she makes use of gauntlets in combat. Her personality is fairly to-the-point and blunt. She can make use of Null fortification magic, specifically the spell **[Boost]**. She loves spicy foods.

Yumina Urnea Belfast
One of Touya's wives.
Princess of the Belfast Kingdom. She was twelve years old in her initial appearance, and her eyes are heterochromatic. The right is blue, while the left is green. She has mystic eyes that can discern the true character of an individual. She has three magical aptitudes: Earth, Wind, and Darkness. She's also extremely proficient with a bow and arrow. She fell in love with Touya at first sight.

Mochizuki Touya
A highschooler who was accidentally murdered by God. He's a no-hassle kind of guy who likes to go with the flow. He's not very good at reading the atmosphere, and typically makes rash decisions that bite him in the ass. His mana pool is limitless, he can flawlessly make use of every magical element, and he can cast any Null spell that he wants. He's currently the Grand Duke of Brunhild.

Sushie Urnea Ortlinde
One of Touya's wives.
She was ten years old in her initial appearance. Her nickname is Sue. The niece of Belfast's king, and Yumina's cousin. Touya saved her from being attacked on the road. She has an innocently adventurous spirit.

Lucia Leah Regulus
One of Touya's wives.
The Third Princess of the Regulus Empire, she's Yumina's age. She fell in love with Touya when he saved her during a coup. She likes to fight with twin blades, and she's on good terms with Yumina.

Kokonoe Yae
One of Touya's wives.
A samurai girl from the far eastern land of Eashen, a country much like Japan. She tends to repeat herself and speak formally, the does. Yae is quite a glutton, eating more than most normal people would dare touch. She's a hard worker, but can sometimes slack off. Her family runs a dojo back in Eashen, and they take great pride in their craft. It's not obvious at first, but her boobs are pretty big.

Linze Silhoueska
One of Touya's wives.
The younger of the twin sisters saved by Touya some time ago. She wields magic, specifically from the schools of Light, Water, and Fire. She finds talking to people difficult due to her own shy nature, but she is known to be surprisingly bold at times. Rumors say she might be the kind of girl who enjoys male on male romance... She loves sweet foods.

Paula
A stuffed toy bear animated by years upon years of the **[Program]** spell. She's the result of two-hundred years of programmed commands, making her seem like a fully aware living being. Paula... Paula's the worst!

Sakura
A mysterious girl Touya rescued in Eashen. She had lost her memories, but has now finally gotten them back. Her true identity is Farnese Forneus, daughter of the Xenoahs Overlord. Currently living a peaceful life in Brunhild, and she has joined the ranks of Touya's wives.

Leen
One of Touya's wives.
Former Clan Matriarch of the Fairies, she now serves as Brunhild's Court Magician. She claims to be six-hundred-and-twelve years old, but looks tremendously young. She can wield every magical element except Darkness, meaning her magical proficiency is that of a genius. Leen is a bit of a light-hearted bully.

Hildegard Minas Lestia
One of Touya's wives
First Princess of the Knight Kingdom Lestia. Her swordplay talents earned her a reputation as a 'Knight Princess'. Touya saved her life when she was attacked by a group of Phrase, and she's loved him ever since. She's a good friend of Yae, and she stammers a bit when flustered.

IN ANOTHER WORLD WITH MY SMARTPHONE: VOLUME 22
by Patora Fuyuhara

Translated by Andrew Hodgson
Edited by DxS
Image Lettering by Stephanie Hii

This book is a work of fiction. Names, characters, places, and incidents are the product of the author's imagination or are used fictitiously. Any resemblance to actual events, locales, or persons, living or dead, is coincidental.

Copyright © 2020 Patora Fuyuhara
Illustrations by Eiji Usatsuka

Original Japanese edition published in 2020 by Hobby Japan
This English edition is published by arrangement with Hobby Japan, Tokyo

English translation © 2020 J-Novel Club LLC

All rights reserved. In accordance with the U.S. Copyright Act of 1976, the scanning, uploading, and electronic sharing of any part of this book without the permission of the publisher is unlawful piracy and theft of the author's intellectual property.

Find more books like this one at www.j-novel.club!

Managing Director: Samuel Pinansky
Light Novel Line Manager: Chi Tran
Managing Editor: Jan Mitsuko Cash
Managing Translator: Kristi Fernandez
QA Manager: Hannah N. Carter
Marketing Manager: Stephanie Hii
Project Manager: Kristine Johnson

ISBN: 978-1-7183-5021-2
Printed in Korea
First Printing: June 2022
10 9 8 7 6 5 4 3 2 1

Contents

Chapter I	A Spot of Matchmaking	13
Interlude	The Crystal Dragon	42
Chapter II	Masquerade	60
Chapter III	Great Expectations	113
Chapter IV	The World of Tomorrow	147
Chapter V	Another Visitor	185

The Story So Far!

Mochizuki Touya, wielding a smartphone customized by God himself, continues to live his life in a new world. After many adventures, Touya, now Grand Duke of a small nation named Brunhild, has joined forces with the other world leaders. Why? To stop the incoming extradimensional threat known as the Phrase. These merciless invaders from another world will stop at nothing until they get what they desire. As Touya continued to investigate potential ways to repel this threat, he found himself falling into another world entirely. This Reverse World was like a mirrored version of the world he knew, and relied on a mysterious mechanical technology known as the Gollems. Now, the fate of two worlds may hang in the balance...

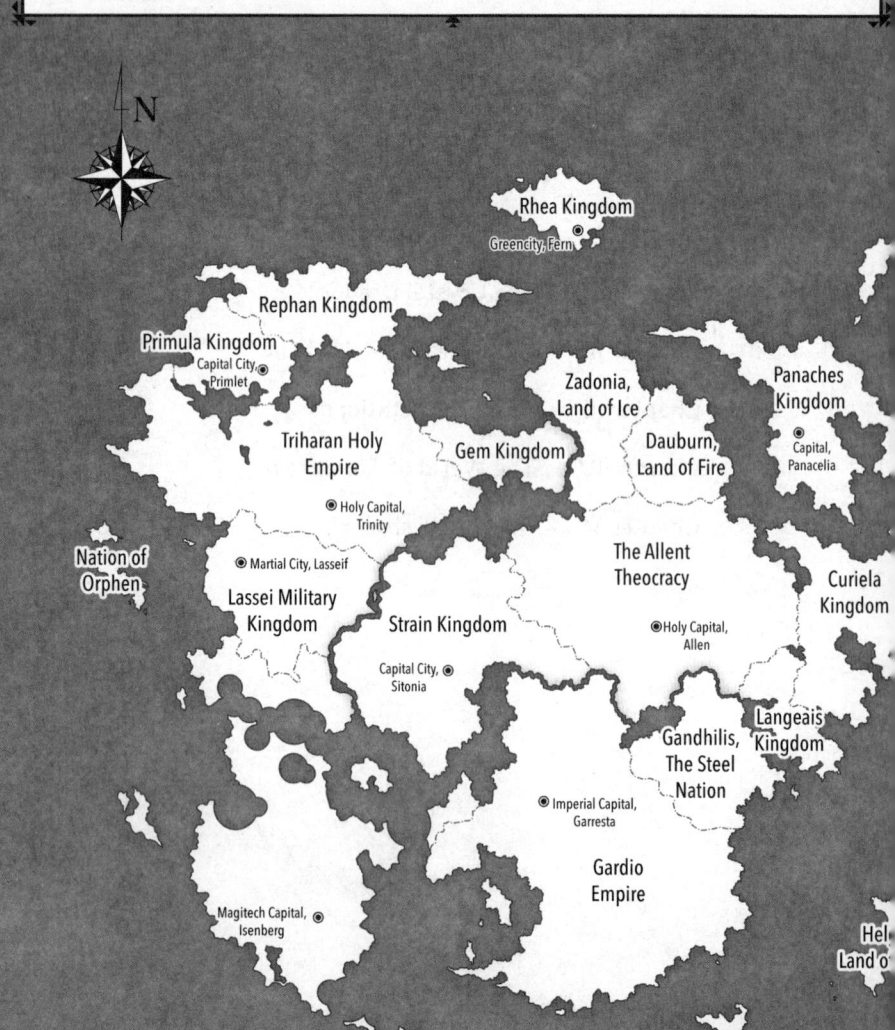

Rhea Kingdom
Greencity, Fern

Rephan Kingdom

Primula Kingdom
Capital City, Primlet

Zadonia, Land of Ice

Panaches Kingdom
Capital, Panacelia

Triharan Holy Empire

Gem Kingdom

Dauburn, Land of Fire

Holy Capital, Trinity

Nation of Orphen

Martial City, Lasseif

The Allent Theocracy

Curiela Kingdom

Lassei Military Kingdom

Strain Kingdom

Holy Capital, Allen

Capital City, Sitonia

Langeais Kingdom

Gandhilis, The Steel Nation

Imperial Capital, Garresta

Gardio Empire

Magitech Capital, Isenberg

Hel
Land o'

The Worlds of In Another World With My Smartphone
World Map

Palerius Island

Capital City, Xenoskull
The Demon Kingdom, Xenoahs

Kingdom of Palouf

Capital City, Slanien
The Kingdom of Elfrau

Capital City, Nimue
The Kingdom of Lihnea

The Kingdom of Hannock — Capital City, Hanookhs

The Nokia Kingdom

Yulong Remnants

Bern, The Imperial City

The Regulus Empire

Gallaria, Heart of the Empire

Divine Nation of Eashen

The Kingdom of Belfast

Alephis, The Royal Capital

The Duchy of Brunhild

The Roadmare Union

Capital City, Falma

The Kingdom of Horn

Reflet

The Holy City, Ills

The Ramissh Theocracy

Capital City, Paneramare

The Kingdom of Felsen

The Kingdom of Mismede

Berge, Capital of Beasts

Capital City, Atryle
The Kingdom of Ryle

Capital City, Lestein

The Sea of Trees

The Knight Kingdom of Lestia

Dragoness Island

The Kingdom of Sandora

Retrobamba

Kyuray, The Sandy Capital

The Kingdom of Egret

New World

Chapter I: A Spot of Matchmaking

"So, what's up?"

"Oh, uh... not much... It's good to see you, by the way. Have a drink and then we'll talk..."

"...Did you hit your head or something?"

Ende was acting a little more docile than usual, which made the whole situation feel weird. We were at the tavern by the guild, meeting up for the first time in quite a while.

I'd recently returned from my honeymoon, so I'd spent the last week and change catching up with affairs I'd missed and taking care of general government busywork. Just when I thought I finally had some free time on my hands, Ende called me up. He should've acted more considerate, given that I was still a newlywed man!

Still, I recognized it was important for guys to bond every now and then. Plus, I hadn't seen Ende in a while, and something about him seemed a little... glum? That was why I decided to hear him out.

"How's uh...? How's your marriage going, man?"

"...You definitely hit your head on something, didn't you."

I wasn't exactly sure why he was so interested in my relationships all of a sudden. Frankly, his out-of-character behavior was a little concerning. Had Uncle Takeru beaten his brains to mush or something? I must've had a strange expression on my face, since Ende suddenly let out a little sigh and began to speak.

"I'm sure you know by now, but marriage as a concept exists in various forms across different cultures. It could be a ceremony to decide your life partner, a contractual agreement to have children, some religious decree, or any other social construct."

"Uh, okay?"

"We Travelers are a transient species, Touya. Few of my kind ever actually get married. Because if we fall in love with something that isn't a fellow Traveler, our journey will end. Those that bind themselves to one world and no longer traverse the boundaries can't very well call themselves Travelers, now can they? Though, I suppose there have been members of my kind who resume their travels after outliving their spouses…"

"Where are you going with this?"

You're spewing a whole bunch of word vomit, dude. Get to the point already!

Ende glanced away from me and took a long gulp of his booze, downing the whole thing in one go. He even drank the ice.

"I'm… gonna… y'know… get hitched too…"

"Huh? Wait… what?!"

Ende's words almost made me drop my glass.

What the hell am I supposed to say to that?! Is this because of the bouquet toss at my wedding?! Or does Karen have something to do with it?!

"Uh… h-hold on a sec… Just to be clear, you mean Melle, right?"

"Obviously. I'm not a playboy like you, Touya."

Tsk… Don't make me leave, asshole! But seriously… Ende? Married? I can't picture it! This is nuts…

"Melle got interested in it after seeing your wedding. There's no such thing as marriage on Phrasia, after all."

"Huh wait, so… how do the Phrase, y'know… couple up?"

Chapter I: A Spot of Matchmaking

The Dominant Constructs had male and female forms. If they didn't group up in the traditional way, then what was the point?

"Dominant Phrase can reproduce asexually semi-regularly."

"Asexually?"

"Yeah. They can spawn their own offspring. And they don't look like babies or anything, either. They're usually born as little cores that grow their own bodies over time."

I asked for some more details, and Ende explained that there was functionally no such thing as a childhood for the Phrase species. They were born as single cores, then evolved rapidly into individual organisms. By the time they became conscious of themselves, they were already fully-grown, living creatures.

A fully-grown Phrase sacrifices its own life energies to create a new core. The more of their lifeforce they use, the more cores they can create. In a sense, the offspring served as replacements for the parent, which would likely eventually die after creating too many.

"Dominant constructs work a bit differently. They can produce cores without sacrificing their life energies, but it ends up creating a degraded copy of the parent, effectively. It's not something they enjoy doing."

"...So then, do they only reproduce asexually? Or can they have children like... together? I dunno."

I wasn't really sure how to phrase my question... Not that I was super interested in the answer to it or anything...

"Well, sort of. Two Phrase lifeforms can fuse their cores to create new life. That's similar enough to human reproduction, right?"

He was sort of right, but not... exactly... It was definitely a fusion of sorts, anyway.

"The Phrase have no concept of marriage. If the intelligent ones want to have kids, they simply use the core of a fellow Phrase they're interested in. But they don't have to be a couple for that to happen.

They don't even have to live near each other. There are some Phrase that live in pairs, but they're few and far between. Most Dominant Constructs don't know both of their parents, so even if they have siblings, they'll likely never know that."

That's... interesting. But I guess it makes sense, given the way their species work and all... I get why Melle would be interested in such an alien concept as marriage ceremonies.

"You know what marriage means, right?"

"I know what it is, Touya. It's when two people love each other very much. They support each other, live together, and maybe even raise kids together..."

That was a fairly basic explanation, but he just about got the gist of it... Stuff like arranged or political marriages also existed, but there was no point bringing that up.

"Could you even have a kid with Melle?"

"Melle crossed through dimensions to be with me, and her body's constantly evolving. Right now she's quite biologically distinct from the Phrase she once was. She's kind of a new species, but one similar to me... As far as our compatibility goes... I think we might be able to try, at least. It's just, well..." Ende looked a little down as he spoke. I was almost afraid to ask what was wrong with him.

"It's not just Melle... Ney and Lycee would be involved too, so..."

"WHAAAT?!"

What the hell?! You just said you're not a playboy like me, right?! Then you come out at me like that?! Harem protagonist-looking ass!

Ende must have seen the fire in my eyes. He quickly waved his arms as if to calm me down.

"Wait, wait. Not me, you idiot. They'd marry Melle. Both of them told me they want to."

Chapter I: A Spot of Matchmaking

"Uhhh..."

The blow to my brain from his words ended up making me speak like an idiot for a half-second. What did he mean?

"Melle wasn't the only one interested in your ceremony, Touya. Ney and Lycee both told me afterward that they want to marry her."

...So Melle's the harem protagonist in this situation? Wild.

"Aren't they girls?"

"So? Why would that matter? Girls on Phrasia can still have children with other girls. It's not as common, since the offspring can't be male in that case, which decreases sexual diversity, but that wouldn't matter much in Melle's case anyway."

Huh, the more you know... Is that really fine, though? Wait, what am I saying! It doesn't really matter whether someone's a boy, girl, or anything else. Love's love, so marriage is fine. Hell, there are plenty of people fighting for that idea to be validated back on Earth, too.

Polygamy was normal in this world, so as long as you had the resources to support your family, you could marry as many people as you wanted. I'd even heard about some duchess someplace with three husbands, actually.

I hadn't exactly heard of any cases of bisexual marriage, but I was sure there was someone out there engaged in it.

"So what did they say about Melle?"

"That they'd be comfortable with all four of us as a family unit. But if Melle said no, then they'd give up."

Hmm... I think Melle will probably say yes. She'll probably see the marriage as solidifying the family she already has. I know she definitely loves Ende, but at the same time... it's not like they have to get married to seal that deal, right?

"How would you feel about those two marrying Melle?"

17

"Uhhh... I'm fine with it, I guess? I've been traveling with Lycee for a while, so I know her well. And living with Ney has made me grow to appreciate her. I'd maybe feel a little jealous, but..." Ende trailed off as he flashed a weak smile.

Hmm...

Ney probably wanted to get married out of her perceived rivalry with Ende, while Lycee was just going with the flow.

"So you'd be fine with the two of them, then?"

"Yeah, I would. I might have a couple concerns, but luckily, I can see you're doing just fine in your own marriage. By the way... take care of Elze, yeah? She's not the kind of girl to be upfront with her feelings, but it's easy to tell when she's down."

What the...? When'd you become her big brother figure, huh?! Sure, you're fellow pupils, but did you guys get that close already?!

"Before you got married, she was really stressed. I basically got used as a punching bag because of how riled up she was! Shouldn't she have been beating on you instead, man?"

"A-Aha... Whoops..."

I didn't think Elze had been relieving her stress like that. She was the kind of girl who easily showed when she was worried, so I thought I'd been on the ball with her problems... Apparently not. Well, either way, Ende was in the same position as Elze once was. He'd be a member of an extended marriage with one spouse in the middle, essentially.

"So, uh... when we get married, we'll probably want to have a similar ceremony to yours. In style, rather than size. That means similar food, of course..."

"Oh..."

Now I get it.

Chapter I: A Spot of Matchmaking

Melle and her fellow Phrase girls were quite fond of the food in this world. They'd certainly chowed down at my wedding. The three of them ate enough for thirty. Hell, they could put away more between them than Yae, of all people. And that was no small feat! I didn't want to think about the kind of bills Ende must have been footing.

Melle and the girls worked part-time here and there, but Ende was a fully-fledged adventurer. He was probably pulling in better pay than me, all things considered.

"I don't mind helping out with food, but brides don't traditionally pig out at the ceremony... You don't think this whole wedding thing could just be an excuse, do you?"

"Yeah... To be honest, I'm a little suspicious myself. They might just want an excuse to eat really well for a day."

"That's not the case. It's a conclusion we all came to after giving the situation proper thought. Please don't cast aspersions upon the girls, Endymion. Neither should you cast aspersions upon me."

I turned around and saw Melle standing there with her hands on her hips. She was pouting a little... Apparently, she'd been eavesdropping for a while.

Her ice-blue eyes, which were the same color as her dazzling hair, were narrowed toward Ende's face. They glowed with an ephemeral light.

"M-Melle?! What're you here for?!"

"I've come to take you home. Are you done with your friend?"

"Oh uh, yeah... Touya said he'll sort the food out for us."

At Ende's apprehensive words, Melle's face lit up like a lamp. She was positively beaming.

"Thank goodness! Oh Touya, thank you so very much! I'd like extra helpings of the meat and dessert dishes, please!"

"Oh, okay... I'll be sure to remember that..."

I had a feeling that her measure for extra helpings was probably a lot more than mine. The number of guests would definitely be smaller, but if all three brides planned on dining, we'd need more food than we'd had at my wedding. I made a mental note to ask Lu to come up with a meal that wouldn't stain any wedding dresses.

"I'll take him from here, Touya. Keep an eye out for the wedding invitation! Come along, Endymion."

"Oh, uh, yup. Sorry, Touya. Can't keep the lady waiting, right? Let's get a drink again some other time."

"Uh, sure... why not."

Ende left the tavern with Melle... Though honestly, it looked more like she was dragging him. As I looked over the food and drink he'd left behind, I heaved a small sigh.

Ende's getting married, huh? Can't say I saw that coming.

Part of me wondered if Karen had been abusing her powers as the love goddess again.

Let me think... The people that caught the bouquets at our wedding... There was Ende, the kid-king from Palouf, Lanz from the knight order... and I think Will? Was he working with Belfast's knights? Oh, and Prince Robert, too, the pumpkin pants guy.

Perhaps Karen had used her powers to ensure those guys got the bouquets... But Robert and the prince of Palouf were already engaged, so that seemed pointless.

"Hum? Touya? Drinking alone, are we?"

"Oh, it's you..."

I turned toward the familiar voice. Just as I'd expected, it was a red-haired girl with a little red Gollem toddling behind her.

She was the leader of the Red Cats, a group of phantom thieves. It was none other than Nia and her companion, Rouge.

Chapter I: A Spot of Matchmaking

Her deputy leader, Est, walked over as well. I looked again and noticed a whole entourage of Red Cats members with them. Euni and Euri were there, even. They all had dirty, ragged clothing, but that was countered by the bright smiles on their faces.

"Hey, barkeep! Bring out enough booze and dragon steak for the lot of us! Tonight, we feast!"

"Hah. Someone's feeling luxurious. Got a little extra cash today?"

Dragon meat was quite rare, so it came at a similarly high price. And obviously the meals made from that meat were even more expensive. That said, this tavern was directly owned and operated by the guild, so the prices were cheaper than in other places. I was also their meat supplier, and I let them have it in bulk.

However, that still didn't make the food cheap, especially not for so many people.

"We found more treasure on those dungeon islands. Two chests that were completely untouched! They were filled to the brim with spellstones and gold! It's a good feeling when you hit paydirt like that," the ponytailed girl, Euni, beamed with pride as she spoke. I was impressed.

Most of the treasures on the dungeon islands were long-lost remnants of the mages who created the place, but some of the treasures were also stuff left behind by ill-equipped adventurers who went in and died.

The monsters of the dungeons would strip the belongings from the adventurers, then store them in places like treasure chests. Some would even sort the items into categories, like by weapon or armor, or by shininess.

Sometimes you could find rare or unusual stuff like enchanted items or unique blades, but every now and then, you bumped into a chest some monster had designated for "shiny things," which was filled to the brim with glittering treasure.

"...I guess if you think about it, you guys are kind of like graverobbers, huh?"

"Don't be a dumbass. We're a band of thieves! Chivalrous phantom thieves! This is simply another way for us to make money. If you see any corrupt merchants, politicians, or nobles... let me know! We'll gladly fill our coffers with their life savings!" Nia chuckled with all her might as she spoke. I just decided to ignore what she said, given that I was the ruler of our country.

She promised she wouldn't have her thieves running any operations within Brunhild, but that didn't rule out other countries... And frankly, that concerned me.

Suddenly, from the corner of my eye, I noticed a person walking over toward us from the entrance to the tavern.

"Oh my... is that little Nia? And my precious Tou... Goodness, are we having a party?"

"Beep."

It was a woman in a traditional-looking purple dress, wearing glasses with purple frames. Standing by her side was another little Gollem that bore a striking resemblance to Rouge.

The woman was Luna Trieste, the former Frenzied Mistress. And the little Gollem was the purple crown, Fanatic Viola.

"Ugh. Purple. What're you doing here? Buzz off, already!"

"So mean... I worked late today, so I came here for dinner, you silly little dear. The food's cheap, and the drink is delectable. Where else would I go?"

Nia scowled over at Luna, attempting to shoo her away in a manner one might apply to a pesky animal. Luna, on the other hand, didn't seem to care. She took a seat opposite me, in the spot Ende had just been. Viola took the seat next to her.

...Wait, why'd you sit at my table?

Chapter I: A Spot of Matchmaking

"What's she doing free, anyway? It's not too late to put her in a jail cell, Touya. Or, you know... a grave?"

"So cruel, little Nia! I'll have you know that Tou gave me a very naughty punishment... No, I suppose it might even be considered a reward... Hehehehe..."

"You disgust me."

Luna smiled, her body shuddering ever-so-slightly with what resembled residual pleasure. Nia just ignored it, so I did the same thing.

"My life's purpose is to help guide the next generation... I love working with children. I can't live without helping people out too... It's like I'm addicted. That's why I often work so late, you know? I can't stop doing good deeds..."

"...That's gotta be a lie, purple," Nia scowled over at Luna, who seemed positively in a daze, as she said that. Contrary to her words, though, I felt that Luna was telling the truth... Probably.

I'd cursed her to derive pleasure from the appreciation of others, instead of the twisted pleasure she used to get from suffering. She couldn't even hurt or kill others anymore. She wasn't exactly harmless, but she was... better than before at least. Viola was also unable to tap into its crown abilities.

"Touuu... Are you drinking alone? Oh my... Oh goodness... Did they kick you out of the castle? Are you getting a divorce? Do you need Mommy Luna to—"

"I don't need anything like that!"

Leave me alone, lady! I just got married! Don't say weird stuff like that, especially not in the middle of a tavern!

"Pfft. Purple might have a point. Did you do something that annoyed your wives? Hassle some of the maids, maybe? Or maybe you walked in on someone changing, like when—"

"That's enough! Stop talking!"

I hurriedly shut Nia up before she got carried away and said something stupid. It was true that I once accidentally used [**Teleport**] and ended up peeping on Nia getting changed, but that was an honest mistake!

Ugh... If she tells the whole story here, there's no doubt all these gruff Red Cat guys'll pile on me and try to kick my ass! Ghhh... I just wanted to enjoy a nice, relaxing evening!

Dammit, this place is getting way too rowdy! I'm out!

I quickly asked the barkeep to hand me my bill.

Wait, this isn't... Shit! Ende, you asshole! You left without paying your share!

I sighed as I pinched the bridge of my nose. It had been one hell of a day.

◇ ◇ ◇

A few days after I learned about Ende's upcoming marriage, I was called upon by a certain someone. Who, might you ask? Well...

"...I'm sorry to turn to you for help so suddenly, but without you, we may well be doomed."

The person in front of me was none other than the first princess of Refreese, Reliel Rehm Refreese herself. We'd received a message from her via the gate mirror in the castle, and once I'd finished reading it, I decided we'd better go to Refreese castle immediately.

I brought Yumina and Linze with me, since the two of them were the closest to Princess Reliel out of all my wives.

"What exactly happened, Rili? You look scarily pale..."

Belfast and Refreese had been allies for a great many years, so it was only natural for Yumina to be worried about the state of Reliel.

Chapter I: A Spot of Matchmaking

They'd been friends since childhood. And Yumina was right, Reliel looked pale as a ghost. I wondered what was wrong. I also wondered whether she'd object to me casting [**Recovery**] and [**Refresh**] on her.

"It's been taken..."

"Hm? What has?"

"My smartphone!"

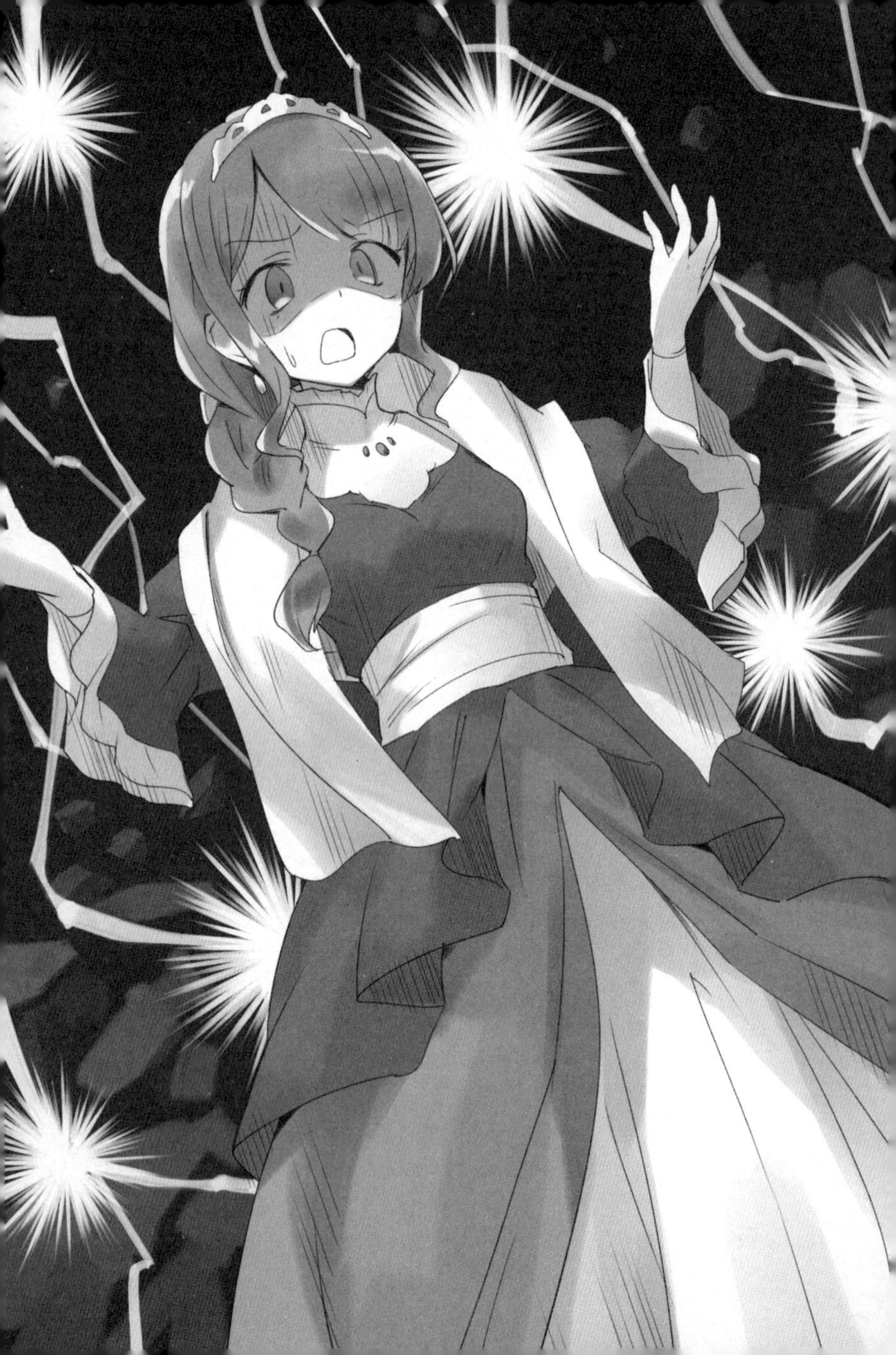

Chapter I: A Spot of Matchmaking

Huh?! Someone stole her phone?!

Doc Babylon had mass-produced rudimentary smartphones using mine as a base, and I'd passed them out to friends and members of foreign royalty. Naturally, I'd given one to Princess Reliel as well, but it seemed like it'd been stolen. I wasn't entirely surprised to learn that, in all honesty. Word had gotten out about the smartphones, and they were regarded as extremely rare magical artifacts. The fact that I hadn't seen the princess in any of our group chats for a while made a lot more sense after learning that.

"Th-That's okay, Princess. Even if your phone's been stolen, Touya can just summon it back. We can get it back in no time! Isn't that right, Touya?"

"R-Really?" Linze's words prompted Reliel's pale visage to perk up a bit.

She was right, of course. I had a failsafe in place on all the mass-produced smartphones. Through a combination of [**Teleport**] and [**Apport**], they'd all been enchanted so that I could recall them to me at any time.

"Yep. Really. I'll summon it right off," I said as I pulled out my phone and scrolled through my notes. Each mass-produced smartphone had its own unique serial ID. I could specify the ID of the phone I wanted to summon, and it'd return to my hand. If the phone was destroyed, it wouldn't work, but we were operating on the assumption that it was a thief who'd stolen it for its value.

Let's see... Reliel's serial code... Hmm...

"Oh, thank goodness... When Father took my phone, I was so worried. I thought I'd—"

"...Hold up. Your dad took it?" I asked as I glanced up from my phone and raised a brow.

"That's right! I was playing around with it during an important ceremony, and he took it away from me! I was booored, so it's not my fault that I had to tune out their droning, is it?"

"...Isn't that just you getting what you deserved, then? I shouldn't take it back from him..."

"Wh-Whaaat?!"

Gimme a break... It wasn't stolen, so I can't just warp it back from your dad on a whim! You can't call on me for your selfish needs willy-nilly! What was that crap about us all being doomed, huh?! Only one doomed here is you!

"Noooooo! You can't just abandon me like that! There's a draft for my next book on there. If Father sees it, it'll be the end of me!"

"Uh... Don't you have a lock on your phone?"

"Sure, but it's just a number lock! He could figure it out!"

Hrmm... I guess... I don't know if the emperor of Refreese is the kind of man to peek at his daughter's phone, but there's also a chance he might snoop if he's wondering why she was on her phone during a ceremonial event.

"What book were you working on...?"

"It was the next one in the Order of the Rose series. It's a more hardcore volume this time around, with two brusque knight captains reprimanding and punishing the newest recruit..."

"I've heard enough. I didn't think you were still writing that series, though..."

It was a huge secret, but the first princess of Refreese was actually an acclaimed writer. For the most part, she wrote about... well... love... A certain kind of love, specifically. Rough love. Between men. Her novels were very popular among a certain audience. Linze happened to be a huge fan, in fact.

Chapter I: A Spot of Matchmaking

"If my father reads my drafts, he'll definitely send me away to a convent... They'll demand I purify my thoughts by praying to the spirits day in and day out! What a horrible life..."

"...Maybe it wouldn't be so bad if your thoughts got a little purified."

Might even be a net positive... Her content's pretty extreme. Ugh... I'm the ruler of all the spirits, too... She's contaminating my purity just by sticking around me.

There was the option to remotely wipe all the data from the phone, like an emergency killswitch. However, when I brought that up with her, she glared daggers right into me.

"No waaay! Do you know how many months of work went into writing that stuff?! I don't even have it printed yet! If I lost everything, I'd just about die!"

"Oh, uh... sorry."

I shrunk back a little when she started yelling at me. Reliel was pretty scary... Not exactly the picture you'd associate with a princess, honestly. Unfortunately, this world didn't have desktop PCs, so it was impossible to save backups of digital data. The only way to save your stuff was to use the printers that I'd handed out to various countries.

For the most part, it was impossible to accidentally lose your data, but you could easily hold the back key too long and erase too much text by mistake. I'd done that a couple of times, myself. For a writer, losing your writing just before completion was probably the worst thing imaginable. Though, I had a feeling Doc Babylon could probably recover data that had been erased at least semi-recently.

"Why not apologize to your father and ask him to return it before he has the chance to look?"

"Well... I could... He already said he'd give it back. There's just one condition..."

Yumina's comment made Reliel frown. She glanced off to the side with a little sigh.

What? He was gonna give it back the whole time? Then why even call us?

"Yumina, you know how you got married? After the wedding, Father kept saying that he wants to see some grandchildren... He's decided it's time I got married, you see..."

"Huh? But didn't you have a fiance already? Or did I just hear wrong? That's what the emperor said a while back, at least..."

As I casually spoke, Yumina suddenly turned toward me with a mortified look on her face. Had I said something wrong?

"...I did have a fiance, yes, but he fell in love with someone else and eloped with her," Princess Reliel spoke quietly, a sober tone overwhelming her voice.

Oh... Crap...

Part of me respected the idea that he'd left a princess for the sake of love, but... seeing the victim of a decision like that up close gave me some seriously mixed feelings. Apparently he was the son of a Belfastian marquis, and he got into a lot of trouble for what he did. Seemed like he was all out of options, though. With it being a political marriage, he could hardly opt out without getting his family's consent. It sounded pretty rough.

It was bad for the guy, bad for his family, and bad for the royals... so he ended up fleeing the country with the girl and was apparently never seen again.

"Pssh. It's no big deal! I didn't really like him that much, and getting married would've been a waste of time! It's no problem at all!" Princess Reliel laughed heartily, but her eyes didn't reflect her tone. She looked immensely sad, as if the incident had left a lasting impression on her. I wondered if she took her writing so seriously as a form of escapism, or something.

Chapter I: A Spot of Matchmaking

Princess Reliel, who'd apparently begun muttering something quietly, turned to Linze and Yumina with a somber expression.

"Is it good, being married? It's not that great, right? You can't be that happy..."

"We're extremely happy!" replied both girls in unison.

"Grrrr!" Reliel growled, then threw a little fit upon seeing the immediate, cheery response from the duo.

G-Geez... You love it that much, huh? I-I'm glad they're feeling confident and all, but I still have a lot of newlywed jitters.

"What kind of person's the best match for you, anyway...? Do you need to pair up with a noble or a royal?"

"Uhm, I don't think my father would mind if I married an adventurer or a merchant, so long as he had a secure future. But it's hard to say for sure, really. When politics come into play, it's never easy to judge intentions. I suppose I could get married to a nobleman from Belfast or Lihnea... Oh, what about your brother, Yumina?"

"No. Not Yamato."

"Oh, o-okay then..." Reliel just about froze up and backed up out of fear in response to Yumina's glare. She was smiling, but there was nothing friendly about her gaze. Frankly, I could understand why. There was a twenty-year age gap, for one... so it wasn't like Yamato would have any say in it... But if Prince Yamato were to grow up and fall for her on his own, that'd be another matter entirely. Though, that would make her related to me through my marriage to Yumina... Didn't exactly know how to feel about that.

"Well, I'm sure Father will hold some kind of formal ball and have the children of relevant nobles attend... I'll be in attendance, of course... With my smartphone being held hostage, there's little else I can do!" Reliel let out a heavy sigh, slumping down in a nearby chair. She sure didn't seem all that pleased.

"B-But maybe you'll meet someone there? You never know."

"Hrmm... I doubt it. I don't think it'll work out well. Besides, I can't just trust anyone with my secret. What if they find out?"

The princess formed a small pout, grumbling softly to herself. I didn't really know what to say. Still, she had no choice in the matter. She had to attend the matchmaking party or she wouldn't get her phone back.

"Wait, why don't you talk to my father? You could explain that I'm sorry and ask him to return my phone."

"Hrmm... I don't feel good about lying, though."

"It wouldn't be a lie! I am sorry! Kinda."

You are not. That "kinda" speaks for itself. Well, whatever... Maybe I can just ask him...

"Goodness me... What a precarious situation. Did my daughter put you up to this, Touya?"

"No, of course not... Ha ha hah..."

Shit. Busted already.

I came to speak with the emperor on Reliel's behalf, but he saw right through me. Apparently, he hadn't looked through her phone yet, as he suspected his daughter of sending text messages to someone during the ceremony.

I'd left Yumina and Linze behind with Reliel. I felt that was fine, since there was no harm in them talking. Plus, Reliel had asked me for ideas for her new book, so I figured getting out of there was the safest decision.

"I fear for my daughter, Touya. If she doesn't decide on a husband soon, she'll become a spinster before long..."

Isn't she only like twenty or something? If you said that back on Earth, people would laugh at you.

The emperor held Reliel's smartphone in his hand, looking it over.

Chapter I: A Spot of Matchmaking

"You'll have to forgive me, but I really can't return this to her. If she keeps getting distracted by this thing, she won't ever find herself a suitable partner. And if that happens, she may well be all alone once Redis gets married."

The emperor leaned back into the couch and let out a soft sigh. Redis was the crown prince, which made him next in line to be emperor. His full name was Redis Reek Refreese, and he was around thirteen. Unlike his sister, Redis was already engaged. His fiancee was princess Thea Frau Mismede, who was around twelve.

Apparently, Refreese was more progressive than I had realized. Not a single noble had rejected the idea of a beastman marrying into their royal line.

Refreese was mostly bordered by water, so it was a maritime nation that prospered on trade. It wasn't quite as old as Belfast, but it still had a storied history. Naturally, they'd dealt with many different ethnicities along the course of this history. And it seemed the royal family had the blood of many races flowing through it, so culturally speaking, they didn't see it as strange or impure for a beastman to join their ranks.

If anything, there'd have been more of an issue if she was a commoner, but she was a princess, so all was well. The marriage was deemed advantageous for both the established nation of Refreese and the blossoming nation of Mismede, so it was a mutually beneficial arrangement.

Honestly, Refreese might have actually been one of the most diverse nations in the world... The people living there certainly seemed happy enough. Plus, it had a special kind of cheer to it. I could definitely see that merry spirit reflected in the emperor himself. But I think that idea, that so long as you were having fun, everything was okay, might have manifested a little too intensely in the princess.

And from what I'd heard, her brother was the complete opposite. He was supposedly a quiet, studious boy.

"When is your son getting married to Princess Thea?"

"Ah... Three years from now at the latest, I imagine. I'll abdicate when he's around twenty, I think. The king of Belfast just had a son, so he won't be ready for retirement by then, but I'll be able to live up my old age with Emperor Regulus."

...Really? Old age? You're like forty, aren't you? Isn't that more middle age?

"At any rate... I need to put together some kind of marriage arrangement for my daughter. I was thinking of a party, but maybe a one-on-one would do... Do you know any eligible young men?"

"Hrmm... I'm not sure..."

Suddenly, a flash of inspiration came to mind.

"Wait. Does it have to be a noble or a royal?"

"I don't personally care about his origin, so long as he can make her happy and takes proper care of her. That said, her marriage is still an important card to play for the interests of the nation. Our noble families likely wouldn't allow her to marry someone who doesn't have anything to offer Refreese."

Hrmm... That complicates things... Wait, I just realized... aren't I gonna have eight or more daughters? Am I gonna have to worry about this kinda thing too? What if one of my daughters wants to marry a commoner or an adventurer... Is that gonna be a problem? Nah, I don't think so. Noble, adventurer, doesn't matter to me. So long as he's a good person, it's fine. If he has ill intent, I won't forgive him... If he's not good enough for her, I'll kick his ass... Whoa... Holy shit. Is that how the overlord of Xenoahs feels about Sakura? Hm... Wait, that reminds me. The first prince of Xenoahs is single, right? He's Sakura's half-brother... so that might be fine? Wait, I think he's a bit of

Chapter I: A Spot of Matchmaking

a meathead, though... There's also Zanbelt from the Lassei Kingdom... I remember he got his ass kicked by Uncle Takeru. Wait. That guy's a meathead, too... Are they the only guys left?

"You don't have any brothers, do you, Touya?"

"Uhhh... I don't think so...?"

"You don't think so? I won't pry any further..."

The emperor stared at me with a raised brow, but he said nothing else. He probably assumed my dad slept around a lot or something. I didn't bother to correct him, either way. I wasn't sure if I'd get any more gods coming down, or any pretending to be my brothers... so I couldn't say for sure.

"I have no other choice, then. I'll just have to host some kind of blind date. But I'm not entirely sure where to start... Maybe all the eligible partners are already taken..."

"Well... the Reverse Worl—Er, the western continent might have some bachelors available. You're connected to one of their countries by the land now, right?"

"Quite right you are! Perhaps Panaches can lend us a hand."

Refreese and Panaches (the pumpkin-pants-prince's country) were joined by a land bridge when the two worlds merged. I'd helped smooth along discussions between the two, establish borders, that kind of stuff. The king of Panaches was a very friendly guy, so I had no doubt he'd be willing to lend his aid.

"If the prince of Panaches didn't have a fiancee, I'd have proposed Reliel take that role... What a shame... Alas, that's how these things go sometimes."

...Really? Now that's an... interesting pairing. Might have even worked out, considering how weird the two of them are. Shame Prince Robert's engaged, honestly. Though his fiancee is a nice girl... Frankly, I think she's too good for him, but I'm not gonna judge if they're happy.

Oh, maybe I can speak to the Strain royalty about this, actually... They might know some guys.

"Hmm... Yes, I quite like the idea of an east-west marriage party. I think every participating nation could get something out of it."

"Yeah, I just hope people treat it with a focus on the bachelors and bachelorettes, instead of an average political event."

If the matchmaking becomes secondary to international networking, I won't be happy... The focus should be on finding partners that mesh well, rather than worrying about stuff like international relations.

"Then..." chimed Karen, "Why don't we make it a masquerade, you know? I think it'll be more interesting and authentic if they all wear masks, you know?!"

"Oh, I see! Yes! Then it won't matter who the person is on the other side, because they won't be recognizable."

"Alright, a masquerade... That's definitely a great idea. I'll be able to prepare the masks for it, so that's fine. Oh, Emperor Refreese, as for the venue... Wait, hold on. Karen, when did you get here?"

I slowly craned my head to the left and saw that my idiotic sister was inexplicably sitting next to me. She was also sipping my tea.

"If something interesting is afoot, it's my time to shine! That's what Mochizuki Karen's all about, you know?"

"You dumbass!"

Don't just wink at me, asshole! Explain yourself! You're supposed to be in Brunhild, so what're you doing warping into a foreign nation's castle?! That's not a good look from an international relations standpoint!

I groaned before turning and bowing to the emperor.

"I'm really sorry... Please forgive my sister for just barging in here!"

Chapter I: A Spot of Matchmaking

"No, I... It's fine... If anything, I'm just a bit confused as to how she actually got here. The castle's supposed to be warded against teleportation techniques... Are my court mages perhaps lacking?"

Shoot, I hope we didn't just get someone fired. I'm sure the wards are enough to block all kinds of regular magic, but people like Karen and Moroha aren't exactly using those spells... Their divine existence allows them to use their own special ability to get around... It's not rooted in magic, so it bypasses stuff like wards...

"I'll make sure this never happens again, honest! It's just a quirk of hers!"

"You sure seem apologetic, you know? Everything okay, Touya?"

"Obviously not! Who do you think I'm apologizing for?!"

Stop chowing down on cookies while I'm apologizing for potentially causing an international incident!

"W-Well, she is your sister, so... I'm sure it's fine... Now, back to the matter at hand. How many people do you think we might be able to gather for this ball?"

"If we use Touya's connections, we can probably gather quite a few people from both continents, you know? Then, we can have the kids get to know each other at the ball. If two of them hit it off, we'll make a little system where pictures of their real faces can be exchanged and they can come together for a follow-up date, you know?"

...My connections? What connections? I only really know the world leaders, so I guess I can start there, but it's not like I immediately know eligible folks...

"Hmm... I'm not quite as well-connected as Touya here, but I should be able to ask a few fellow monarchs for their aid. I shall draw up the invitations at once... I suppose I'll be quite busy for a while," Emperor Refreese smiled warmly as he said that, perhaps because he felt his daughter's problems were about to be solved at last.

We finished up, and apparently Reliel was allowed to have her phone back on the condition that she attended the ball. I was honestly a little worried about her prospects... She was a special kind of eccentric, so she needed to find an equally unique guy.

In the meantime, I decided to focus on figuring out attendees. Fortunately, I knew a few folks in Brunhild who'd be interested in the idea. We didn't have nobles in my country, but I didn't see the harm in inviting a few knights and other interesting commonfolk to the party.

Hmm... Maybe this masquerade won't be so bad after all. It's not like I'll be forcing anyone to attend, at least.

◇ ◇ ◇

"And that's that..." I said as I finished stacking up the last mask and disengaged my [**Modeling**] spell. There were lots of different masks to choose from, but in the end, I went with the typical domino style, which covered half your face. It was the kind you either associated with phantom thieves or dominatrixes, depending on the situation.

Apparently, the name of the game of dominoes was actually derived from these masks, but that wasn't exactly an important detail or anything.

I'd used my phone to look up various designs, then set to work making some different ones. There were animal-style ones that resembled cats or birds, some were decorated with feathered plumes, some of them were simple monochrome designs, and some were unnecessarily flashy.

They weren't just regular masks, either. Each and every one of them came with specialized functions to anonymize the wearer.

Chapter I: A Spot of Matchmaking

After all, it would be easy enough to identify someone by their voice even if you couldn't see their face... That was why I made sure they all had voice-modifying functions enabled by default.

I also decided to make fake animal ears and tails for the venue, to make it impossible to know whether you were talking to an authentic beastman or not. It was all shaping up to be a real anonymous masquerade.

I tossed all the masks into **[Storage]** and headed out into the prep area. When I got there, I found several tailors from Fashion King Zanac making their final adjustments to the tuxedos and formalwear to be used for the party.

"Ah, Your Highness. I've finished drilling some manners into the men. Taught them some basic etiquette and whatnot, so they should get by well enough," Vice-Commander Nikola said that as he approached me. He was part of one of the biggest mercantile families in all of Mismede, so this kind of event wasn't too unfamiliar for him. It was his first time at an actual masquerade, though. He looked pretty good in his black tux, and his foxy ears looked just a bit more well-groomed than usual.

It was a bit rough figuring out Brunhild's attendees, since so many people wanted in on it. That was why I'd asked Nikola to participate in the ball to keep everyone unified. I couldn't exactly participate in this one personally like I did during the knight recruitment exam, after all.

Nikola was tough, though. He was treating this like any other combat excursion. In a way, maybe I was wrong to deploy such a fearsome force of politeness and propriety...

"Maybe you'll find yourself a partner tomorrow, huh?"

"Ah... I'm really trying my best not to think about anything like that... I'll mostly be keeping my attention on ensuring that Brunhild isn't made an international disgrace."

Nikola was quite popular among the maids who worked in the castle. That wasn't too surprising, given his capable skills and his well-established position in our military. He was a little bit too serious, though... He never quite smiled too often, but apparently that just added to his charm and mystique. I swear, women are hard to understand.

"How're the girls doing?"

"Fairly fine, I'm sure. Take a look at the picture Nore just sent me," Nikola said as he held out his smartphone and showed me an image on the screen. What I saw was a picture of Commander Lain in a beautiful white dress. The image had a translucent black bar covering it with the text, "Look at how cute Lain is!" on it. She was the very picture of a white bunny.

"I'm a little concerned, honestly... Hopefully nobody messes anything up at the party."

"It'll be fine, Nikola... Just keep a close eye on Nore and Lain, especially. If you can recognize them, at least..."

The masks inhibited facial recognition, but if you knew what a person was wearing beforehand, you'd at least be able to track them based on that. At the very least, attendees from the same country would probably know who their fellow nationals were.

The female participants from Brunhild were Lain, Nore, head guardswoman Rebecca, our intel trio (Homura, Shizuku, Nagi), and Lakshy the Alraune demonkin. Tsubaki was invited, but she'd declined. Said she didn't want to stand out.

Chapter I: A Spot of Matchmaking

I hoped that everyone would have a good time, romantic prospects aside. Though, that actually worried me, a little... What if someone important ended up falling for someone at the party? They'd have to leave Brunhild! Although, if it was a second or third child of a smaller noble family, they could probably drag him over here...

It'd be sad to see anyone go, but if they really fell for someone, I'd see them off with a smile. Better they live a happy life elsewhere than one pining for what-ifs in Brunhild.

The event itself was rapidly approaching... All I had to do was sit back and hope that nothing would go disastrously wrong!

▎▎▎ Interlude: The Crystal Dragon

"What, you're saying the Phrase are back?!"

"That's what the eyewitnesses say, at least. One showed up in Roadmare, apparently," Ende claimed as he shrugged and slurped his fruity water through a straw.

Preparations for the masquerade were in full swing, so I asked Ende if it'd be okay to postpone his wedding for a little bit. In the end, I called him and the three brides-to-be over for a drink at the Parent Cafe.

As the three Phrase girls munched down on various treats I'd purchased as an apology, I raised my brow due to the topic Ende had brought up.

"I thought the Phrase were all gone, though."

"Sure, in this world. But it's not like Phrasia stopped existing or anything."

The Phrase that Yula had brought to this world were corrupted by the wicked god and turned into mutants, but I was fairly certain we'd hunted down and exterminated the lot of them... Maybe it was a situation where a strong one had escaped being mutated?

"Nope, I don't think so. We would've noticed if it was something like that. Mutant or not, we'd sense it. It's probably just a misunderstanding."

The Phrase constantly emitted sounds that were imperceptible to the human ear. However, Melle, the other Dominant Constructs,

Interlude: The Crystal Dragon

and Ende could perceive those noises from anywhere in the world. And apparently, they couldn't hear anything, so this crystal monster was probably just a case of mistaken identity.

"But can't that sound be hidden through special means? Isn't that what I did to Melle's frequency?"

In order to prevent the mutants from finding Melle, I used [Prison] to confine her core. Surely it would be possible to block off another Phrase's frequency through similar means.

"I mean, sure, but how many people in this world can raise barriers as strong as yours? Hell, why would a regular Phrase want to seal off its frequency, anyway?"

"Yeah, I guess you've got a point there... It's just a little weird."

Hrmm... I'm at a loss here. Is it really just a misunderstanding? Something feels off. If it is, though... are there even any monsters out there that resemble the Phrase? They're pretty distinct creatures.

"I should probably run a search."

I projected a map of the world above the table and searched for "Phrase," but there were no hits at all. Well, that wasn't exactly true. There were three hits right next to me, but they weren't the Phrase I was looking for.

Hm... Fake news, I guess... Wait, no. If it's a fake Phrase, I won't recognize it as a real one, so let me try that search again...

"Run search. Uh... Something resembling a Phrase...?"

"Searching... One result found."

"Oho."

This time I was right on target. It seemed it really was just a beast or monster that resembled the crystal menace. It was in Roadmare... so presumably, that was the one that'd been sighted.

"What're you gonna do?"

"I should probably go verify what it is. Better safe than sorry and all that jazz."

Luckily, it's pretty far from any settled areas... I'll go check it out tomorrow, after I get permission from the doge, of course.

◇ ◇ ◇

"It's around here, I think..."

"Sure it isn't in those woods over there?"

"Or that lake, maybe?"

I stood atop a cliff with Sue and Sakura right behind me. They each gave their opinions on where the monster might be hiding. They'd asked to tag along since they were bored, but it wasn't like I'd come to have fun...

The mountainous region we were in was part of Roadmare's territory, but it was quite out of the way. As such, there weren't any settlements in the area. The information I got from the adventurer's guild said it was spotted around here, but I couldn't see anything.

I expanded the search range on my map and zoomed it out. The most confusing thing was that my map said it was... right there. Like, right where we were standing. But I couldn't see a thing.

Invisibility magic, maybe?

"Sakura, can you use your vocal magic to track it, maybe?"

"I can try..." Sakura mumbled, then began to sing toward the cliff's edge. Sakura's vocal magic would hopefully be able to figure out the location of the enemy.

She sang for a while but abruptly halted. Her brow raised. Perhaps she'd found something.

"...Grand Duke, it's below us."

"Huh?"

Interlude: The Crystal Dragon

Right after Sakura finished saying that, the cliff's edge began to crumble as if something was emerging from below.

"Watch out!" I roared as I used [**Fly**], grabbing the girls just in time to keep us from falling off the side. While floating there, I saw the creature emerge from beneath the ground. It gleamed in the sunlight, its crystal body reflecting the rays all around. For a split-second, I definitely thought it was a Phrase, but it wasn't. It was a Dragon made out of pure crystal.

Sure, it certainly resembled a Phrase at face value, but I knew after taking a good look at it that it couldn't be one. Its body was simply too different in appearance and structure. Dominant Constructs aside, the Phrase looked distinctly inorganic. They resembled carvings, or cut gems, as they were angular like they'd been designed to fit a mold. However, the Dragon I was looking at was very clearly a living organism.

So it's a Crystal Dragon, then... Wait, is that even an actual type of Dragon? I've never heard of those.

"Luli!"

"...You called, my lord? Ah... Hm?"

I called on Luli in her blue baby form. Right after addressing me, she cast an inquisitive glance over at the Crystal Dragon.

"Is this one of yours?"

"It's not. It doesn't fall under my species' domain. It's similar in form, but it has no life to it," Luli proclaimed, sounding almost disgusted as she looked down at the crystal creature. What did she mean about it having no life?

"She's right, Grand Duke... It's like it's lifeless... There's no breath nor heartbeat..." Sakura, who was tucked under my arm, spoke quietly.

"Wait, huh?"

Like it's lifeless? So wait, it's not a crystal creature, then...

"That's right, my lord. It's a magical construct akin to a Golem or Gargoyle. Likely a familiar constructed by a sorcerer from ancient times. It may look similar to my kind, but it's far different from my grand and noble species. That much I can assure you."

A familiar... So it's an artificial lifeform constructed out of magic, then.

Luli mentioned Golems, and they were definitely the most common example found across the world. There were also fake treasure chest monsters called Mimics.

Thankfully, it wasn't a Phrase, but what was a familiar doing out in the open? They were usually conjured up by humans (or demi-human species like elves) and made to follow extremely specific directives, obeying the last order given.

The most obvious examples were Gargoyles who acted as gatekeepers and Golems that guarded ancient ruins. They usually followed ancient orders like "protect this treasure" or "kill any intruders." Bearing that in mind, I could only conclude that this Crystal Dragon was following orders of some kind.

"Is it guarding something, maybe...?"

"It might be! Maybe someone broke in someplace and activated it?"

Sakura and Sue were already hypothesizing the same thing, it seemed.

"—————!"

"Gh... [**Teleport**]!"

The Crystal Dragon opened its maw and launched a shock wave in our direction. Right before it hit us, I used [**Teleport**] to move us all out of the way. A large boulder behind us crumbled apart. It clearly viewed us as enemies... or even trespassers.

"My lord. Please leave this to me."

Interlude: The Crystal Dragon

"Uh... Sure... I guess?"

"My thanks to you."

After gaining my permission, Luli transformed into her full-sized sapphire form. Thus, the stage was set. Dragon vs Dragon... even if only one of them was actually a Dragon.

"If you must hold a grudge, then hold one against your creator for giving you such a maligned form!" Luli bellowed loudly, seemingly enraged.

Ugh... I know you're mad at that thing, but please dial down the volume.

The Crystal Dragon was completely fearless in the face of Luli's roar. Given that it was basically like a robot, that wasn't too surprising.

The familiar's mouth opened wide, preparing to launch another shock wave. Luli didn't move at all, tanking the attack head-on. A massive crashing sound rang out as the blast slammed into her body, but she was completely unscathed.

"Pathetic. Even Kohaku's attacks are stronger than that. You dare imitate a Dragon with such pitiful strength?"

Damn, she's really mad... Maybe I shouldn't have summoned her. She's pretty quick to get heated, too. Though, given that she spends most of her time bickering with Kohaku, I shouldn't be surprised. She's extremely proud at heart. I bet she's insulted that something like this has the shape of a Dragon... I should probably warn Doc Babylon and Elluka not to make any Dragon-shaped Gollems. The Dragoon's probably safe since it's not a Dragon... right?

Apparently, the Crystal Dragon wasn't deterred, as it launched three or four more shock waves. Luli tanked all of those hits head-on once more. I wondered if she was okay... Why was she holding back so much? The only sound for miles around was the thudding crash of blast after blast striking Luli.

47

"...Pathetic!"

Oh, she snapped.

Just as the Crystal Dragon geared up for further attacks, Luli spewed a deluge of blue flames from her mouth.

"—————!"

In a matter of seconds, the Crystal Dragon's upper body melted like glass. Only the construct's lower body remained, flailing around aimlessly without its upper portion. Eventually, it collapsed completely.

Holy shit. I was kind of planning to power it down and bring it back for Doc Babylon, but it just got blasted to hell. Maybe she'd still like the bottom half?

Satisfied with the damage she'd inflicted, Luli returned to her miniature form.

"I won't make Luli angry if I can avoid it..." Sue couldn't help but mutter those words to herself.

Before the heat spread to the nearby woodland, I used [**Storage**] to stash the Crystal Dragon's lower half. Being responsible for a forest fire was not something I wanted added to my list of crimes against nature, after all.

"Well, that takes care of the fake Phrase. Though, if this thing was a gatekeeper or guard, maybe there's some ancient dungeon or ruins around here..."

It'd probably be easy to find something like that by firing up [Search].

"Grand Duke, look..." Sakura said as she pointed toward a little outcropping in the cliff face.

"Hm?"

It was mostly just crumbling rock, but I could see some kind of man-made gate a little further in the crevice. It'd been long obscured

Interlude: The Crystal Dragon

by rockfalls and other such natural blockages, only being finally exposed now. That was probably what the Crystal Dragon had been guarding... Maybe it was some kind of dungeon. If that was the case, I'd need to inform the doge right away.

Dungeons made good national attractions, after all. I'd been permitted to hunt the Crystal Dragon, but I wasn't allowed to perform any archaeological searches within Roadmare's territory... But then again, there was no guarantee this was a dungeon.

I flew down toward the entrance and found bodies. Fresh ones, even. They were probably people who'd found the place, accidentally awakening the Crystal Dragon in the process. I dug a small hole with Earth magic and buried them in it.

"It's huge... Did someone hollow out the mountain, maybe?"

Sue's words made me glance up at the entrance. It was less like a gateway and more like the entrance to a great stone temple. Some ruins back on Earth looked similar... If I remembered right, it was called Petra.

I cast **[Light Orb]** and headed into the structure. We passed through a straight passage and eventually came out into an open hallway. The orb of light illuminated the room, prompting Sakura and Sue to gasp out in surprise.

The room was filled with statues of all shapes and sizes. An armored warrior, a woman in a fancy dress, a pegasus with spread wings, a wolf mid-leap, and a nude woman on her side. And all the statues were carved from shining crystals.

Perhaps because protective magic had been cast on them, not a single statue had lost its luster. They all looked brand new. The sight was like something out of a dream, resulting in us standing there transfixed in the dark for a while.

"What is this, a museum? Or maybe a private workshop."

49

"Wow... It's like they're alive..."

Sakura's words startled me a little, since it made me consider the possibility that these were familiars or magical constructs like the Crystal Dragon. I walked over to the statue of a little dog, then activated [**Analyze**] to be on the safe side. There was no magical flow in any of them, which confirmed that they were simply carvings.

They were certainly the work of exquisite craftsmanship, though. It was as if people and creatures had simply become crystal themselves. The statue of the nude woman was especially realistic... Her breasts, for example, sagged in a way that was consistent with gravity. They were quite large, too...

As I stood there, admiring the statue of the woman, I felt two piercing gazes bear down on me from behind.

"...Tsk. Some nerve you have, ogling some naked statue when you've got two of your wives right here, Touya."

"...I hope you're not comparing our sizes, Grand Duke... Or do you want to cause a family argument...?"

"N-No, wait! Sorry!"

I felt scared after hearing the two of them, so I immediately backed off. I didn't want them saying anything to the other girls and causing some kind of weird misunderstanding... If I could put out a fire while it was still an ember, that was the best course of action. Fortunately, they seemed to accept my apology, so my ears remained un-nagged.

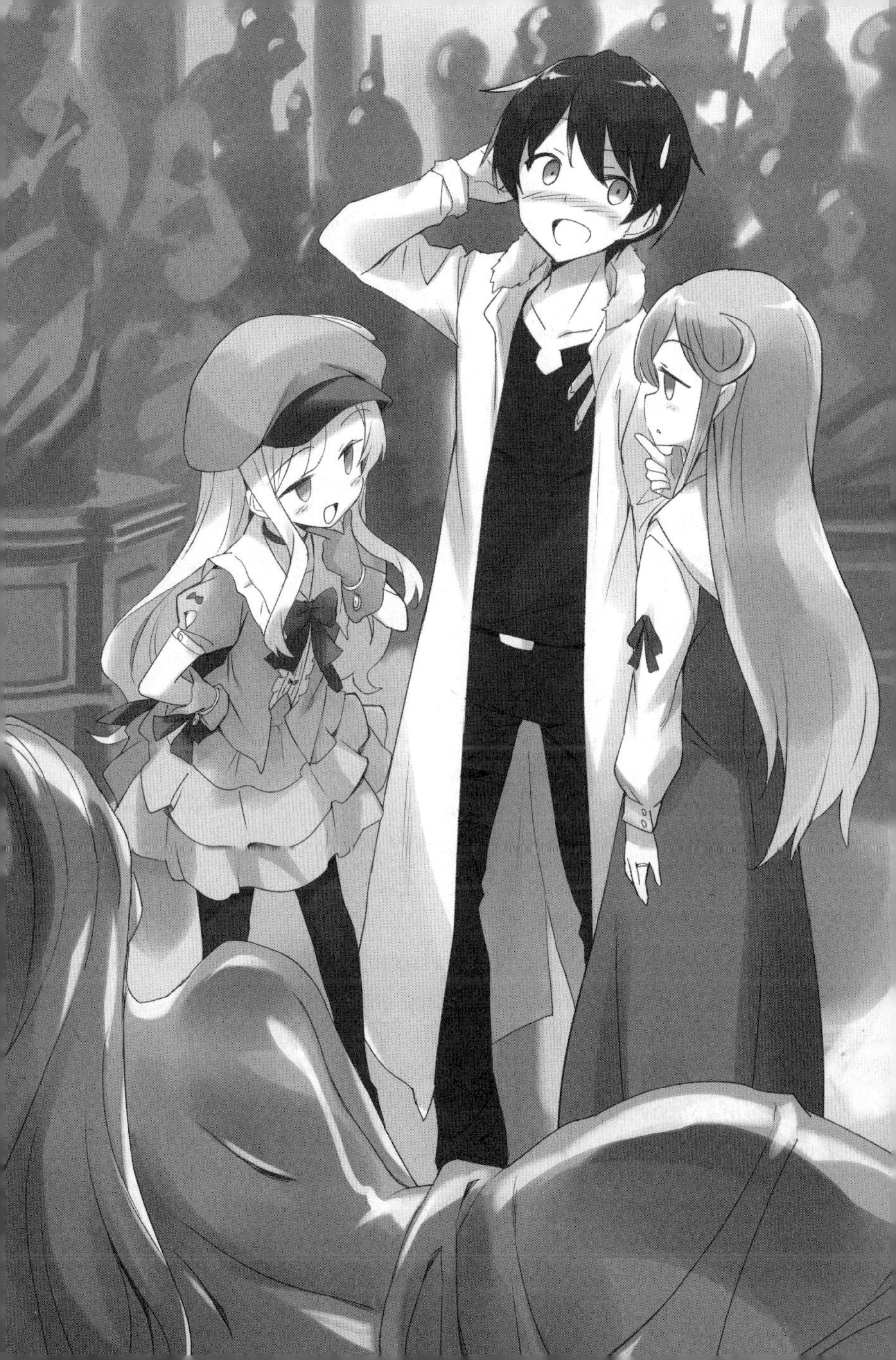

"There's a lot of them, huh? You gonna bring them all back, Touya?"

"Nah, I'll just report the discovery to Roadmare. I don't think it'd be right to just take the stuff without asking."

If this was some sort of ancient Roadmarian treasure trove, it'd be morally wrong for me to plunder it. A nation's cultural heritage belonged to them, and them alone, after all.

It was possible they'd reward me for finding it, though, which seemed like a fine alternative. In any case, for the time being, I decided to message the government of Roadmare. I had to report what happened to the Crystal Dragon too.

I whipped out my phone and called up the Doge.

◇ ◇ ◇

"Oho! What an incredible find! I never thought we'd uncover so many of Reginabyln's great works! What a miracle!"

The doge of Roadmare seemed awash with excitement. In fact, it was a little unnerving how amazed she was. I didn't really get why it was such a big deal.

Upon seeing my confused expression, the doge decided to explain the situation to me.

"Reginabyln is a great genius from the past. They were an artist, an alchemist, an accomplished professor of magic, and a true prodigy. Very few of their works survived to the modern-day, so those that have are tremendously valuable!"

Huh? So what, this person was like Leonardo da Vinci? I guess we've got a genius like that in the modern era, but she's an awful pervert...

"So then, how much is this stuff worth?"

Interlude: The Crystal Dragon

"Honestly, I'm unsure. Perhaps its weight in orichalcum?"

Wait, what?! That's way more expensive than I thought! Maybe if I find a large enough crystal, I could try crafting something with [Modeling] myself...? I'm not much of an artist, though.

"They would certainly fetch a high amount on auction. But... they're works of art. Cultural treasures! We can't simply sell this collection off. If possible, I'd prefer to display it in a museum here in Roadmare."

The doge seemed quite passionate about the subject. Typically, adventurers owned anything they found while out on a mission, but plundering cultural treasures from ruins in a country's borders was probably a little much... Archaeological sites and ruins were under the jurisdiction of the country they were found in, so a person would, at most, get a finder's fee.

Technically, it was possible to just sneak off with the treasure, but that would make you look like a huge asshole. You'd also probably make yourself a known enemy of whatever country you decided to steal from. It was just sort of a big unspoken rule among adventurers, like how you needed permission to enter a specific country's dungeon and earn its spoils. Other adventurers would probably view you negatively, too, so the trade-off usually wasn't worth the potential gain.

Under most circumstances, when I came across stuff like this, I just negotiated my way into getting something I could make better use of. Artifacts or weapons were more valuable to me than statues, anyway. I personally didn't have much of an eye for art, so I didn't care enough to claim it even if it was some great stuff.

"I'm perfectly fine with donating the find to Roadmare."

"Thank you so much!"

In the end, the Roadmarian government gave me a ton of money, I couldn't believe the statues were worth that much... I didn't understand art at all, but if people wanted to spend crazy amounts of money on sculptures, more power to them.

All that said, it was a nice little cash bonus for me and Brunhild. And so, I headed home with my newfound riches.

◇ ◇ ◇

"Oh, Reginabyln? You must mean Doctor Babylon's pseudonym. She only used that name for a little while, but it seems to have stood the test of time longer than her real one."

"Wait, what?!"

I was explaining the day's events over dinner when Cesca, who was halfway through pouring some tea, shocked the hell out of me with her casual commentary.

"Wait... Wait... Then that crystal stuff was made by Doc Babylon?"

"Crystal...? Oh, yes! She was quite into that material for a while. It only lasted about a week, as I recall. She's a woman of many tastes, and she often gets very distracted. I think her crystal workshop's probably out there somewhere..."

Reginabyln. Regina Babylon. The names certainly were similar... But that meant the Crystal Dragon was created by her, too.

"She seriously made art, too?"

"Back in Partheno, she was considered a jack-of-all-trades."

Seriously? Is there anything she can't do? This is a little much. I guess there's a fine line between genius and insanity... Though in her case, maybe it's perversion and genius.

Interlude: The Crystal Dragon

"Then doesn't that mean all those statues belong to Touya? Doctor Babylon's his property, right?"

"Hey, don't say something so ridiculous, Sue..." I quickly brushed off the girl's comment.

It was true that Doc Babylon was a gynoid and part of the Babylon Numbers like Cesca, and I was their master, but, well... I wasn't exactly going to tell the doge of Roadmare something like that. It wasn't a huge deal anyway, and if her art made some people happy, that was fine. Yumina lifted a cup of tea, sipped it, and then spoke up.

"What will you do with the money you received, then?"

"I was thinking of dividing it into bonuses for everyone in the knight order."

"Bonus? Like an extra payment?"

...Yeah, basically.

I'd given bonuses to the knights a few times before. The knight order was funded solely by me, rather than the state, so it made sense to pay them out this way.

Sometimes, when I came into an unexpected windfall of cash, I'd just give it out to the people who worked for Brunhild. It'd been a while since I paid out the last one, so this seemed like the right time.

"I don't think we should just hand them money for nothing. Why don't we give them some kind of incentive, instead? Or use it to pay for a prize of some sorts?" Moroha raised her brow as she spoke across the table. I wondered what she meant by prize.

"We could host a tournament, then give out prizes to the top contenders. Or perhaps we could give the money out to knights who've served Brunhild the best in recent weeks."

That sounds like a pretty fun idea, actually. It might help motivate them, too. Hmm... I do have a lot of cash to spare, so why not do both? It might be good to float the message that if you work hard, you'll be duly rewarded. Now, how to go about this...?

◇ ◇ ◇

"Hmm? Crystals? I don't remember anything like that..."

"You don't?"

The next morning, I spoke to Regina Babylon, AKA Reginabyln, about what I'd found.

"Ahhh... Haaah... D-Don't you remember, Doctor? You even made a Crystal Dragon to guard the place, mhhh..."

"A Crystal Dragon, you say...? Oh... Ohhh... I totally forgot about those."

Tica, the gynoid assigned to the research laboratory, jogged the doc's memories.

"That's right! At the time, there were a lot of Phrase sightings, so I started dabbling with a little crystal crafting of my own."

"Oh, so the sight of them inspired you to make your own?"

I was a little surprised by that revelation.

"Indeed. But as the Phrase sightings became more synonymous with death and destruction, I decided that the crystal constructs were in poor taste. And so, I ended up having the facility condemned. Where was it located again?"

"Mfh... Haaah... It should be facility twenty-six... It's... ahhh... around where Roadmare is now, as I recall..." Tica stated. That was right where I'd discovered it.

Interlude: The Crystal Dragon

Apparently it got sealed away, and she'd forgotten all about the sculptures by the time she started working on the floating islands project.

"You don't need those statues for anything, do you?" I'd already sold the statues to Roadmare, so there was no point asking, but I hoped for a favorable answer.

"Nope. They were just a side project to kill time."

...Being remembered as a renowned artist for your side projects is pretty amazing, Doc. Wait, if I ask her to make some new ones I can pretend I found more and make a killing...

"I'm not interested in making more, either. It'd be a waste of time mass-producing something solely for aesthetic purposes. I don't consider them worth the effort."

I knew a lot of people considered the statues worth their time, but apparently the artist disagreed. The mental image of a sculptor smashing his half-finished vase into the ground out of dissatisfaction flashed through my mind. This was fine, though. I had a feeling people would get suspicious if I suddenly found a ton of priceless antique artworks. It'd be in my best interests not to invoke that kind of scrutiny.

I left Babylon and headed to the Brunhild training grounds. All our knights were there, except those assigned to guard duty or patrol. When Lain, the leader of the knights, told everyone about the upcoming bonus, they just about jumped for joy.

I was happy to hear them so excited, but part of it felt a little backhanded, like I wasn't paying them enough regularly or something...

Maybe Brunhild paid a bit less than the knight orders of other countries, but still...

"Now then, we'll be hosting a tournament with a special cash reward! Are you all ready?!"

The knights cheered to the heavens, raising their fists with joy as Moroha gave the announcement. They all seemed really fired up.

"But I think we should make it a little more interesting, no? Let's divide the tournament into various categories. That'll allow your different strengths to shine. Some can throw better, some can dodge better, some have more endurance, and some are better at getting past obstacles... Whoever comes in first place in these categories will receive a prize from Touya! Do well enough and you may even qualify for multiple prizes!"

That makes sense. Some might not excel just at swordplay, so turning it into a more general athletic meet gives everyone a chance to win. I like that.

In the end, we threw in an obstacle course and a bread-eating competition as well. That way the paper-pushing members of the knight order had a chance as well. We also decided to split everyone up into two teams, east and west. The team that earned the most points would get a collective prize, which allowed us to have both team-based and individual events... But it also meant I'd be paying out a lot more than initially intended... Whoops.

"Alright! Time for the race! Those who want to participate, line up!"

This race was initially a simple one-hundred-meter dash. But since there were so many participants, we decided to set it up like a relay instead.

"Hey, Touya? Shouldn't we make this an event for the townsfolk to watch? They had stuff like this in your homeworld, right?" Sue, who was idly watching by my side, made a small suggestion. She was referring to a track and field event we'd watched on TV during our honeymoon. This was a little different, but similar in principle. She had a point. Athletic events were more exciting with spectators, so I'd definitely consider it.

I asked Sakura to make Mr. Mittens and his friends go around town telling people about it. A few people ended up wandering over, and by the time the race finished, there was quite a large crowd.

The second event was an egg-and-spoon race, which was one of those novelty races where you had to balance a boiled egg on a spoon and beat everyone else.

The crowd went wild, cheering whenever a knight dropped or picked up his egg. It was surprisingly engaging.

"It's nice doing this every once in a while, huh?"

"Hm… I wish I could participate in this, I do."

Elze and Yae looked on with slight envy. I had to stop them from joining in. Otherwise, I'd definitely just win all my money back.

I started to wonder if it'd be a good idea to host this kind of event on a more regular basis. It'd be a good way for everyone to take a load off. Plus, making it a public attraction could be good for tourism. Though, if I had to give out prizes every single time, I'd probably drain my coffers pretty quick.

Well, maybe we'll try this again next time I have a little extra pocket change.

Chapter II: Masquerade

"Wow... This is such a big venue..." Linze quietly mumbled as she glanced around the ballroom.

There were dazzling decorations all over the place and a huge chandelier dangling from the ceiling. It was a custom-made dwarven creation with a [**Light Orb**] enchantment. I wondered how much it must have cost.

The ballroom's second floor had a large balcony dining area, which offered an astonishing view of Refreese's coastline. The deep blue of the sea complemented the light blue of the sky and the white of the city brought the spectacle together. The view was so breathtaking that I couldn't help but snap a shot on my phone.

"It's quite similar to that Mediterranean Sea we visited, Touya."

"That's actually what I thought the first time I arrived here."

Leen smiled softly at my response. It was nice that we could share little thoughts like that now. It really made me thankful that I'd brought the girls around Earth with me.

"There is a garden below, there is."

Yae was peeking over the balcony railing, so I joined her and looked below. There was a beautiful blooming bed of flowers right below us. A little brick road passed through the bushes, flanked by little water fountains and benches. There was a nice little clearing, too. Looked like a perfect spot for a picnic.

Chapter II: Masquerade

Hilde seemed to think so as well, given how much she was admiring the place.

"I think the idea must be that if you find a partner at the ball, you can come out here to get a little more privacy..."

"Yeah, that sounds about right. If you can find a partner, at least."

Even though I'd designed the masks to disguise identity, I hadn't really considered the issue of clothing, so there wasn't really a limit on that. I had a feeling the more gaudily-dressed people would be more popular. If you wore something fancy, people would know you were filthy rich, after all. Still, people who flocked to others because of that would also show their character that way. It might even be a good way to discern someone's intentions.

As I pondered the matter, Sue scurried up to me from behind.

"Hey Touya, where's Lu?"

"Hm? Pretty sure she's in the kitchen."

Last I recalled, she'd gone off with the Refreese Castle's head chef.

"Isn't it strange for one of Brunhild's grand duchesses to be cooking for a foreign country?" Sue said as she sighed a little and shook her head in disbelief.

Hey, wait. There's a reasonable explanation for this.

Lu published weekly recipes through her blog on the Cookery app that was on everyone's smartphones. The pictures of strange dishes and tasty treats immediately captured the hearts and minds of the royals who saw them. So naturally, they passed the recipe information on to their chefs, resulting in Lu becoming somewhat of a legendary chef among the royal kitchen staff.

The head chef at Refreese Castle was a particularly avid fan of Lu's blog. The emperor knew about this, so he petitioned me directly to ask if she'd be able to help mentor his staff.

"Lu's food is amazing, it's no wonder people go crazy for it."

"That might not be a good thing…"

Sakura had a point. If the attendees got too engrossed in their meals, they might spend more time eating than chatting. But hey, maybe people would get to know each other over their shared love of food. That could be a bonus.

Suddenly, Yumina clapped her hands together. The shock made me jump for a moment.

"It's time for all of us to get ready! This is our first formal event as grand duchesses of Brunhild!"

"Uh, wait… Yumina… Do we have to?" Elze muttered in response to Yumina's decree. She seemed nervous, as did Linze, Yae, and Sakura.

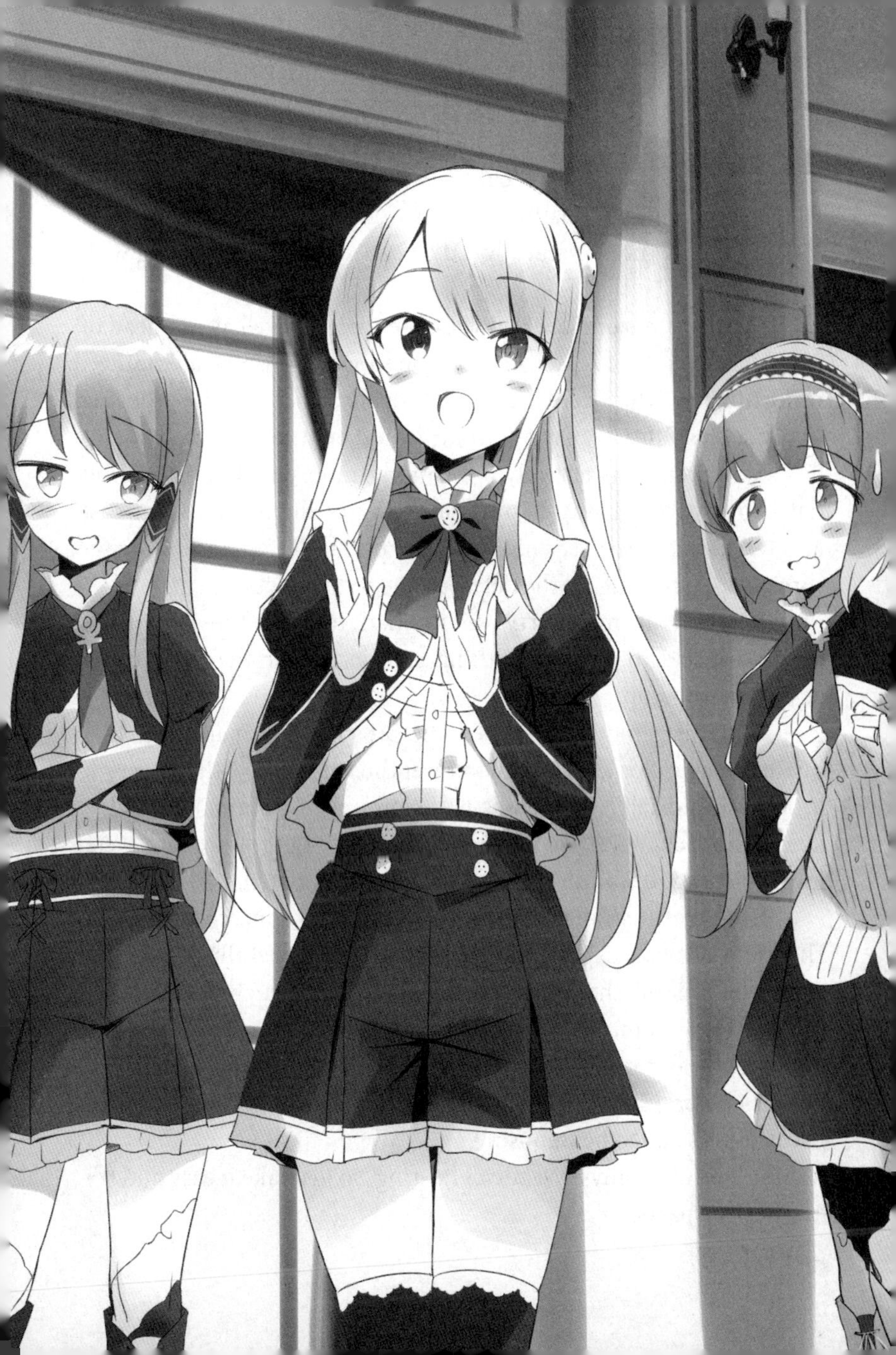

While the blind matchmaking was going on, the second floor would be hosting a separate event for nobles and dignitaries who were already in relationships, as well as those too young to be looking for partners. Naturally, I'd be expected to attend along with my wives.

Prime Minister Kousaka would be there, as well as our head of infrastructure, Naito. Moroha and Karen would also be attending... unfortunately. They were technically royalty, since they were posing as my sisters, after all. Granny Tokie would be staying home, though.

This event was actually a lot more important than the blind date downstairs. It was a royal gathering of dignitaries from east and west, so it'd be a very high-security event. Refreese asked me for some help in beefing up the defenses due to that fact.

It was a formal party, so we had to look the part. That meant we had to wear something a little fancier than our usual adventuring getup.

When it came to my wives, the prospect of a party like this divided them. Some of them were enthused, while others were a little uncomfortable. There was no helping that. Yumina, Lu, Hilde, Leen, and Sue were used to formal events, but the others were inexperienced. It was no wonder they felt intimidated.

I thought it strange that they were still so concerned, though. They had a lot of experience with royals, so hopefully, this party would be a good chance for them to deepen their bonds in high society. Then again, they were probably just concerned about making their debut as formal members of a royal family. They were my fiancees before, sure... but now they were full-on grand duchesses. The prospect had to be imposing.

"It'll be okay, guys. We're not hosting, so just take it easy and try to enjoy the party."

Chapter II: Masquerade

"Easy for you to say... Can't I just work security instead?" Elze asked. It sounded like she was joking, but I had a feeling she wasn't. Unfortunately for her, royal wives couldn't be seen doing something like that!

Yae grumbled a bit alongside Elze, then suddenly raised a brow as she noticed something behind me. I turned to see what she was looking at.

"Sakura-dono... Is that not the overlord, is it not?"

"...Ugh," Sakura noticed her father, then let out a small, disgusted noise.

The overlord of Xenoahs was wandering down the hall in our general direction. A few demonkin guardsmen were walking with him. Among those guards was a familiar face. It was Sirius. His daughter, Spica, was a member of our knight order. He looked young as ever, which was unsurprising given that he was a dark elf. Even the overlord looked like he was in his twenties, but he was actually over a hundred.

Hm? Who are the other two guards? Do I know them?

"Oh, if it isn't the grand duke of Brunhild. You're here already?"

The overlord gave me a little wave as he addressed me, but he was only looking at his daughter. That was rather rude...

I'd gone to all the invited nations the night before to place [Gate] portals for ease of access at the appointed time. The first one to arrive appeared to be the Xenoahs party.

The overlord smiled toward Sakura and gave her a timid wave.

"Er... H-How's my little Farnese these days?"

"...Fine."

"How's married life? No problems, I take it?"

"...I'm very happy. Don't worry about it."

"I-Is that right..."

Things between them still felt awkward. Not at all what you'd expect from a father and daughter... Sakura was far too curt with him, and he was just awful at knowing how to respond.

Sirius, who seemed to be fidgeting impatiently, suddenly leaned in and whispered something to the overlord.

"Your wickedness... The introductions, remember?"

"O-Oh, right! Doy! My bad! Hey, you guys. I have to introduce these two to you. C'mere, both of you."

The two young men behind Sirius and the overlord stepped forward. One of them was a dark-skinned young man who stood well over six feet. He had bulging muscles, even on his neck, as well as long, fiery-red hair and eyes that burned with passion. A little smirk sat on his face. The other was a thin young man with round glasses. He was closer to my height. His eyes were a lot less intense than the other guy's... In fact, he looked a little bored. His hair was the same red as the muscular guy's, but his skin tone wasn't quite as dark. He had a bit of a nerdy vibe about him, honestly.

However, the most distinctive feature about both of them was the horns sprouting from the sides of their heads... They were clearly identifiable as the same types of horns the overlord had.

The overlord's horns were a signifier of his lineage, which could only mean one thing...

"These are my sons, Faron and Farese. They don't share the same mother as Farnese, but they're her brothers nonetheless."

That explained why they seemed vaguely familiar. They were the first and second princes of Xenoahs, Sakura's elder brothers. That also made them my brothers-in-law. I'd heard about them in the past.

I sure had a lot of brothers-in-law, though... There was Yae's brother, Jutaro... Reinhard, Hilde's brother... Lu had a brother, probably... Yeah, he was called Lux. Barely ever saw him, though.

Chapter II: Masquerade

There were a few more here and there, too. And now Faron and Farese had entered the fray... Though, I suppose this was inevitable. I had a lot of wives, after all.

Prince Faron walked up to Sakura. There was a considerable height difference between the two, prompting him to crouch a bit to look down at her. For whatever reason, he was also striking a flashy pose at the same time.

"This is the first time we've ever met, little sis! But I'm yer big bro, Faron!"

"...Are you as stupid as you look?"

"What kind of opener is that?!"

Sakura had said exactly what I was wondering, but that sure was a cold way to address one's brother. Then again, she probably didn't think of him as family or anything.

"She has a point, brother. Your introduction was unnecessarily flashy and boorish."

"Not you too, Farese!"

Poor Faron slumped his shoulders after taking the double-pronged attack. This was one of those times where you'd say "like father, like son..." He looked just like the overlord did whenever Sakura gave him a rough time.

It was the glasses-wearing prince's turn to introduce himself.

"I'm Farese, as you just heard. I'm sure you know, but I'm the second prince of Xenoahs. I've forfeited any and all rights to the throne, however... I apologize for the trouble my mother's family caused you... I don't believe it's something that can ever be forgiven, but I feel as though I have to let it be known all the same."

Farese bowed his head to Sakura. Sakura blinked in surprise at the sudden apology, and I had no idea what he was talking about... but then I quickly remembered.

Sakura had once been the target of a malicious, life-threatening plot. In Xenoahs, the one who holds the overlord's horns and has the most magical power is the de-facto ruler of the country. Sakura was raised away from the royal family because her horns never manifested, but once she got older, they started to grow in... and she also possessed a deep reservoir of magical potential. In accordance with tradition, that made her the next heir to Xenoahs' throne. But the second prince's uncle, a man named Severus, conspired to kill her by hiring Yulongese assassins.

Sakura was gravely injured and lost many of her memories as a result. But after she got them back, we tracked down the one responsible for the attack, and the entire conspiracy was unraveled. The second prince didn't actually have any part of this, but it seemed like part of him felt responsible for it due to his mother's brother being the one pulling the strings.

"It's fine... If I never got attacked, I wouldn't have met the grand duke or the others... You needn't mind, Farese."

"Very well... Quite bold, aren't you?"

"Mhm."

Farese smiled a little at Sakura. He had a point. Calling him by name like that even though he was a foreign prince wasn't exactly normal protocol. Then again, they were siblings, so it was probably okay... Though there was one person nearby who seemed to have an issue.

"Hey... Aren't you getting a little too friendly with him, Farnese?! What about me?!"

"Father... Please don't take it personally, okay? Just calm down."

"Hmph... You're annoying..."

"Oh, now you're both gonna hassle me?!"

Chapter II: Masquerade

The overlord sighed quietly as both his son and daughter spoke back to him. He was a lost cause, it seemed...

"Uh... Overlord? Will your sons be attending the matchmaking event?"

"Huh? Oh, right... They will, yes. Neither of them have wives yet, after all."

"I'm a little surprised. They're not even engaged?"

"They're too picky... Frankly, it's pathetic that they don't have a partner at their age. They could stand to learn a bit from you, Grand Duke."

...C'mon, man. Gimme a break. One of my wives is your daughter!

"Hrmph... I'm just a busy, important guy, you know? I could get a wife or two if I really wanted..."

"Could not... You're just lazy..."

"Grr!"

Sakura was being completely merciless as far as Faron was concerned. She was treating the poor guy about as badly as she treated her dad. I'd assumed that his position as prince would've meant he'd be married off by now, but apparently things worked a bit differently in Xenoahs. Demonkin like him had long lifespans, so there was less immediate pressure to get married. It was also seen as a rite of passage to find a spouse on your own.

"What about you, Farese?"

"I'm not exactly interested in marriage. I was simply dragged here by my brother. That said, I am grateful for the opportunity to visit Refreese, and finding a partner here might not be the worst thing in the world."

"Mmm... Give it your best and take it slow. You'll find the right person for you eventually..."

"...Hey, aren't you treating him a little different?"

While she'd had nothing but scorn-filled words for Faron, Sakura was surprisingly calm and supportive when it came to Farese.

Hrm... I guess Faron's similar to the overlord in personality, so maybe Sakura finds that part of him annoying...

As I was pondering, Prince Farese called out to me.

"By the way, Grand Duke... Father told me that Brunhild is home to an exceptional library."

"Huh? Oh, yes. That's right. I can use teleportation magic, so there are books from all around the world in my personal library."

For a moment, I thought he was referring to Babylon's library, but thankfully that secret hadn't leaked. He was just talking about the regular one in my castle.

I'd shown some of the other world leaders during a league of nations meeting once, so the overlord probably mentioned it to him after that or something.

Most of the books in Babylon's library were in ancient languages, and some others contained forbidden knowledge that was best kept secret. On the other hand, there were plenty of regular, interesting, and inoffensive stories there as well, so I'd copied them for the castle library. There were also some rare books I'd collected from around the world at the behest of Fam, terminal gynoid of the library.

"Apologies, but might I come to Brunhild to see it someday? I haven't been able to stop thinking about it ever since my father brought it up..."

"Are you an avid reader?"

"I am, yes. Sometimes I read to the point that I neglect eating. But there's little better in life than the pleasures of books, don't you think?"

Huh...? This guy's a bit of an intellectual, especially when compared to his brother. If he's into books, maybe that'd make him a

Chapter II: Masquerade

good match for Princess Reliel? Then again, there's no guarantee he'd like her particular brand of novels...

There was no issue with the prince visiting my castle library, so I said he could at a later date.

After that, the Xenoahs party went off to change into their proper outfits for the evening. The overlord tried to stay behind to talk to Sakura some more, but he was dragged off by his sons before long.

Shit, that reminds me... I've gotta get ready too. I haven't worn a tux since my wedding day...

I parted with Yumina and the others, making my way toward the changing room set aside for Brunhild's men.

◇ ◇ ◇

The melodic rhythm rang through the ballroom, and the guests finally started to dance with one another. The majority of the guests were the children of nobles, after all, so they were all instructed in dancing, and I made sure that the attendees from Brunhild at least received some degree of instruction as well.

It was a masquerade ball, but dancing was optional. That said, Yumina and Lu told me that to prevent any embarrassment, everyone from Brunhild had to at least be willing to get up and dance if invited.

Most of the people dancing now were those I recognized as nobles, while everyone else was either sitting around the hall or outside the venue in the garden. And because everyone was wearing masks, people were forced to talk to one another. That could often lead to either dance invites, or walks in the garden.

From what I could see, though, people were sticking more closely to those from their own countries. Maybe that was unavoidable.

"It's nice to see people chatting here and there. Oho, isn't that one of ours?"

The king of Lihnea looked down over the hall, peeking through his opera glasses. Apparently, all the countries had some kind of identifier that marked them as members of their own country. Brooches, cufflinks, stuff like that.

"Cloud... Do you really think you should be snooping like that? They're probably nervous down there, you know?"

"Oh, you're right... Apologies. I was just a little curious."

After a little chastisement from his fiancee, King Cloud handed the opera glasses back to me.

The girl in question was Princess Lucienne Dia Palouf. She was the elder sister of King Ernest of Palouf, and in a few months, she'd become the queen of Lihnea. I liked her a lot, she had a very gentle temperament to her.

Princess Lucienne's comment got me glancing around, and I noticed that Cloud wasn't the only one peering at the hall below.

I suppose it made sense when you considered that the guests were family or friends of the royals and nobles up here. It would only be natural to be a little curious.

I glanced around the second floor and saw all the important dignitaries of each nation chatting to one another, clinking champagne glasses in their hands. The actual royals, myself included, weren't quite as eagerly schmoozing our way through the crowd, however. That said, some of the royals and nobles from the Reverse World... or rather, the western continent, were fresh faces to the royals of the eastern continent. I was the only person from this side of the world who'd had much experience over there, so I had

Chapter II: Masquerade

to adopt a kind of mediator role while letting everyone get to know each other better. In all honesty, it was kind of a drag, but I gave it my best anyway.

I was done giving the introductions now, though, so it was just a case of kicking back and relaxing.

I glanced back to Lucienne, who was looking over at the dining room.

"It's been a long time since Ernest has been able to talk with children his age."

"Yeah, I'd imagine so. I'm sure he's more comfortable hanging out with them than us."

King Ernest was sitting by his fiancee, Rachael. They were happily chatting with Remza and Alba, the first and second princes of Mismede. Nearby were First Princess Lilac and Second Princess Milneah of Hannock, as well as Lucrecion, the former heir to Gardio and now the count of Lowe.

They were all roughly ten, so it was nice to see them getting along. I glanced over and saw the newly-crowned King of Dauburn talking to my brother-in-law, Reinhard, who'd also been recently crowned Knight King of Lestia. It was nice to see new leaders bonding so quickly. Then again, I was a fairly new leader too. Same went for Cloud, really.

Yumina and the other girls were mingling with the foreign queens and princesses, likely asking for advice about life as a state figurehead. Elze, Linze, and Yae were uncertain about how to act, judging from the stiff smiles on their faces. But that was only natural, really. I was sure they'd learn how to handle themselves in due time.

The kings, emperors, and other male leaders were all grouped up and chatting. So far, things seemed to be going without a hitch, so I decided to do a little looking around myself.

I said my byes to Cloud and headed out to the balcony. From there, I could see what was happening down below in the gardens. Some men were nervously chatting up women, while others were sitting at a table and sharing a nice pot of tea. Everyone was enjoying themselves in their own way. It was nice to see, but that was all...

It'd be wrong of me to say I hadn't expected this, though. This wasn't supposed to be a particularly exciting event. Curiously, however, there was a strange gathering of muscleheads on the balcony. The leaders of Mismede, Felsen, Lassei, and Egret were all chattering amongst themselves. I hadn't taken them to be the type to care much about other peoples' romance.

They seemed awfully merry, though, and they kept looking down over the balcony... For some reason, I had a bad feeling.

"Oho! There you are, Grand Duke! Here to watch?"

"...Watch what?"

The beastking waved his champagne at me, spilling a little in the process.

What exactly were they watching? I hadn't booked any live performances. Unless they were just... people-watching. That seemed rather dull, however.

I glanced around a little more and suddenly noticed a few members of the Refreese royal infirmary standing by. Was someone sick, or something?

"Uh... What's going on?"

"Oh, you'll see in a minute, lad!"

The king of Felsen grinned slyly as he winked at the beastking.

"It's inevitable at gatherings like this. Watch and learn."

I didn't understand what was going on at all, but that didn't stop the king of Egret from tapping me on the shoulder. It was very unusual to see him in a formal tux instead of his Native American-esque tribal outfit, but he certainly pulled it off. That didn't surprise

Chapter II: Masquerade

me, though. He was remarkably popular with women for a reason... It was no wonder he had seven wives.

"You've never attended a gathering like this, I take it?"

"I mean... I was an adventurer before I met my wives. I've only really been to a few fancy parties like this, so I haven't had a chance to attend any courtship-oriented events, no."

"They're young, you know? Youngsters don't tend to yield. And when two unyielding forces meet, well..."

As if to interrupt the king of Egret, a voice rang out from the courtyard below. I wondered what was going on.

"Looks like the first one of the night."

"First what?"

I looked down and saw two masked men glaring at each other. Well, they were more masked teens, but still... The two of them looked incredibly tense, drawing in concerned glances from onlookers.

"Huh? A fight?"

"But of course. This kind of thing's bound to happen. Usually, if it gets too intense, the parents of the youngsters will come out and put a stop to it, or the host will. But at times, it escalates into a duel."

"A what?!"

Aren't those usually to the death?! That doesn't sound very smart!

"Worry not, Grand Duke. Those boys won't be losing their lives today. In cases like this, we set out rules and have them compete against one another. No matter who wins, what's important is that there's no bad blood left behind. Anyone who acts out after the conflict's over tends to lose a little face among their peers, so it's not really worth it."

"Wait... you guys make them compete? Like what, horse racing or something."

"Mm... Not usually, no... Though I have heard of a few cases where they settled their differences over a horse race, so it's not unprecedented. It's generally peaceful, though."

Peaceful sounded good to me. Better than dueling to the death, at least... It was smart of them to think ahead and prevent feuding teens from seriously hurting each other. I was of the opinion that disputes were best solved without conflict, anyway.

"Anyway, we'll probably have these two fistfight or something."

"What's 'generally peaceful' about that, exactly...?"

That's violent as hell, man!

Noticing my surprised reaction, the king of Felsen laughed out loud.

"It's better to handle things this way when they're young. Good for one's soul to vent your feelings through your fists in honorable combat than to let your feelings fester. Plus, we have healers on standby, so it's all good!"

So that's what they're here for?! That's crazy! Is this kind of thing really that common at parties like this?! You're making me regret arranging this thing, man...

"Those masks won't come off so easy, right?"

"Huh? Oh, they shouldn't. Even if you get knocked around, they won't come off without me uttering the proper keyword."

"Most interesting... Usually, fights like these get called off and mediated if the two men aren't of the same social status, but it seems with these masks a commoner could even fight a prince."

"Hmph. That's good, if you ask me. Social status shouldn't matter at all when it comes to the path of the fist. Only thing that counts is how you swing."

The Beastking nodded at the ruler of Lassei, and the two eagerly looked down over the balcony.

If you're sure this is okay, I guess...

Chapter II: Masquerade

An independent observer stepped between the two men, and it looked as though the brawl was about to begin. But then, they suddenly headed deeper into the garden area, followed by a small entourage of onlookers.

"Looks like they realized the spectacle they're making and took their fight deeper in. Time to follow, eh?"

"...You guys really just wanna watch a fight, huh?"

"Wahahaha! Come on, lad. The main event at parties like this is the passionate clash between two men, not the will-they-won't-they nonsense of romance!"

The brawny men all filed out of the balcony area, eager to see the fight. I stayed behind.

...Pretty sure romance is supposed to be the main event here, guys.

"Geez..."

Some of the bystanders followed to see the fight, but most remained in the courtyard and resumed their business. A lot of them seemed focused on their partners, which was nice.

I saw some groups where several men fawned over the same woman and even vice versa. The masks generally blocked the physical features of the guests, but some people just had natural charisma that transcended looks. Conversation, gestures, mannerisms, and general responses... Those were the best ways to find out about a person's real character.

"Hm?"

A figure down in the courtyard caught my eye. She stood alone, away from the other partygoers. She was leaning against a tree. Some might call her a wallflower, a girl who was simply too introverted or shy to speak to others. But I knew better. She was away from the other partygoers because she was busy with her phone, frantically typing on it at high speeds.

Not many people in the world had smartphones. They were specially made by Doc Babylon, after all. Only the heads of nations, their closest staff and family, as well as my personal friends had them. And I knew for a fact that most of those people were up on the second floor, talking amongst themselves. Which could only mean one thing. This girl was Princess Reliel.

She wasn't inside, dancing in the ballroom. Nor was she chatting with the others outside. The only dance was the waltz of her fingers against the screen. She was definitely writing some new sordid novel on there.

What an idiot!

If the emperor of Refreese saw her typing away like that, he'd obviously take it from her again.

"Oho. Nice to see you out here, Touya."

"Waugh?!"

"Hm? Have I bothered you?"

Speak of the devil!

I turned around to see the emperor of Refreese, the king of Belfast, and the queen of Elfrau smiling my way.

"N-No! Not at all! I'm having a great time! Isn't this fun?!"

"Hm? Oh, well... I'm glad you're enjoying yourself..."

I laughed nervously, walking forward and trying to grab their attention. He was Reliel's dad, so I didn't want to risk him seeing her down there. I didn't think a mask would keep him from identifying his daughter. Even I knew it was her at a glance, after all.

"H-Hey, uh... where's Prince Redis? How's he doing these days?"

"Oh, Redis? He's over there, but..."

"Over there, huh?! Amazing! I wanna give him an engagement gift! Could you take me to him?!"

Chapter II: Masquerade

I was being pretty pushy, but I needed to get the emperor the hell away from the balcony. Reliel's little brother, Prince Redis, got engaged to Princess Thea of Mismede a while back, but I'd never given them anything to commemorate the event. Well, we did on a national level, but I hadn't done anything personal.

"Hoho. A gift from you, of all people? It must be something interesting."

"Yep, it really is. It's a rare treasure I found on my honeymoon. I think the prince is gonna love it."

King Belfast chimed in, so I nodded really quickly and prompted the three of them to follow me into the nearby hallway.

...Wait, why did all three of you come?

Before long, we found Redis and Thea, so I wasted no further time in opening up my **[Storage]** and pulling out some interesting items for them.

"Wow!"

"It's so pretty!"

I took out two small glass spheres filled with liquid and fake snow. Inside was a small diorama scene with a brick house and a reindeer. The little glittering flakes danced around the area as I shook them.

It was a simple trinket back on Earth, known as a snow globe. Luckily, I'd bought quite a few of them at the landmarks I'd visited.

The two of them looked positively ecstatic as I handed the snow globes over. The little prince immediately started shaking his around.

"Is this from Elfrau?"

"Er, no... It's from a, uh... different country."

I didn't exactly want to ignore King Belfast's question, but I wasn't ready for the baggage that'd come with explaining it was from another world entirely. Another cool feature about these snow globes was the fact that they'd been enchanted with **[Program]**, so you didn't have to shake them to make the snow float around in there.

"Hm... This is quite the wonderful little trinket. It shows the beauty of snow, even where there's no snow to be found. This may sell..." Queen Elfrau mumbled as she gazed at the snow globe even more intently than the two kids. Her expression was scary. It kind of reminded me of Guildmaster Relisha.

I had a feeling Elfrau would probably begin producing snow globes at some point in the near future.

◇ ◇ ◇

"Ugh... Why do I have to be here? This suuucks!"

At least I've got my phone, I can still make my deadline... So long as I finish writing this by tomorrow morning, it'll be okay. I'll finish writing my story, get it printed off, and hand it over to my editor. Easy... I don't have much time left, though... Dad ruined everything by taking my phone away, and then I had to deal with all this party nonsense. The costume fitting, the boring old nobles... Ugh!

Calm down, calm down... Geez. I'm making typos now. More typos mean more time spent proofreading. I'm getting angrier and angrier, but what else am I supposed to do?

"Excuse me, are you alone?"

"I am. What do you want?"

Another one. Another champagne-wielding wannabe lover. Great. Just what I need. This is the fourth time tonight. A golden mask this time around. How fancy. I thought I'd escape this by leaving the damn hall. Why are you even talking to me? I'm wearing a mask, hello!

"Would you mind if we chatted a little?"

Chapter II: Masquerade

"I would mind. Begone."

"Hahaha, how standoffish."

Huh? He's staying by my side? I got rid of the other three like this, so why's he hanging around? What's he peeking at, exactly? He's just being a pain in my behind!

"That's an artifact created by Brunhild, isn't it? Are you perhaps from that country?"

"No, I'm not. I'm from... Oh."

"Oh my."

Oh no. I just messed up. These phone things are limited to royals and higher-ups, right? I basically just outed myself as a big deal.

Now I get it... These creeps keep approaching me because of my phone!

"I've had enough of you, sir. Can you go away?"

"Hey, don't be like that. How about we have a little drink together? There's some tasty punch at that table over there."

...Screw it. I'm outta here. Phone off, into pocket. If he won't leave, I will. Off I go and—Did he just grab my arm?

"H-Hey! Let go of me!"

"C'mon, little lady. Just one drink, yeah? I'll make sure we have fun together."

What's with that attitude? I feel sick just looking at him. I can't tell his expression, since the mask's covering his face, but I don't like this one bit... It feels like he's smirking at me. It's scary. He's practically squeezing my arm... I could call for help, or reveal my identity... b-but that'd ruin the party. Or maybe people would think I was being hysterical. Plus, people might think less of my dad if I kick up a fuss here...

"How about we go somewhere a little more private, mm? Relax, okay? Just trust me. We're all friends here."

"Get off me!"

I-I can't overpower him... He's gonna drag me away! Stop! Someone, please help!

"I don't think the lady likes that, mister."

"Hm?"

Who said that? Oh... Another man? This one's in a black mask and a tuxedo...

"Shut up, white knight. Don't get in my way."

"Oh, I don't intend to get in anyone's way. It just seems to me that the lady doesn't want your company. Or am I mistaken?"

He's turning to me now... I'm saved. That's it... Shake your head, shake this guy off, and run to this guy... It'll be okay now.

"Are you alright, milady?"

"Y-Yeah..."

I can barely speak... At least I managed that... Th-That was too scary...

"She doesn't seem to be too fond of your company, friend. Why don't you pursue someone else, hm?"

"Don't just muscle in on my mark, man! You piece of—! Hngh?!"

Wait... what just happened? The golden-masked guy's on the floor already? But I barely saw anything happen... The black-masked man moved, grabbed him by the arm, and then... C-Could it be that... this black-masked man is a trained knight?

"...Do you really want to take this any further, friend?"

"Screw you... Get off me!"

Oh, he actually let him go... Ah, and now the golden-masked man is running off... Thank goodness... If the black-masked guy hadn't shown up just now, ugh... I'm just glad they didn't escalate into a duel. That would've been ugly... Now I just... Ah!

"Careful, ma'am!"

Chapter II: Masquerade

"O-Oh!"

I must've slumped over without realizing... He's holding me now... But I don't feel disgusted like I did when the other guy had me in his grasp... What is this feeling? I've never felt this way before... C-Calm down, let's just sit on this bench.

"Are you okay? Do you need some water?"

"N-No, I'm fine. Thank you for saving me..."

...It feels like he's smiling, but I can't see it because of his mask... How annoying, I want to see his smile... Wait, why do I care?

"Now then, I'll be on my way. Please excuse me, ma'am."

"N-No, wait! C-Could you maybe stay a little longer? H-He might come back..."

Wait... why did I just try to get him to stay? O-Oh, geez... My tone sounded so girly there, too. How embarrassing...

"Very well, then. I'll sit with you a little longer."

"A-Ah...! Thank you so much!"

O-Oh, now he's sitting right next to me... I feel like I should say something. But I can't think of anything... Aren't I a writer? Why can't I come up with something as easy as small talk? U-Uhm Let me think...

"The weather sure is nice today, isn't it?"

"It is."

The weather?! All these ideas in your head... and you bring up the weather?! A-Agh! Another topic! Come on, you can do this! My head's spinning... Why can't I come up with something?! What am I even doing here? Augh, I suck at this... I-I'm pathetic... I can't even hold a conversation. Ugh... Now I'm starting to cry... This is the worst... Huh? He's offering me a handkerchief?

"Don't push yourself. It's okay. I'll stay here as long as you want."

"Sh-Showwy..."

He probably thinks I'm crying about the man from before. Well, I'll wipe my tears with the handkerchief, at least... It'd be rude to reject his offer... Maybe I'll just stay sitting here all night... Maybe gazing up at the sky from here isn't all that bad...

◇ ◇ ◇

"Ah. Excuse me a moment."

I was talking to a few other world leaders, but my smartphone suddenly started going off. It was due to a text message, apparently. I shuffled off to a less crowded corner to check it out.

Let's see here... Huh, Shizuku sent me something? Why's she sending me texts now, of all times?

Shizuku was one of the three kunoichi girls under Tsubaki's command. She was also attending the party. I gave the message a look, out of curiosity.

The message header read "Interesting Find," and had a picture attached to it. The image showed a woman in a peach-colored dress and a red domino mask. At a glance, she looked completely ordinary... What exactly was so interesting about her?

"Hm? What's got your face so weird-looking?"

I looked up from the picture and saw Elze walking over to me... I didn't think my face looked especially weird, but Elze probably had a better grasp of it than I did.

"Oh, nothing in particular. I just got this weird text."

I didn't have anything to hide, so I showed the image to Elze. I thought perhaps a woman's set of eyes might notice something I hadn't.

"Those boobs... They're a little big, aren't they? Padded, perhaps?"

Chapter II: Masquerade

"...That's a pretty random observation, but okay."

Elze stared at the image with curious eyes. Sure, the lady's boobs were big, but that couldn't have been the reason...

Then again, Shizuku's boobs are pretty lacking, same as Elze's, so...

"Yeowch!"

"Were you thinking something rude just now?"

Augh! My arm! You're gonna break it! Guh... My wives are getting way too good at reading my mind. Bah, whatever. I'm not gonna call her in the middle of a party, so I'll just go down and find her.

Fortunately, my clothes were fancy, so all I needed to do was slip on a mask to blend in with all the others down there.

"I'll be back soon, alright?"

"H-Hold up! I wanna tag along!"

...She's that keen to escape her social obligations, huh? I can understand it to an extent, but you should at least try a little harder...

I glanced back at Elze, who seemed to be a single step away from begging. Her eyes were pleading.

"Pleaaaaaase. Just for a little while?"

"...Fine."

"Woo!"

Damn you, Elze. You know I can't say no when you make a face like that... When'd you get so good at using your womanly wiles, anyway?

I felt a little bad about leaving the other girls behind, but I figured it wouldn't hurt to take only Elze if we weren't out long. Right as we turned to leave the gathering, Sakura suddenly shuffled toward me at a rapid pace.

"...No fair... You can't just sneak off... Take me too..."

"You heard us, huh?"

"Hehehe... You know my ears are the best in the world... That's your fault, Grand Duke."

Sakura had a smug expression on her face as she said that. It was pretty cute, honestly. She was right, though. Her heightened hearing had manifested as a trait because she benefited from my divinity.

"I wanna get out of here for a little while, anyway... The overlord won't leave me alone..."

"Ah... That makes sense. He keeps trying to butt in under the pretense of national interest, I bet."

It was a rare opportunity for the overlord to talk freely with his daughter in an official capacity, so I couldn't exactly blame him for trying...

"Shall we go, then? Before the overlord finds us, I mean."

"Yep."

I hoped that the overlord wouldn't be mad at me for whisking his daughter away, but part of me felt it was already much too late for that.

I triggered [**Teleport**] and transported the three of us to the first floor. It wasn't necessarily a problem, but Sakura and Elze looked a little too flashy in their dresses, so I used [**Mirage**] to make their looks more subdued.

"Now then, Shizuku..."

I used my phone's search function to trace her, and it told me she was out in the courtyard. It was hard to identify people because of the masks, so my phone definitely helped.

We walked into a nearby corridor and headed out into the main ballroom, making our way past the dancers until we were out in the garden area. As we walked, a male guest attempted to approach Elze.

Chapter II: Masquerade

She spotted him and clung to my arm, shutting him down before he even had a shot.

"I-It's better if we walk like this, okay? We're married, so it's not weird!" Elze couldn't help but blush as she spoke. She seemed to have forgotten that this was a matchmaking party, so there'd be no way for onlookers to tell we were married... But I didn't really mind, to be honest.

"Me too..." Sakura mumbled as she grabbed my unaccosted side. I hoped people didn't get a bad impression, especially since we were all anonymous.

Out in the courtyard and garden area, the attendees seemed to be enjoying themselves. Princess Reliel wasn't in the spot I'd seen her at earlier, though. Wherever she went, hopefully she didn't bump into Emperor Refreese... Didn't want him catching her on her phone.

"Oho, that's Shizuku over there."

"Is it? I can't tell because of the mask..."

The girl standing by the water fountain was Shizuku, there was no doubt about it. Or at least, that was what my gut told me. The disruptive effects of the mask were still in place, so I used my divine sight to confirm.

"Psst. Shizuku."

"Hm? Who's saying my name out here...? Ah! Your highness!"

I quickly slipped my mask off, revealing my identity to the kunoichi. The mask couldn't be knocked off or forced off, but you were capable of removing it yourself fairly easily.

"I got your text. Ah, Elze and Sakura tagged along as well."

"Oh, I see. Sorry to bother you..."

"It's fine. I felt like coming down anyway. What's the deal with the person you buzzed me about?"

"Look over there."

I followed her gaze and saw a group of around five people. There was a woman there, wearing the same peach dress I'd seen in the photo. Her blonde hair was tied up in a bun. Age-wise, she didn't look all that older than me. Early twenties, most likely. She wore a pearl necklace about her neck and had a pair of sapphire earrings. She seemed like a fairly ordinary woman, all things considered... Though she definitely had a large pair of boobs on her...

"What's so interesting about her, exactly?"

"Don't you see it? Look, when I go out and spy in other nations, I often have to disguise myself to get information."

That's true, I remember you being good at disguising in general. In fact, I'm pretty sure I've seen it firsthand. It's crazy how well she can disguise herself without using magic...

"Disguising isn't just about your clothing. It involves adjusting your manners, your gestures, and the way you speak. The slightest mistake can expose you, after all. That's why I've found myself fixated on the mannerisms of other people, and... I noticed there's something up with that woman."

Upon Shizuku's insistence, I took a closer look at the woman. Nothing really stood out, but... there was something a little off about her. Still, I couldn't place it.

"...She's too pretty and proper."

"Pretty? But she's wearing a mask."

"She doesn't mean her looks, Touya. She means her motions. There's no deviation when she moves. She always makes the exact same gestures in the exact same way. It's like she's repeating them over and over again."

Elze's words prompted me to take a closer look, which clued me in on the issue. The way she spoke, the way she laughed, and the way she gestured or moved her body all felt rather rigid and pre-prepared.

Chapter II: Masquerade

Though, there was always the possibility that we were jumping to conclusions for no reason.

"...Grand Duke... She's not right..."

"Did you notice something, Sakura?"

...Am I really the only one not picking up on this? I've been called slow on the uptake before, but c'mon...

"I can't hear it... Her heartbeat, I mean..."

"Huh?!"

No heartbeat? Don't tell me she's a zombie or something... No, she's moving too fast to be one of those... Plus, she's talking casually, too. Can't be undead. What the hell is she, then...? No heartbeat, but walking and talking like a person. Life-like, but not actually alive...

At that moment, a thought popped into my mind.

Don't tell me she's...

I used my divine sight to see through her mask. A beautiful face lurked beneath, there was no contesting that. But then I focused my gaze even harder, peering beneath her flesh. Ordinarily, I hated focusing my divine sight in this way, since I didn't like seeing the people around me as horrible walking skeletons with flesh and muscle clinging on to them, but I had to test my theory...

"I knew it!"

"Knew what? Did you see something?" Elze asked. She'd stared into my eyes as they flashed gold, so she clearly knew what I'd just done.

"That's no human. That's a Gollem."

Both of my wives stood utterly dumbfounded, confused by the revelation... That woman was a Gollem. Namely, a simulacrum model built to imitate a human.

There were many different types of Gollem out in the world. Autonomous models, who acted on their own, were the most prevalent type. However, even those were fairly diverse. There were humanoid models, miniaturized bipedal models, and animal models. The crown Gollems and Elluka's Gollem, Fenrir, fit into that category. They were contracted to a master and performed better based on how well they meshed with a person. Some could talk, like Fenrir, but those were rarer than others.

Then there were the vehicular models. They were the kind you could ride inside, controlling them either directly or indirectly. Some semi-autonomous models could move on their own. They included things like tanks, trailers, minibuses, and most any carrier with legs or wheels. Sancho, the merchant from Allent, had one of them. His was a large bus shaped like a crab. Those types didn't need a contract, but they did require keys to operate. Some could be found in ancient ruins, but they were considerably rarer.

Drone models came next. They were similar to the vehicular ones, except they were controlled either via remote control or voice commands. They had no will of their own and couldn't make decisions for themselves, so they were generally lacking in skill compared to autonomous Gollems. Military Gollems fell into this category.

Ordinance models were after that. They were Gollems that could be worn by their masters or wielded like weapons. Some could transform, while others had rigid shapes. They could take the form of either armor or weapons. Some even resembled power armor like in sci-fi. They were essentially a derivative of the autonomous models, really. I'd fought someone who'd used one back in Isengard, but I couldn't remember much about it. Most of them were mass-produced, which was why they were given the factory-type designation.

Chapter II: Masquerade

Last, but certainly not least, there were the Simulacrums. They were allegedly created in the image of humans to act as companions, but the truth of their origins wasn't entirely clear. My Gollems from the etoile series fell into this category. Though Ruby, Saph, and Emerl didn't really resemble humans in appearance.

Still, the body double the witch-king of Isengard had used looked just like a real human. Same with Norn's maid, Elfrau... which meant some models were truly indistinguishable from human beings. Such models were insanely rare, though...

What's she doing at this masquerade?

"What will you do, Grand Duke...?"

"What can I do...?"

"It's not like we have a 'no Gollems' rule, right?"

Fair point, Elze, but... I doubt she's here to find love.

It was true that she hadn't done anything dangerous, but that didn't rule out the possibility of her being here for nefarious purposes.

"Maybe I should inform Emperor Refreese... It's his party, after all..."

Oh, but first...

I quickly employed [**Drawing**] to sketch out the face I'd seen beneath the mask. If I asked around, I could probably get an answer about her identity.

I left Elze, Shizuku, and Sakura behind to keep an eye out, then used [**Teleport**] to report my findings to the emperor.

"There's no doubt in my mind... This is the face of Miss Imelda, but... I had no idea she was a Gollem. Are you sure there's no mistake here, Grand Duke?" Lucrecion, former prince of Gardio, now count of Lowe, looked utterly baffled as he glanced over the paper.

"Unfortunately it seems to be true... Did you know about this, Emperor Gardio?"

I turned to Lancelet Rig Gardio, the young emperor standing next to Lucrecion.

"I can't say I did, no. I don't understand..." Emperor Gardio replied as he shook his head.

I glanced over at the pope of Ramissh, who responded with a little nod. That meant her mystic eye had told her he was telling the truth. That was a relief, at least.

If that was the case, then... She could have been planted by her family. Imelda Tryus was the daughter of a noble in Gardio.

"I can think of three possibilities here, darling. The first is that Imelda was a Gollem from the very start, meaning she never existed to begin with. Then there's the second possibility, which is that Imelda was born as a person, but she got swapped out for a Gollem at some point. That's the idea I find most plausible. Though I don't know if the switch was to infiltrate this party or the Tryus family at large. And the final option is... that my husband is wrong, and she's just a normal person..."

"It can't be that, Leen! Sakura couldn't hear her heartbeat, remember?"

"I know, I know... It's just a possibility, silly," Leen replied. She couldn't help but grin as I grumbled at her hypothesis.

"I've known Imelda since I was a child, so I don't think it's the first one. Gollems don't grow like people, after all. Therefore, we must conclude that Imelda was a real person at one point."

The emperor was a member of high society, so it made sense that he'd have met nobles like the Tryus family throughout his life. That meant there'd been a switch at some point. Was this the work

Chapter II: Masquerade

of the Tryus family, or a third party...? Was the original Imelda even alive anymore?

"We should take the fake Imelda into custody. Gardio can't overlook this."

"Hrm... As emperor of Refreese, I understand your feelings, but making a big fuss in the middle of the party could be messy. We don't want to create an incident."

"We can't leave her as-is, either. It's true that Gollems of her model don't have skills and aren't as combat-capable as others, but they can still be dangerous. We must act while there's still time..."

Emperor Gardio and Emperor Refreese both seemed troubled by the matter. I could understand why. It was a bad idea to sour the evening with a big, flashy arrest... but it'd be even worse for Emperor Refreese if it called the party off, since he was doing this for his daughter.

Weapons weren't permitted in the ballroom, and my previous scan of her body didn't reveal any hidden weapons, either. But if she wanted to, I was sure she could kill at least one person around her... You could say the same of just about any attendee, though.

"Hey, darling."

"Hm? What's up?"

Leen beckoned to me, then whispered a suggestion into my ear.

Oho. I like that. It might actually work...

"I'll be back soon, okay?"

"Hehehe... Good luck, darling."

I nodded to Leen, then used [**Teleport**] to return to Elze, Sakura, and Shizuku.

"...All's well that ends well, eh?" Elze said, grinning as she glanced at Imelda, who was now slung over my shoulder.

Leen's plan was simple enough. First, Sakura and Elze would go over and get the Gollem's attention. Then, while she was distracted, I'd use [Invisible] to sneak up behind her, touch her neck, and use [Cracking] to sever the neural magic circuits connecting her Q-Crystal to her brain. With the connection severed, she'd be unable to move. Then, once she's collapsed, Elze and Sakura would get close to her and mention how she looked faint or anemic. At that point, I'd come back, fully visible again, and valiantly offer to carry her to the infirmary on my back. Mission accomplished.

Even though she was a Gollem, she barely weighed anything at all.

These types are authentic, huh? It feels like I'm actually carrying a girl... The two things pressed up against my back are so accurate... Heh... I wonder what they're made of...

"Grand Duke... Are you thinking something indecent...?"

"What?! Me?! No way! Not at a time like this!"

"That's right. Touya wouldn't be thinking anything about sizes or softness when he has his two beautiful wives right next to him, isn't that right?"

"Th-That's right!"

Elze looked terrifying.

I'm not comparing, I'm just curious!

I was sweating buckets, but I managed to covertly open up a [Gate] to the castle infirmary.

◇ ◇ ◇

As far as this Gollem was concerned, I needed an expert opinion. Thus, I contacted Babylon and called in our engineer, Elluka. Doc Babylon herself accompanied her, unfortunately. Fenrir was doing a routine maintenance checkup, so he stayed home.

Chapter II: Masquerade

When I returned to the Refreese infirmary with the scholarly duo, I found Lucrecion, Emperor Gardio, and Emperor Refreese waiting for me, along with their guards.

Imelda (or at least the Gollem that resembled her) remained on the bed. She was still unconscious. She really did look human at a glance.

Elluka forced open the Gollem's eyelids, shining a light into them. She then traced her fingers along her throat.

"This is definitely a simulacrum Gollem. Quite the elaborate one, too. One from the fleurage series, perhaps? Yes, it seems so..." Elluka mumbled as she rubbed a damp cloth against the Gollem's collarbone, revealing a faint flower-like mark. Apparently, it'd been covered up by some makeup.

Next, Elluka took hold of Imelda's wrist. She used a thin needle-like object to prod at the skin, which made a little hissing sound ring out. Within seconds, the back of Imelda's hand opened. Inside were various transparent threads of light flowing along her body, as well as a little round spellstone aspected to water. There was no doubt about it... This girl was absolutely a Gollem.

As an aside, I had Kohaku use a group of summoned beasts to covertly check for any other Gollems at the party. They were the best ones for the job, since they could easily identify non-humans by scent. Thankfully, there weren't any more of them.

"So she's really a Gollem, then..."

"But why? What was the purpose in sending such a life-like Gollem to our party?"

Lucrecion looked completely confused, while Emperor Refreese glanced suspiciously toward Emperor Gardio. The Ramissh pope had already cleared Gardio's ruler of suspicion, but he'd still brought the Gollem with him.

"I'm having this investigated at once. I've already sent a team to the Tryus estate in our capital. We'll get to the bottom of this…"

As Emperor Gardio spoke, his phone began to vibrate. He stood up and walked a short distance away, talking to the person on the other side. The mass-produced smartphones had been presented to the rulers of every nation, and they came in handy during incidents like this. I'd heard a lot of stories about how rulers, nobles, and cabinet members had become a lot busier since they'd received their smartphones, but it was an unavoidable situation.

Eventually, Emperor Gardio returned to us.

"That was my investigation team. They found Ms. Imelda in the closet of her bedroom. She wasn't injured, she's simply unconscious right now. Though I think we can safely conclude that the Gollem swap had nothing to do with her family."

Hrm… There's the chance her family did all that to cover this up, though. Then again, why would they?

"Tell me more about the Tryus family, would you?"

"They've been loyal to Gardio for generations. The head of their family is also a stand-up gentleman. He's in charge of all educational institutions in the capital."

"E-Er, lemme uh… Sorry, let me add something here. When I was crown prince, I met Earl Tryus many times. He was always a true gentleman who took his duties very seriously. I doubt he was involved in this situation, personally."

Emperor Gardio's comment was followed up by Lucrecion's own account. Given both of their testimonies, I had to assume that the earl was innocent. For now, at least…

Elze quietly looked over Imelda's face as she "slept."

"…Can Gollems like this have their faces changed easily or something?"

Chapter II: Masquerade

"To an extent, yes. While humans can augment their looks with makeup, Gollems of this type can tweak their skeletal structure, facial shape, proportions, and so on."

Elze and Sakura quietly stared at Imelda, their eyes glazed over with some measure of annoyance as they took in Elluka's explanation.

"...No fair."

"It's not fair..."

...Please stop worrying about her breasts. Ugh, this is a pain in the ass. Gotta change the topic somehow.

I turned to Emperor Gardio, hoping to somehow change the flow of the conversation.

"S-So, you had no idea she was a fake? Wasn't there any difference in her mannerisms?"

"Miss Imelda is known as something of an introvert. In fact, I haven't actually seen her in five years, so pretty much everything about her was different. I just took it as a given that she was the real deal, as I had no reason to suspect otherwise."

Not very sociable, huh? That could be why she was targeted, right? It would make sense to switch someone who wasn't very well-connected.

"Hm... We should get the information from the Gollem itself, I say." Doc Babylon stated as she rolled her pipe around in her mouth, looking over the sleeping Gollem all the while.

"Is it safe to reboot her? Might she just attack us?"

"It's always a possibility, but the fleurage Gollems aren't known for their combat capabilities. If you're worried, we could tie her up."

After Babylon voiced her concern, Elluka produced a length of rope from her toolbox. Why did she have that on hand, exactly?

"Can't we just override her master control authority before waking her back up?" I threw my own suggestion out there for them to consider. If we bound her to a new master, then we'd be able to gain any information we needed and there'd be no risk of her attacking us.

"Hmhmhm... So you want us to take out her G-Cube, Touya? That's what you're saying?"

"Huh? I mean, yeah, but..."

"No, no. I totally get it. I understand. I wanna see what kind of boobs a Gollem like this has, too."

"Wh—?! That's not what I meant! Don't lump me in with you!"

Sure, Doc Babylon was right. To access a Gollem's G-cube, you needed to open a hatch on its chest, but that was just a means to an end! I wasn't thinking about it like that!

"...Touya, sweetie... Can we have a little chat?"

"...Grand Duke... You can't act like this in front of your wives..."

"W-Wait! Both of you, no! Please!"

Elze and Sakura both grabbed me from either side, squeezing me just a little too tightly for comfort.

Just then, Elluka came in from behind Doc Babylon and delivered a swift karate chop to her head.

"Hey, Regina. No teasing the newlyweds, yeah?"

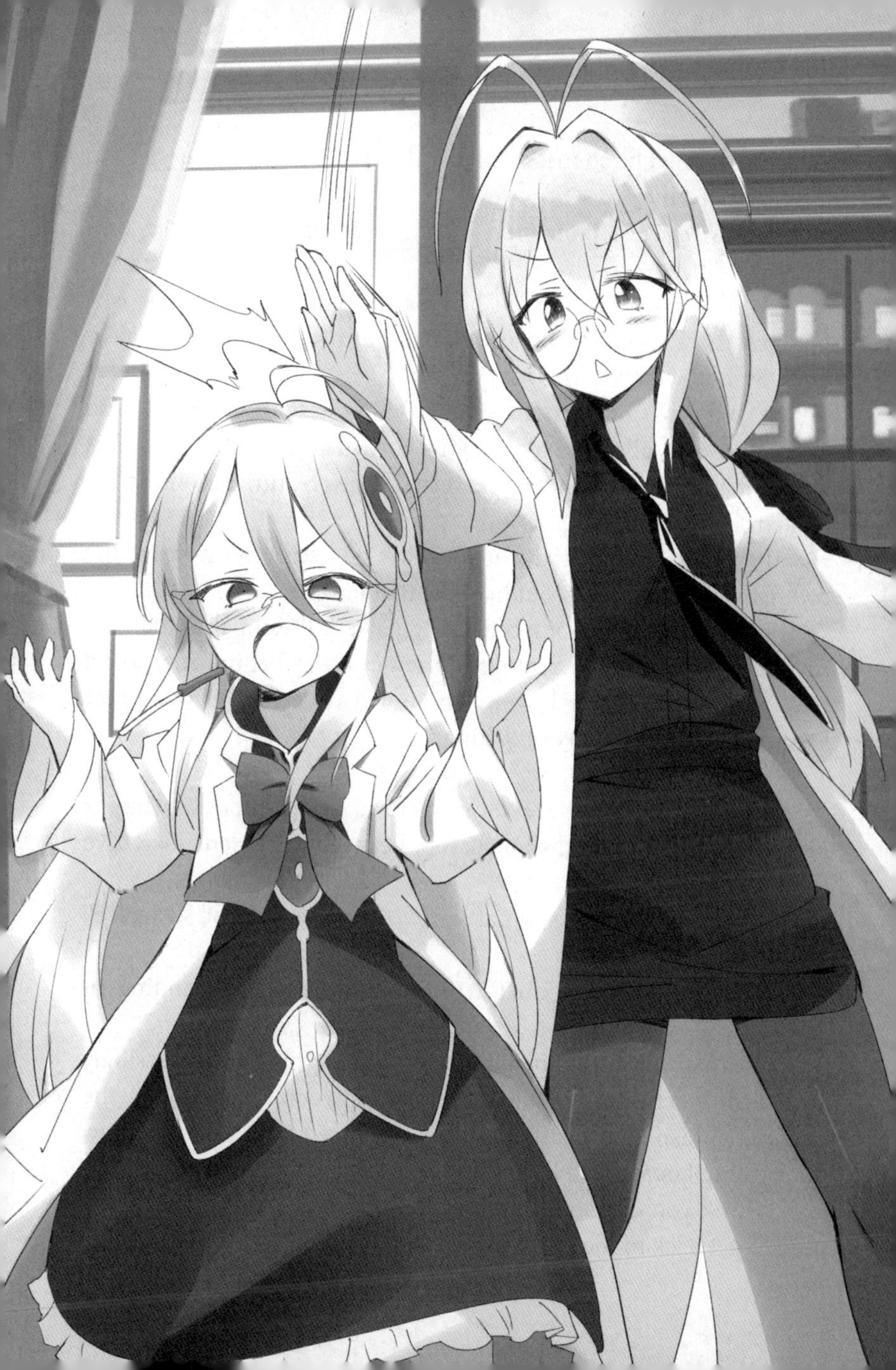

"Geez, don't be so mean... I just thought I'd add a little spice to their married life."

That's no spice, you little witch... it's poison! Don't toy with me, dammit!

"Well, I can make myself her master temporarily. Fenrir isn't here, so there shouldn't be any signal jamming issues. Look away, boys. Synthetic or not, this isn't for you."

At Elluka's command, I, Emperor Refreese, Emperor Gardio, Lucrecion, and all the male knights turned to face the wall. This was probably better than that perverted little creature becoming the Gollem's master, at least.

Part of me wondered if it wouldn't be better to just leave the room, but apparently it wouldn't take that long.

I heard the sound of fabric being parted. Presumably, that was Imelda's clothing being removed. The door was behind me, so I'd have to turn around to leave... There was no escape at this point. I would have to listen to everything.

"Whoa!"

"Hot damn. These are some melons, huh? Almost as big as Flora's... Hm... Soft to the touch, too. Very realistic. Here, Elze, give them a squeeze."

"A-Ah! W-Wow... What are these made of, exactly?! They're unreal!"

"Heavy... Guh... I can't win... Not with these standing in my way..."

The conversation behind me was growing increasingly awkward. I definitely should have left the room while I had the chance. It wasn't too bad for me, but I glanced to the side and saw poor young Lucrecion. He was burning red right up to his ears.

"Think you can speed up a little? The emperor and the others need to get back to the party, remember?"

Chapter II: Masquerade

"Oh yeah, you're right. Okie... Lessee here... Open sesame."

After Elluka spoke, I heard the sound of hissing air. She must have opened the chest hatch. Seconds later, I heard the sounds of mechanical tinkering. Presumably, that was the sound of them removing the G-Cube and overwriting the master control.

Even if they placed the G-Cube back after rewriting it, Imelda wouldn't wake up until I used [**Cracking**] to repair the pathways I'd severed.

"There we go. Now we just need to dress her again... Hmm... We can forget the bra, though. Too much effort."

"Hey now..." I voiced my irritation, still facing the wall. Poor young Lucrecion was mumbling to himself. His eyes were shut and he was doing his best to drown out whatever he was hearing. I was legitimately concerned for his mental health after all this.

"Fiiine. I understand how it could be damaging to the young folk. Let's get this thing back on her, then. Ugh... How heavy... Squishy, too... These heaving breasts... So voluptuous. My hands sink right into them..."

Please stop narrating. Please. Stop. Narrating.

When the girls eventually finished redressing Imelda, we turned back around. I glanced over at the Gollem. She looked about the same as before, though her necklace was now on the bedside countertop and her outfit looked a little more disheveled.

"Alright, Touya. Can you reconnect her neural lines?"

"Sure thing."

I put my hand on the back of Imelda's neck and activated my [**Cracking**] spell to reconnect what I'd severed earlier. Her entire body suddenly shuddered and her eyes shot open. But those eyes of hers seemed completely devoid of light. Her gaze was muddled and unfocused. Her entire body began convulsing as if she was having a seizure.

"I-Is she okay?"

"Give her a minute. Her neural pathways just got restored, so she's processing. She'll be okay soon."

If you say so... It's a little scary seeing such a life-like Gollem thrash around, though.

Eventually, Imelda stopped convulsing and opened her mouth. What came out of it was a cold, mechanical voice.

"Model Number FR-006, Hydrangea has recovered from an unexpected shutdown. No operational issues detected. Master registration has been modified. Previous master records will be expunged from—"

"Crap! Touya, sever her circuits again! Quick!"

"Huh?! O-Okay!"

I hurriedly touched my hand to her neck and reversed the last thing I did with **[Cracking]**. Imelda immediately slumped back, as if fainting.

"Records... to be... expunnnggged..."

Though she'd stopped moving, she still spoke slowly.

"I screwed up. I didn't think they'd tamper with her Q-Crystal, but it makes sense if you consider her a spy model. It's only natural to put some kind of insurance policy in place if you're using a Gollem for recon. Damn it, why didn't I think of this earlier?" Elluka growled quietly, furrowing her brow. I wasn't sure what she meant.

"Legacy Gollems have their memories stored in the Q-Crystal in their foreheads, yeah? The crystal's like their brain. It has several layers of memories, including personal memory, foundational memory for behavior control, and accumulated knowledge. You can't erase stuff like their base directive to obey their masters or their self-preservation instinct, since that stuff's written in on their most fundamental levels. But the data pertaining to their masters,

Chapter II: Masquerade

personal memories, and directives could be stored in a separate block..."

"Ohhh, I see. And that block could be easily erased under the right circumstances, hm? Seems like this Gollem was set to erase her memories upon having her ownership transferred. Likely a defensive mechanism for whoever sent her." Doc Babylon said, nodding to Elluka with a grin on her face.

Huh? So she's programmed to reset her memory?!

"This is most abnormal, though. On a human level, it'd be tantamount to erasing all the experiences you've had over the years. On top of that, there are only a handful of people who could even set about tampering with Q-Crystals to begin with. This is quite concerning."

Legacy Gollems were usually found in ancient ruins, having remained dormant for many years. The general memory portions of their Q-Crystals would be the first thing to go after being inactive for so long, so most excavated Gollems had no memories of the ancient eras in which they'd been built. Some of the higher-tier models, like the crowns, kept their memories intact. Yumina's crown, Albus, was like that.

In Albus' case, if anyone other than the person who controlled it opened up its hatch, it would trigger its reset ability. It was a similar principle of self-preservation.

"...Does that mean we're back to square one?"

"I'm really sorry. This was a total flub on my part. I should've thought about this before rushing on ahead."

Hrmm... I'm the one who suggested taking ownership of her, though. I feel a little responsible.

"But this might help us narrow down the culprit. There are very few Gollem technologists who can actually tamper with Q-Crystals like this. They could've easily been blackmailed or threatened into assisting, but..."

"Then you think it could be one of the five great gollemancers?"

Elluka nodded in response to Emperor Gardio's question. Apparently, Lucrecion could tell how confused I was, as he began explaining.

"In our world... oh, uh... our continent... there are five incredibly talented Gollem technologists who are known as the five great gollemancers. Miss Elluka here is one of them! She's known as the Restoration Queen. There are only three others at the moment, however, since one of them died recently."

"Oh, really?"

"Why do you sound so surprised? You caused his death, didn't you?"

"Huh?! I did?!"

Elluka's words confused the hell out of me. When had I done anything like that?

"The witch-king of Isengard, genius. That old fart was one of my foremost peers."

...*Oh, yeah. That'll do it. I guess it makes sense that he'd be one of the top five Gollem technologists in the Reverse World, especially when you take into account that massive Gollem he had control over. Plus, he had that sophisticated body double as well.*

"Who are the others, aside from you and the witch-king?"

"Well, there's the professor. You've met him before, Touya."

She was referring to the old man who'd been kidnapped by Yulong. It was true that he was pretty talented. He'd been able to create a lot out of very little. I heard he'd gone traveling after

Chapter II: Masquerade

that incident, but I wondered where he'd gone after that. Had he been captured and made to work for evil again, perhaps?

"I don't think he's involved here. He's currently in Panaches, helping their royal family out with some maintenance work."

Oh, so he's with pumpkin-pants. Gotcha.

The blue crown, Distortion Blau, apparently needed pretty intense maintenance. It made sense that they'd seek an expert like him for that.

The number of people who could tweak legacy Gollems was limited, and the number of people who could tweak crowns was an even smaller subset of that number. Even Nia relied on Elluka to fix up Rouge when it got all busted up.

"And the other two?"

"I'm not sure where either of them are. The Maestro is a bit of a misanthrope, so he's pretty secluded from all the kingdoms and empires... And the other one is, well... more of a group than a single person. They're called the Seekers and they roam around, so they're hard to pinpoint..."

Either way, it stood to reason that one of them was involved in the great Imelda switcheroo. And I couldn't discount that they'd been threatened or blackmailed, either.

"That's the only lead we have for now... I suppose we should at least consider ourselves lucky that no damage was done." Emperor Refreese said as he let out a small, regretful sigh. I tried getting more information from Elluka so I could look up the other technologists with my smartphone, but I got no hits. They probably had some kind of protective measures to keep tracking-oriented Gollems from finding them.

I could understand not wanting to stand out. If you were someone that skilled, then every country would want you. I definitely couldn't bear being hounded sometimes.

"Nothing else we can do, then. We'll have to look into this later. For now, I still have a party to host."

"O-Oh, uhm…"

As Emperor Refreese got up to leave, Lucrecion raised his hand. I wondered what he wanted.

"I-I might be able to help get some information."

"Hm? How do you…? Oh, I see!"

I'd completely forgotten, but the former crown prince had a mystic eye. He could view the residual memories on an object that were left behind when someone had touched it. It was also known as psychometry. If he used that power, he could maybe see who touched Imelda. Even if he only gave us fragments of information to work with, it was better than nothing.

"You could've mentioned this sooner…"

"My mystic eye doesn't always work, and it usually needs me to touch a major area of focus… s-so I probably have to touch around Miss Imelda's hatch…"

"Oh. Her boobs. I get it now. That makes sense… You're a young man, after all."

"Wh-What does that mean?! Aren't you younger?!"

Doc Babylon, who looked very much like a little girl, smirked mischievously over at Lucrecion. The poor kid had no idea that she was the oldest person in the room.

I wasn't entirely sure about having Lucrecion touch up her chest, but it wasn't like she was human or anything. It couldn't be sexual harassment if the target was an object, right?

Chapter II: Masquerade

Emperor Gardio was a little more reluctant, however. He'd been entrusted by the former emperor to look out for Lucrecion, so something like this was... well... indecent. It was a tricky situation.

"Then do it this way." Elze untied the ribbon that was binding her hair and used it to cover Lucrecion's eyes.

His ability was called a mystic eye, but he didn't actually need to see to use it. So long as he could touch, even being blindfolded wouldn't deter him.

Emperor Gardio seemed a little more okay with this approach, too.

"Alrighty... Men, turn around."

"Ugh..."

As I turned around, I heard Lucrecion mutter something about something being surprisingly soft. I began to regret everything all at once. I wondered if this really was a good idea. A blindfold might just make his imagination run wild, after all.

"Ah! I see it! I can... Oh!" Lucrecion said, seemingly getting a grasp on something. Hopefully, his mystic eye wasn't picking up the intense, surely lascivious thoughts that Babylon had had upon touching that chest earlier... I didn't want her corruptive influence ruining further generations, especially such an innocent young man.

"I didn't see everything, but I caught something."

As I quietly worried, the psychometry session came to an end. I swiftly turned back around. Lucrecion's blindfold was off and Imelda's clothes were fixed up again.

"So? What'd you see?"

"What I saw... or felt, rather... was brief. Voices, flashes of imagery in my head. But what stood out the most was a pile of Gollems... and two crossed hammers on a flag."

"What?!" Emperor Gardio seemed concerned by the news, and Lucrecion merely responded with a somber nod.

"Hammers on a flag?"

"...Dumbass. Aren't you a world leader? Why don't you know your national flags?" Elluka complained as she scowled at me.

"...My bad."

Gimme a break... There are a lot of countries, you know?

"Only one nation has a flag like that. It's the nation right next to Gardio... One that was second only to Isengard when it came to magical engineering..."

"Gandhilis, the Steel Nation..." Lucrecion's quiet words echoed out into the room as if to finish Emperor Gardio's sentence.

◇ ◇ ◇

"Gandhilis? The Steel Nation?"

It was a country to the east of Gardio and south of Allent, if I recalled correctly. I hadn't been there yet, but the crossed hammers were a feature of its flag.

"Gandhilis is home to many mines and natural mineral deposits. That's why it's known as the Steel Nation. They have plenty of trade with Gardio. Most of our Gollems are made from their mineral exports, in fact."

A mining nation, huh? Makes sense. You need a good deal of rare metals like adamantite and orichalcum to manufacture Gollems. Wait, are there any orichalcum Gollems on the western continent? If not, that might be a good thing for the east to start exporting. Wait, what's Gandhilis' relationship with Allent and Gardio, anyway? I've never heard much about that...

As if picking up my curiosity, Emperor Gardio spoke up.

Chapter II: Masquerade

"We're neighbors, so we obviously have some formal relationship... but I'm not so sure it's friendly. We've had a few clashes in the past, after all. Count Lowe's grandfather was quite a brutal man. He took covert action against Gandhilis and its mines many times."

So it's like that, huh? That old emperor sure was a piece of work... Didn't he team up with Isengard to invade Lowe, too? He's the maternal grandfather of the current emperor and the non-blood-related paternal grandfather to Lucrecion... What a mess he's left behind.

As I quietly mused to myself, Emperor Gardio spoke up. He sounded troubled.

"I still don't understand any of this..."

"What's wrong?"

"Well, the iron king's a pretty friendly, respectable man. I never really took him for a schemer. But I suppose any nation would have subterfuge or intelligence divisions."

That much was true. Even Brunhild had Tsubaki and her agents. Hell, they were at the party! Belfast also had that secret agent unit, Espion, which reported directly to the king. I wondered if any of those agents were in attendance.

Information, ultimately, was a weapon, being a schemer had nothing to do with it, and sometimes you needed it to protect your country.

That being said, we had no idea if Gandhilis' iron king was involved in this. It could've easily been a member of his cabinet or a prominent minister.

"This was no attempt at subterfuge or an assassination. A Gollem like that isn't capable of much more than intel-gathering.

Still, we can't overlook the fact that the real Imelda suffered as a result."

That's not entirely true. The capability part, I mean. She could've sabotaged something or poisoned someone... Still, just about anyone in attendance could've done that, so it's a moot point.

Elze turned to look at the Gollem Imelda.

"Hmm... But they went out of their way not to hurt the real one, right?"

"What do you mean?"

"Well, think about it, Touya. Since they didn't kill her, it would've been obvious that there was a fake Imelda sent to this party. The real one would wake up eventually, yeah? I'm saying it would've made way more sense to kill her."

Now that you mention it, that is weird. They don't care about being found out right after the party? Just offing the real Imelda and burying her somewhere would've been the safer play, since people would assume she went missing right after the party. Maybe they didn't want to kill her? Or maybe... they were ordered not to? I wonder what the deal is here...

Emperor Refreese turned to Emperor Gardio.

"How do you plan to proceed with Gandhilis?"

"It's a difficult situation. The mystic eye's testimony isn't really hard proof, nor would it be enough to level an accusation. We also have no physical evidence that Gandhilis is responsible."

"But the flag the boy saw must have been Gandhilis', no?"

It'll probably be worth checking again, just to be safe. If we end up accusing them and they're not related to it, that'd be a whole mess of trouble.

Chapter II: Masquerade

"It definitely is. I saw that flag many times as a young boy. But you're right, there's no hard evidence. Me seeing that flag doesn't mean it was Gandhilise people behind it, even. That said…"

"Hm? Was there anything else?"

"There was a voice. I could barely make it out, but it was a woman's. The words I could make out included, er… 'Emperor Gardio,' 'in the way,' and 'must be eliminated'…"

"What?!"

Eliminated? Are they planning on assassinating the emperor?! It's not super unusual for heads of state to be targeted like that, I guess… I've had it happen to me a few times. But thankfully, there aren't just shadowy assassination squads. Each nation has its secretive defense forces as well. It's not that easy to kill a world leader. Even right now, there are personal guards for the royals in here. Emperor Gardio has protective Gollems with him too. Something tells me that nurse sitting in the corner of the room probably isn't a pushover, either. I bet she could kick the Imelda Gollem's ass if it tried anything.

"Are there any women in high positions in Gandhilis?"

"Not as far as I recall, no… But this makes me uneasy. The woman he heard may not even be related to the iron king. She could be anyone."

Hrm… We don't really have a leg to stand on here. At the very least, we know this is likely an assassination attempt… and the person behind it had the real Imelda incapacitated.

"Ugh. We can't make a case against Gandhilis like this. It may be best to simply examine the situation further for the time being."

"That's right. If we keep an eye open and spot signs of civil unrest, we can plan accordingly."

111

At least we had the fake Imelda in our custody. Or, well, in Elluka's custody. Hopefully a more thorough inspection could bring us some more answers.

I sent Babylon, Elluka, and the fake Imelda back to Brunhild before returning to the party. The event continued as usual. Some people coupled up, while others didn't. On the whole, it could be called a modest success.

Personally, I wondered what had happened with Princess Reliel, but I was sure I'd hear about it from her father one way or the other. I didn't expect much from her, though... She'd spent most of the party on her phone from what I'd seen.

Having a daughter sure sounded rough... The fact that I knew I would have at least eight wasn't exactly reassuring, either.

I returned to Brunhild, quietly worrying about my own future as a parent.

Chapter III: Great Expectations

"Why didn't you ask him for his name?"

"Ugh... W-Well, I just didn't think of it... I wanted to, it just... It never ended up happening."

Princess Reliel sat down opposite me. She was clutching a handkerchief in her hand, which was given to her by her black-masked savior. Yumina, Linze, and I were the only ones in the room other than her. The emperor had summoned me here for a private chat, but I hadn't expected this.

Everyone in the ballroom wore masks, so even if you hit it off with someone, you wouldn't know who they were. That was why there was a system in place where you could secretly tell the other person your real name in order to get in contact later.

Of course, that was a bit of an issue. If it was one-sided, then you'd be outing yourself, so the guys were expected to take the lead in that regard. Plus, if you just gave your name out like hotcakes, you'd look pretty desperate.

"Can you do something about this, Touya?"

"Maybe, but I dunno..."

Even though Linze was just about pleading for help, I wasn't entirely sure what to do.

If a black mask's the only clue, that doesn't give me much to go off. We distributed the masks across all the countries, so each nation had at least one black-masked person... Even discounting women from that list, that still leaves no shortage of people.

113

"Oh, we could maybe rule out Xenoahs or Mismede... The person didn't have any beastman traits, right? No tail or horns?"

"Actually, Yumina... some of the black masks I gave out erased beastman features, since that helped keep anonymity."

Upon hearing my response, Yumina's smile vanished.

Look, it's better this way... I don't want people to judge others by appearance alone. Mismedean beastmen, Xenoahs demonkin, or Lassei dragonewts get discriminated against fairly regularly. I want people to pick their partners for their personalities, not their pedigree... Not everyone can retract their horns like Sakura and her half-brothers.

"There's a record of everyone who got the black masks, so I should be able to narrow it down. I'll just have to go over them carefully..." I grumbled quietly as I thumbed over the participant list on my phone. If I questioned them, I wondered if they'd be honest with me... They could have their own agendas, after all.

"...You definitely want me to find the guy?"

"I do. I wish to talk to him again, so please..." Princess Reliel mumbled as she squeezed the handkerchief tightly. She seemed surprisingly desperate.

"If I don't see him again, I won't be able to finish my latest book! I can't make any progress at all because I keep thinking about him! It's interfering with my writing, so please help me get out of this funk!"

...What? This girl's something else, man...

I beckoned Yumina over toward me, whispering to her in a hushed tone of voice.

"What's going on with her, exactly?"

"I'm not sure. I've never seen Reli like this in my life... I don't know if she's realized her own feelings yet."

Chapter III: Great Expectations

This delusional princess... Why can't things be simple with her for once? Still, I guess love can bloom in the strangest of places... Even if this is an especially strange place.

"That person saved her, so I suppose it's natural she'd get hung up over him. I've never heard of Reli being interested in matters of love, so we'll just have to see how things go with her."

"I see... Well, you've known her since you were little, so I'll trust you on this."

"Thank you... I'll have you know I wasn't too different myself."

My wife cast a sly grin in my direction as she spoke. She wasn't technically the one I saved during our first meeting, though... Still, the situation was close enough. Reliel was a princess, much like Yumina, and now it seemed she was facing love for the first time.

I went through the list and narrowed it down to people with black masks, then cut the women out. That still brought the number to thirty-eight, however.

What a pain in the ass.

"We should start with the people we know."

"Mhm. Brunhild's up first, then."

"Let's see... Three Brunhild citizens had black masks. Our knights Lushade, Charon, and... oh, Vice Commander Nikola."

Lushade was a vampire from Xenoahs. The funniest thing about him was that he had an aversion to blood! He was one of the earliest members of our knight order.

He was a bit of a pushover, but also a kind young man for the most part. Well... young man in looks, at least. He was actually over sixty.

Charon was from Belfast, and his parents were pharmacists. He had a great deal of knowledge about medicinal plants and was contributing to our farmland development. Uncle Kousuke, the god of agriculture, had taken quite a shine to him. As a result, he'd received a small amount of agricultural divinity, even if he didn't know it. Though that didn't mean he'd manifest an ability like Yumina's foresight or anything, it just meant that his abilities would be slightly beyond that of his peers.

Nikola needed no introduction, he was the vice commander of the entire knight order. Originally from Mismede, he was a fox beastman.

Wait... Did I give him a race-concealing mask? I can't remember. Well, whatever. Let's go get their alibis... Wait, is alibi the right word? It's not like I'm investigating a crime or anything.

"Lushade and Charon are in the clear..."

"...In the what?" Yumina asked as she tilted her head, apparently curious about my choice of words. I couldn't help but feel like a detective like this.

I didn't want to directly mention princess Reliel, so I simply told Lushade and Charon that a woman had been rescued by a black-masked man, and she wanted to thank him. If either of them had said yes, I'd planned to bring up the handkerchief to test if they were lying or not. I didn't think any of my knights would do that, though.

Lushade apparently spent the evening dancing with a woman, while Charon was too busy eating Refreesian cuisine to care about romance. Obviously I had to take them at their word, but there was no reason not to trust them. They weren't the ones who'd saved the princess. That said, I could've probably stood to put some more rigorous methods in place.

The keither polygraph or the Ramissh pope's mystic eye would probably do the trick, but I didn't feel like invoking those against someone who hadn't done anything wrong.

Chapter III: Great Expectations

Honestly, this whole situation was plain annoying. Just as I was pondering using [**Recall**] to delve into the potential peoples' memories, I felt a gaze burning into me.

"You can't do that, Touya. No using [**Recall**]."

"I-I'd n-never even think of doing that!"

Linze had somehow figured out exactly what I was thinking... She was too damn sharp. In all fairness, [**Recall**] couldn't show me memories that a person wanted to hide, so I couldn't go that route anyway. Though... if I used my divinity to amplify the spell...

N-No, bad Touya. Stop.

I headed out to the training grounds to speak to Nikola. All the knights were hard at work, which was good to know. They were all suffering under the intense training regimen that Moroha had put together, but the hard work was beginning to pay off.

In the early days of this training, I saw plenty of beaten men without any stamina left, but nowadays I barely saw any collapsed guys at all. It was a testament to how well they were doing.

Strength-wise, they were probably all equivalent to red-rank adventurers... But the skill set between knights and adventurers was still pretty different, so it wasn't a fair comparison. None of my knights were trained in things like disarming traps on treasure chests, for example.

"Oh, heya Touya. What's up?" Elze asked as she waved over to me from nearby. She was sitting on a bench, dabbing sweat from her brow with a towel. Even becoming a duchess wasn't enough to stop her, it seemed.

"I'm looking for Nikola. You seen him?"

"The vice commander? He's over there," Elze replied, pointed right to the middle of the training ground. There, two individuals were clashing. One jabbed forward with a wooden spear, while the other slashed with a wooden sword.

Nikola's spear was just a little bit slow, however, and the wooden sword swished upward to knock it away. The sudden disarming stunned Nikola and allowed his enemy, Yae, to close the distance in seconds. She swung forward with her training weapon.

"Gah!"

Just like that, the vice commander was brought to his knees.

...I-Is he okay?

"Game set. Can you stand?"

"Y-Yes... I-I'm fine, thank you," Nikola replied while wearily nodding toward Hilde, who seemed to be acting as the judge for the bout.

It wasn't that he was by any means weak, Yae was just... no longer in the realm of reasonable human standards. But even she was no match for Moroha. Nobody in our knight order could hold a candle to her. That didn't seem to bother most people, though. As Uncle Takeru often said, he who spends all his time comparing himself to others may never grow.

"I am ready for the next one, I am!"

"Let's go!"

Nikola stepped aside, allowing the next in a long line of would-be challengers to face Yae.

The vice commander came over to the bench near me, sitting down on it before wiping his brow and sipping some water. I felt a little bad about pulling him aside when he was so worn out, but I didn't want to waste much more time.

"Could I have a moment?"

"Your Highness? Of course."

He tried to stand up, but I told him to stay seated. Then I asked him about the situation without letting on that the girl was Princess Reliel.

Chapter III: Great Expectations

"O-Oh, no... I'm afraid I don't know what you're talking about..."

"Damn..."

Hrmm... Well, this sucks. It would've been real convenient if it was someone from Brunhild. Guess I gotta go through the list, then. What a pain in the ass...

Apparently, the black-masked man wasn't from Refreese, either. The two men with black masks from that nation were both a bit chubby, so it didn't match up with the description she'd given. The masks couldn't very well mask body type, after all.

Left with no other choice, I had to go to the different world leaders and meet all the black-masked people one by one.

"Hm... This is kinda sus... isn't it?"

"Sus? Like suspicious? What is?" Elze had noticed me muttering, so she shuffled along the bench and spoke up.

"I mean... this is love, right? Where's Karen...? Usually, she'd pop up outta nowhere and start yelling about how she's gonna take charge, but nothing..."

"Maybe she's just busy with something?" Yumina responded with a sickeningly sweet smile. Perhaps a little too sweet...

I was very confused. She was the one who was all for the ball to begin with, so why wouldn't she involve herself in a big scoop like this? But then I thought of something that worried me a little... The only reason why Karen might not have been all over it was because their love was doomed from the start. The masquerade had been open to single, unmarried folks. I was sure most of the guests were there by their own will, but some might've been there reluctantly. Perhaps some of the nobles even had boyfriends or girlfriends, but still had to go for appearance's sake. That'd be pretty rough... Hopefully it wasn't the case with the black-masked guy.

I didn't want to have to tell Princess Reliel that, at least. The more I thought about it, the messier the potential of the situation got.

I sighed a little bit and decided there was no point moping. I then called up King Belfast to see about questioning the black-masks from his entourage.

"Nobody? You're telling me nobody was involved in the princess' situation?"

"Yep. I asked everyone, and nobody knew what I was talking about. Ugh..." I muttered as I slumped down onto the couch with Leen sitting opposite me. I'd just got done explaining the situation to her. I'd gone around the whole world and asked every black-masked individual about Reliel, but nobody had come forward. In other words, the person responsible had to be lying for some reason.

The situation felt more hopeless to me by the minute. I didn't really think forcing the guy to admit it was fair. He surely had his reasons for keeping himself concealed.

"First the damn Gollem, now this... I've got way too much going on because of that damn party."

"Come now, darling. Where's your spirit? Are you not the man who rushes headlong into danger? You should accept your lot and run with it."

Well, I guess that's fair... It's not like the black-masked guy did anything wrong, anyway.

Still, I had no idea what to do. I could easily just report in with a simple apology for not being able to resolve things, but then Princess Reliel's situation would be left completely open-ended. I'd also feel bad about messing with her feelings that way, too. It was clear she was at an important precipice where she didn't quite know if she was in love or not. Still, at the end of the day, I couldn't force the situation one way or another. It hinged on Reliel's feelings.

Chapter III: Great Expectations

I wanna help her, but...

As I let out a little yawn, my smartphone started ringing.

Who's calling me now? I don't want any more trouble, dammit...

I grumbled quietly as I looked at the display. The incoming caller said Ariattie Tis Allent.

Uhhh, is she the holy king of Allent's granddaughter? Something like that, right? Pretty sure she's rumored to be engaged to Zadonia's new leader, Frost.

I'm pretty sure she got a smartphone after the Holy King and King Frost bugged me about it, right? Never had a call from her before, though.

"Uh... 'Sup? Is this Ariattie?"

"Oh, yes. Is this the grand duke of Brunhild? I'm terribly sorry to call you out of the blue... but I need your help with an urgent matter..."

"Pffffft..." Leen, who was sitting opposite me, started laughing so hard she spat out some of her tea. Apparently, my expression gave away the fact that I was about to become an errand boy again.

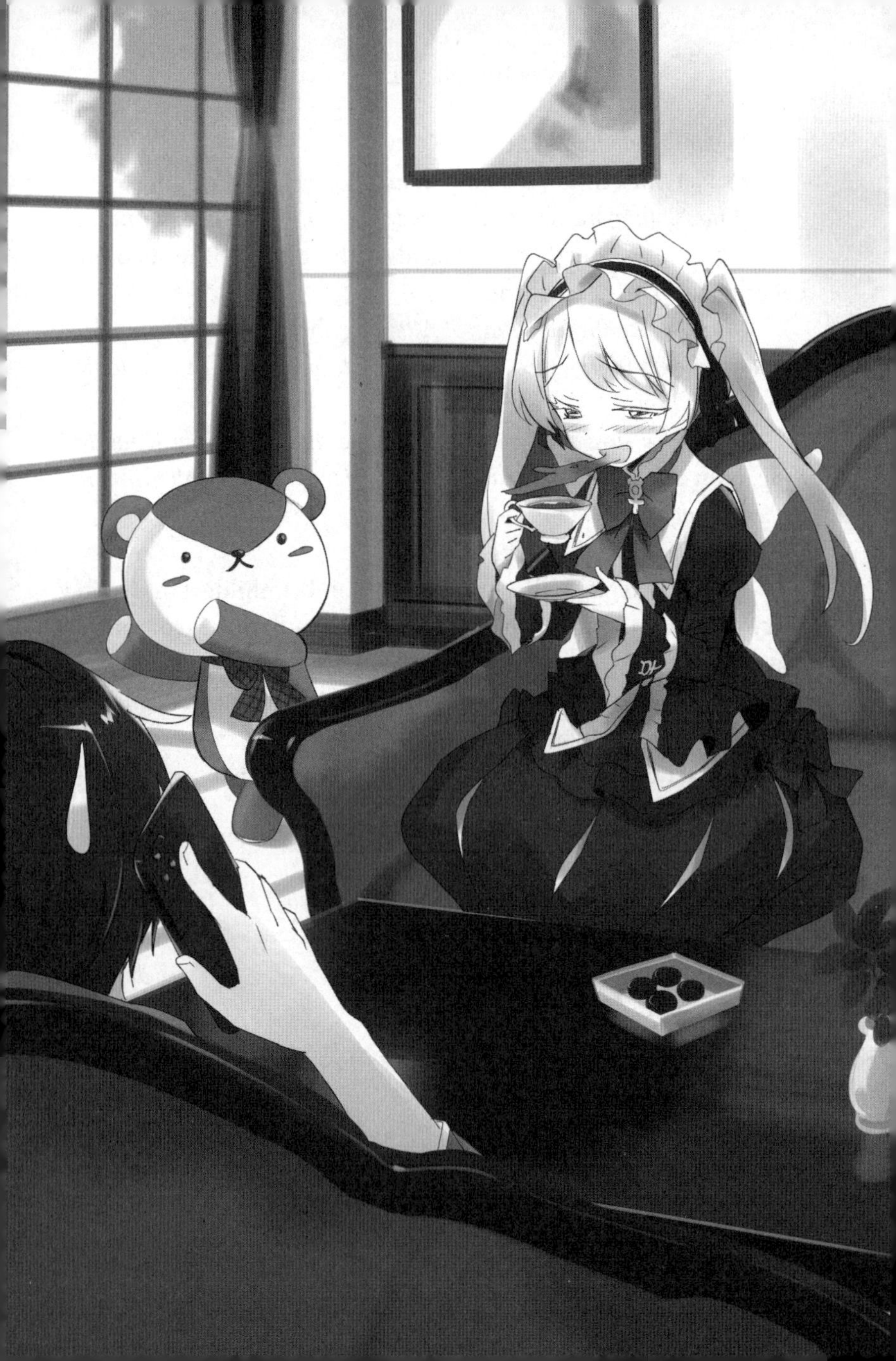

Chapter III: Great Expectations

Aw, c'mon, what is it now? Can't a guy rest for five minutes? And... dammit, Leen! Don't laugh at me! This isn't fair...

"Oh, uh... sorry about that. What did you want to talk about?"

"Well, I'm calling on behalf of someone who wishes to meet with you in private... They're from Gandhilis..."

...Oh?

◇ ◇ ◇

"I'm really, truly sorry!"

"Er, I don't really think you need to be sorry?"

The woman across the table from me just wouldn't stop bowing her head. She was about the same age as me. She wore a lovely light green dress and had a glittering tiara atop her head.

We were in Allent's royal palace. Or more specifically, a gazebo in the rose garden. Princess Ariattie had called on me to help with an urgent matter, so I'd brought Yumina and Sue along to meet her. Once there, I found the second princess of Gandhilis waiting for me. Her name was Cordelia Terra Gandhilis.

Much like the Great Gau River on the eastern continent, the Sebra River separated a few nations on the western continent. Most notably, the Sebra ran south of Allent and north of Gandhilis.

Unlike Gardio, who had a historically antagonistic relationship with Gandhilis, it would seem that Allent and the steel nation were rather cordial.

It wasn't unusual for neighboring countries to have communication between royals, but I never expected to see a princess from Gandhilis in the Allent palace. The biggest thing confusing me, however, was why the princess was apologizing so profusely.

"Really! I didn't mean for any of this to happen! The situation at the party was all my fault!"

In other words... she meant the situation with the fake Imelda. Princess Cordelia was effectively confessing to being the person behind that situation. But she definitely wasn't the mastermind, that much was clear. The real one was the person standing behind her.

"H-Hey, Parullel! You need to apologize as well!"

"I am sorry," the maid, Parullel, said as she bowed her head in apology. Her expression was timid and tinged with guilt. She was an intelligent-looking young woman, perhaps in her twenties or so. Her hair was tied up in a ponytail and she wore round glasses.

According to Princess Cordelia, her maid was the one who'd incapacitated Imelda and had the fake Gollem attend the party in her place.

"What was your aim here?"

"To protect the emperor of Gardio, sir."

Huh? Protecting Emperor Gardio? But he had like... soldiers with him? What was one weak Gollem based on a noble girl going to do, exactly? And why would Gandhilis be protecting the emperor, anyway? Gardio's hardly an ally.

"Wh-What she means is... to protect him from... any women who might have approached him at the party, hahaha..."

"What?"

As I pondered the peculiarities of the situation, Princess Ariattie flashed a weak smile and spoke up. Upon hearing her words, Princess Cordelia went beet red and glanced to the side.

Wait, don't tell me...

"Well, you see... a few years ago, Sir Lancelet was invited to a series of parties in Gandhilis... He wasn't in line to be emperor at the time, he only had his noble station... a-and we talked quite intimately a few times, and, well... I..." she trailed off,

Chapter III: Great Expectations

but I wasn't stupid. I could be a blockhead sometimes, but I knew what the second princess of Gandhilis was getting at.

The current emperor of Gardio was once named Lancelet Olcott. He was the son of the prime minister, Lancelo Olcott. Lancelet's mother was the sister of the former emperor, so after Lucrecion renounced his claim to the throne, Lancelet was next in line.

The previous emperor was trying to mend relations with Gandhilis, so Lancelet must have visited the steel nation several times in the past before becoming emperor. And that was how he'd met the second princess.

Sue, who was standing nearby, let out a little giggle as she realized the situation.

"I see... But how did that turn into... this?"

"Well, I heard that there was to be a matchmaking party in Refreese, with royals and nobles in attendance. And I heard that Sir Lancelet would be in attendance as well..."

"You must have misunderstood. While it's true that Emperor Gardio attended, he was only there as a monarch. He wasn't actually involved in the matchmaking itself," Yumina spoke up, correcting Cordelia's account. Reliel was forced to participate, but everyone else was free to opt in or out. The same went for royals as well, and Emperor Gardio elected not to join. After all, he was already a head of state. He couldn't join in something like that so casually.

"That's right... Lady Ariattie told me about that recently. In my panic, I made a hasty mistake. I was so worried about Sir Lancelet potentially meeting someone there that I accidentally complained about it in front of Parullel..."

Now it makes sense. She thought Emperor Gardio was trying to find a partner there. I guess it's not too unreasonable. Princess Reliel participated, as well as the princes from Xenoahs. So I guess the maid,

Parullel, just took matters into her own hands after hearing about her mistress' love woes, huh? That's pretty extreme...

"The thing is, Parullel's parents own a Gollem engineering guild known as the Seekers... so I believe they had a hand in this."

A familiar term stood out among Princess Cordelia's apologetic words.

The Seekers... I've heard that before. They're part of the whole five great gollemancers thing, right? That's what Elluka mentioned, at least. If they're a husband and wife, I guess they're a package deal.

"The Seekers are a group of engineers that travel the world seeking out ancient ruins, excavating the ancient world, and repairing any Gollems they come across. They're not just engineers, however. They also sell and trade the Gollems they refurbish, operating as a fairly proficient mercantile group," Parullel explained it fairly concisely, but the idea of a roving group of archaeological merchants was a little weird to me.

But hey, if a group like that could be self-sufficient, that was pretty cool as well. It was only logical to live in that way if you could.

"So how did the daughter of the two Seeker leaders end up working as a maid in Gandhilis?"

"The Seekers have been roving around Gandhilis' ruins for several years now. At her family's behest, my father took Parullel in, and she's been working as my personal attendant ever since. I'm sure her parents asked that she not be left among the common rabble."

Cordelia's explanation made sense. The Seekers clearly had a strong relationship with Gandhilis, and it was easy to see why. If the steel nation produced a ton of metal and ore, it was obvious they'd be the main pitstop of a roving group of excavators who worked with metal. They were the most natural pair-up possible, really.

Chapter III: Great Expectations

"I asked my father to repair, rebuild, and restore the Gollem used to infiltrate the party... It's a cattleya model. I also had the Seekers craft its current appearance, but I didn't explain what I was going to use it for. My parents are completely innocent in this. It goes without saying that the princess is also free of culpability. This was all my doing, and I'm ready to accept whatever punishment is deemed appropriate," Parullel said as she looked right at me. It was clear she was remorseful for going over the princess' head.

Hrmm... Why's she asking me to punish her, anyway? I don't have the authority to do that. Plus, I'm hardly the victim here.

The biggest victims in this situation were the real Imelda, who was incapacitated and missed the party, the Gardio Empire, which was thrown into a crisis, and Refreese, which lost honor for allowing a foreign agent into their formal event.

"Nay, it is I who should be apologizing! This wouldn't have happened if not for my shortcomings. Please, Grand Duke... Please give me a chance to apologize to everyone!"

Princess Cordelia was bowing on her knees at that point, while Parullel kept up her bowing display right behind her. Frankly... I felt relieved. I thought this was some kind of heinous plot, but it was just a simple misunderstanding.

Those words Lucrecion had heard about the emperor eliminating anything in his way was probably meant to be something like:

"If any women get in the way of Emperor Gardio, then they must be eliminated."

To be honest, that was kind of scary in its own way, but who was I to judge.

"What should we do, Touya?"

"Well, it's not really up to me. I need to inform the people involved."

"That means you're gonna have to tell them about Princess Cordelia's feelings, right? I wonder what he'll think when he finds out..." I paused for a moment. Sue raised a very good point.

Personally, I thought that a princess pairing up with a neighboring emperor was fine, but I wasn't the one who got to decide that.

Hm, what to do...?

As I glanced upward, Yumina suddenly started speaking to Princess Cordelia.

"You and the Emperor were close, no?"

"Hm? Oh, well... I think so? Sir Lancelet was always kind enough to speak to me, and would even buy me presents on my birthday..."

"If he's been buying you birthday gifts, then he must've at least been thinking a little about you."

"I-I-If that's really true, I would be most happy..."

Yumina was relentless in her questioning. Sue came up from behind her and joined in as well.

"How come you never told him your feelings? Didn't you have the chance?"

"Well, I... It was difficult for me at the time on account of my position... A-And then Lancelet became the emperor, of all things, and I didn't want to give off the impression I only wanted to be empress..."

"I think you worried too much. It's not like you were strangers. And if he was still getting you stuff for your birthday, isn't that a good sign? Yumina'd say so too."

"I-Is that so...?"

Chapter III: Great Expectations

This entire royal situation was just about to make my head spin. Why couldn't people just talk to each other?

It was pretty rare for a romance to start with two-sided affection right off the bat. Most of the time it was something one-sided that blossomed into something more. In that sense, Princess Cordelia's feelings already had a little bit of a head start due to her history with the emperor.

"I guess now we have to see how the emperor reacts to finding out about the mess you caused, huh?"

"Agh!" Prince Cordelia's groaned, her expression twisted into one of misery in response to my words. Yumina shot a menacing glare my way.

Oh, crap... I didn't mean it!

"The real Imelda's a problem, too. Surely she won't stay silent forever."

"...Actually, Ms. Imelda won't be an issue. She consented to this. I doubt her family will kick up much of a fuss, either."

"...Wait, huh? What?"

Parullel's words confused me. What was that about consent? Was Imelda actually in league with them?!

"Ms. Imelda has a spouse in mind already, but her parents insisted she attend the party. Thus, she petitioned me for help. She wished to stage it so that her arrival at the party was halted by a mysterious interloper, allowing us to take her place in the process."

"Wh-What?! I never heard about this!" Princess Cordelia suddenly spoke up, apparently astonished by this piece of information.

How'd she even get in touch with a foreign noble like Imelda?

"The Seekers have members and former members all over the world, so getting into contact with her was a trifling matter.

As was drugging her into a comatose state the night of the party. Things ended up working out well for Ms. Imelda, as well."

The situation was slowly revealed to have been orchestrated by this maid. But it all added up so far, at least. If Imelda had rejected some high-ranking noble she'd met at the party, it could've turned ugly for her family.

These Seekers, though... They were really something else. I had a feeling that if they teamed up with Olba Strand's company, they could spread Gollem tech across the eastern continent in no time at all.

Maybe I could take advantage of the situation and have Parullel introduce me...? No, no... That won't do...

"When you say things went well for Imelda, what do you mean?"

"Oh, well... The man she loves is her family's doctor, and he took care of her when she was in her comatose state. It was apparently the push the two of them needed to confirm their feelings for each other and tell her parents. They seem to be set in a relationship now."

Everyone in the room seemed charmed by the story, but I felt like we were getting a little off-track.

"As I said earlier, every single part of this plan is on me. The princess had no part in this whatsoever. I shall shoulder any punishment deemed necessary."

"W-Wait! I must share at least some of the blame. It was through my negligence that—"

"Nay. It was wrong of me to grow tired of your inability to make a move, Princess. It's not your fault for being timid or inexperienced..."

"H-Hey, do you have to put it like that?!"

"...Yes, sort of."

What a mess of a situation. But I guess it's always like this when love gets involved. Okay, but seriously... Where's Karen? This is her

Chapter III: Great Expectations

thing, isn't it? I haven't heard from her in a few days, either. I guess if Moroha's not worried, I'm not worried, but still...

"Well, we're not the only parties involved here. I need to speak to the emperors of Gardio and Refreese about this. If you still feel the need to apologize, then it's them you need to say sorry to... Okay?"

"...Very well."

"I understand."

Cordelia and Parullel both nodded slowly.

If Imelda really was complicit in this, then the situation wasn't all that bad, but the two men could still take it poorly. I was especially curious as to what Emperor Gardio would think.

I wasn't entirely sure how to convey Princess Cordelia's feelings... nor did I understand how or why I'd become some kind of love messenger.

I heaved a small sigh, burdened by another new responsibility. There was nothing else to do, so I decided to just be honest.

◇ ◇ ◇

"Well... Refreese didn't come to any harm. If Gandhilis feels it owes us a debt, we'd be happy to accept the princess' apology. If the Gollems are to spread over to our continent, then forging ties with Gollem-rich nations seems like a wise idea to me. We may well make contact with the Seekers through this, as well."

The emperor of Refreese didn't really seem all that bothered. Frankly, I was impressed. If I ever became half the pragmatist he was, I'd be doing well.

"Well, that seems fine for Refreese, then. What about Gardio?"

"..." Emperor Gardio remained silent, staring blankly. I didn't know what was up with him.

Count Lowe waved a hand in front of the emperor's face.

"...Your Majesty? Emperor?"

"H-Huh? O-Oh, wh-what?!"

"Are you okay? We were talking about the Gandhilis issue..."

"O-Oh, yes... Well, it's as Emperor Refreese said. We'll let them handle the princess. I'll speak with Imelda, as well. I doubt there'll be any major issues. We've been working toward a friendlier relationship with Gandhilis, so I'd prefer not to rock the boat."

Well, at least the guy was listening. Hm... I guess that's the end of that...? I'm not so sure, though.

I told Emperor Gardio about Princess Cordelia's feelings, but he seemed completely stunned. I wonder how he felt.

"...Emperor Gardio, what are your thoughts on Princess Cordelia?" Emperor Refreese suddenly spoke up, asking exactly what was on my mind.

"H-Huh?!"

How bold! Guess that's the power of age for you.

We were in a room in Brunhild Castle. There was only me, Emperor Gardio, Emperor Refreese, Count Lowe, and a couple of guards present. Yumina, Sue, and the others wanted to find out more about the romantic aspect of the situation, but I didn't think it was fair to have them sit in. There were some things you could only talk about with fellow men.

"Oh, well... I'll confess that I'm flattered by her feelings... However, her actions did cause some measure of inconvenience. I can't let that slide, and therefore it makes answering her feelings more difficult to..."

"Stop considering things like that. I'm asking how you feel about her, regardless of the political landscape."

Chapter III: Great Expectations

"...H-How I feel?" Emperor Gardio's cheeks burned bright red as he mumbled those words. It was pretty clear that he felt something. The way she talked about their old interactions made it seem that way, at least.

I was grinning as I watched Emperor Gardio squirm. The emperor of Refreese was grinning as well.

"W-Well! I... Th-This is rather sudden, no?! I-I'm obviously as flustered as I am flattered, but I need to consider my status as well! I-I'm not just a nobleman's son anymore, I'm the head of a state! I can't simply respond to her so casually, can I? O-Oh, Grand Duke! You've proposed nine times, haven't you?! G-Give me some guidance here, please!"

"Just go with the flow."

"What's that supposed to mean?!"

The young emperor was panicking, but I didn't know what advice to give him... With all my wives, we simply came to care for each other and it just kind of worked out.

"Gandhilis used to be on bad terms with Gardio, did it not? Would it not then be smart to nurture more close relations as a gesture of your willingness to commit to a brighter future?"

Emperor Refreese had a point. If the princess of Gandhilis married the emperor of Gardio, it'd be a strong symbol of their national union. That was often how royal marriages worked, anyway.

My marriages to Yumina, Lu, and Hilde were symbols of my strong relations with their home countries. Though in Yumina's case, I wasn't actually a world leader when we got together.

"B-But this is still an international incident, isn't it? Should I just wave it off like that...?"

"That's not relevant right now. Think about what's really important here. If you can't shoulder the feelings of one woman, princess or not, how can you hope to shoulder the burdens of an entire nation? Look at the grand duke. He's shouldering nine wives," Emperor Refreese stated, bursting out laughing a second later.

Ghhh... Don't bully me, you old fart!

"Well, I suppose I could offer you my daughter's hand if all else fails."

"Uh, no... I'm good, thank you..."

"Hahahaha, I'm just joking," Emperor Refreese was laughing, but I couldn't bring myself to join him.

Your daughter's in a bit of an odd love story of her own, you know?!

Either way, I agreed with Emperor Refreese in this situation.

"It might be an opportunity for you, you know? The goddess of love would say something about timing being important here."

"Hoh... The goddess of love, you say?" Emperor Gardio asked, raising his brow at my words. He didn't know it, but that goddess happened to be my sister.

Either way, while Parullel's actions were rather rash, it opened up a chance for him to voice his feelings for a woman who clearly cared for him. This was probably the kind of ideal situation Karen always talked about. Though Emperor Gardio was still a little concerned, it was clear that the Gollem issue had been resolved. Now I just had to chase things up with Princess Reliel.

Who could this black-masked guy be? I've questioned every last guy I can think of, and I just... can't...

Suddenly, a thought occurred to me. I'd only questioned all the **men** in black masks.

Wait, don't tell me...

◇ ◇ ◇

Chapter III: Great Expectations

Both Yumina and Linze were completely taken aback by what I said to them. I wasn't surprised, since the idea had shocked even myself.

"Uh... Touya... What do you mean, exactly? The person who rescued Reli is..."

"A woman?"

For now, I wanted to keep the information quiet, so I'd only shared it with these two. I hadn't told Reliel yet, and frankly, I wasn't sure how to. Hence coming to the two wives most involved in the situation.

"But Reli said the other party was a man, no?"

"Are you saying it's possible it was a woman using a concealing spell like [Mirage]?"

"No, that's not it. They were simply dressed in a man's outfit."

It had never even occurred to me that someone would register as a female attendee and then wear a man's formal outfit. The changing room was within the venue itself, so it wasn't like anyone was keeping an eye on who was dressing into what. Plus, the masks were designed to obscure faces from the start. The woman I asked about it confessed to doing as such, anyway... It was just a matter of telling Reliel.

"Anyway, yeah. I've already followed it up, and the person I asked admitted to it."

"But why?"

"Well... apparently, she was uncomfortable wearing a fluffy dress. She said she felt quite shy in that kind of attire."

I wasn't exactly sure what was so embarrassing about a formal dress when everyone was anonymous, though. But hey, everyone had different hangups.

"S-So, who was the one dressed as the black-masked man?"

"Princess Listis Le Triharan, from Triharan. She was posing as a prince way back when, if you guys remember..."

"Oh, that's right. Back when Ende got mind-controlled... That adds up."

Princess Listis Le Triharan was raised as a prince in order to trick the senate, who'd robbed all power from the royal family and was ruling the nation as they saw fit. Since she was raised that way, her personality wasn't stereotypically girlish. She looked and acted like the kind of prince you'd see in a shoujo manga, frankly.

Even without the mask, it'd be easy to mistake her for a handsome man. Her mannerisms weren't in the least bit girlish. That didn't mean she was brash or anything, she was just an example of the perfect gentleman.

Oh... I guess from that perspective, it'd be really embarrassing to wear a dress, huh? That must have been why.

"She was a frontline fighter in the war against Primula, wasn't she?"

"That's right. She's no stranger to the battlefield, either."

Incidentally, her brother, Prince Lupheus, was a total bookworm who was more interested in studying magical engineering. They were polar opposites in terms of presentation and interests.

Lupheus was engaged to be married to Princess Berlietta of Strain thanks to the race we hosted a while back. Perhaps Listis had some kind of pressure on her to get married as a result of that pairing...

"Are you sure it was her?"

"She knew about the handkerchief, so why wouldn't it be?"

Part of me wanted to be wrong, but the story was already convoluted enough.

"Well, hmm..."

"What now...?"

Chapter III: Great Expectations

Yumina and Linze exchanged furtive glances. I understood how they felt.

"Well, we have two choices here. You can either tell Princess Reliel the truth or keep it from her. You could say that you simply couldn't find the one responsible and leave it at that, but..."

"But I don't think you should take away her agency like that. Reli deserves to know the truth. She can do with it what she wishes."

I thought so too. No matter how it ended, honesty was the best policy. Linze made a funny, almost pensive, face. I wondered what that meant.

"Well... it's just... she writes that kind of thing too, you know...?"

"Hm?"

"Her Order of the Rose books, which feature romantic stories between a male-only cast, are obviously her most popular works, but... she has an all-female spin-off story as well. It's called Defenders of the Lily..."

Wow, the more you know. She even writes stuff like that? I guess she's a pretty varied writer, so it makes sense to dabble a bit.

"It's a love story about a senior knight commander and her feelings for a young girl from the countryside.. It has some pretty intense scenes in it, if you know what I mean... B-But now I'm wondering, do you think she might be open to that kind of thing?"

The second half of what Linze had said was a little muffled, but Yumina heard enough for her cheeks to turn bright pink. Frankly, I was a little curious about what she might have imagined at that moment, but I let it be.

Linze sort of had a point, but one could easily write about something without it being a reflection of their real-life preferences... Then again, I couldn't really bear the thought of writing something that didn't interest me.

Anyway, I wasn't sure how to tell the princess that her mystery man was actually a mystery woman. I just didn't have the heart.

"Well, maybe we can bring Princess Listis with us to meet Reliel? She might not believe us otherwise."

"Y-Yes, that might work... If the two of them talk, it'll be easier to know for sure, too..."

I'm pretty certain Listis was the black-masked person, so I dunno about needing to confirm things... but whatever.

While quietly wondering just what kind of situation was about to unfold, I took out my smartphone and called up Princess Reliel.

◇ ◇ ◇

"S-So... Did you find him?! Wh-Who is he?!"

"Hey, hey. Calm down. Just take it easy and have a seat, okay? Deep breaths."

"Don't treat me like a child!"

I tried to calm down Princess Reliel, who was so frantic she'd already knocked her chair over. I wondered if this would really be okay... I glanced to my side, at Yumina and Linze. They were both wearing forced smiles, suggesting that it was far too late to back out.

This was Refreese Castle's private courtyard, where even members of the extended royal family couldn't enter without permission. Thus, we could speak freely without any risk of being overheard.

"Well... I could bring your black-masked suitor here now, if you like."

"Ah?! R-R-Right here?! B-But I'm not ready!"

I'd never seen Princess Reliel act so flustered before... It made me concerned about how she'd react, and with good reason.

Chapter III: Great Expectations

I whispered over to Yumina and Linze.

"Shouldn't we tell her before dropping the bombshell? I feel like we might break her brain..."

"Mmm... Maybe? But I'm not sure..."

"It should be fine to just introduce them, no?"

I groaned quietly. They were supposed to be the experts here, not me...

"I'm sure she'll handle it better than you're expecting her to. Let's just do it..."

"Well, I'll call her over then. I don't wanna keep her waiting."

"Her...?"

I ignored Reliel's confusion and cast **[Gate]**, connecting it to the other side. Most castles had wards in place to prevent this kind of magic, but Reliel had the nearest one temporarily disabled.

"Oh, finally. I certainly waited long enough."

The girl entered through the portal, giving a little bow and a curtsy as she clutched the hem of her dress. She was evidently not used to wearing something so frilly. Her golden hair was a little longer than it'd been the first time I'd met her, and she was even wearing a little makeup. We'd had maids assigned to her in order to bring out a little more of her feminine side, and the result was surprisingly sweet.

The outfit she wore wasn't an overly gaudy dress, so it actually suited her pretty well. Though, the two maids that came with her couldn't help but giggle. They'd had to work a miracle on her.

She'd said that she wasn't used to wearing girlish clothing, but it was clear to me that they suited her nicely.

"Uh... who is this?" Reliel seemed puzzled, probably because a woman had come through the portal rather than the man she'd expected to meet.

"Well, this is Listis Le Triharan, Princess of Triharan. And Listis, this is Reliel Rehm Refreese, Imperial Princess of Refreese."

Princess Listis gave another curtsy upon being introduced.

"Thank you kindly for your cordial invitation, Princess Reliel. It's a pleasure to meet you, on behalf of Triharan. Thank you once more."

"Oh... Uh... Invitation? Uhm... I-I'm Reliel Rehm Refreese... Welcome to my country...?"

Reliel gave a little curtsy back, but she was clearly confused. Her eyes gave away her lack of understanding, the little orbs dancing around with curious glances here and there.

Yumina suddenly turned to Reliel, raising her voice a little, and said, "Reli, listen... And be calm, okay? This person is your black-masked savior."

"...What?" Reliel looked flabbergasted. I could almost hear her internally screaming in confusion.

Princess Reliel suddenly tiptoed over toward the three of us and spoke in a low voice, saying, "The black-masked person who saved me was a man..."

"She was just dressed as a man at the party. It was actually a girl all along."

"Linze... I'm not going to fall for your tricks. Can't you get your kicks from my books instead?"

We're getting nowhere...

I sighed and reached into my pocket, turning away from the princess-in-denial, then called over to Listis.

"Princess Listis. You were the one who helped Princess Reliel at the party the other day, right? This handkerchief... Do you recognize it?"

Chapter III: Great Expectations

"Hm? Ohhh! You mean she's the girl from back then?! I didn't realize! She looked quite different from behind the mask... Though I imagine I must have looked different as well. But yes, that's my handkerchief!"

"...WHAT?!"

Another few moments of stunned silence passed before an eruption of confusion resounded. Reliel's expression was half-frozen. She looked completely blindsided.

"G-Grand Duke... Is the imperial princess okay? She seems to be seizing up..." Princess Listis was somewhat startled by Reliel's outburst, so she turned to ask me out of concern. I wasn't too surprised that Reliel felt this way, even if she was reacting a bit strongly. Clearly, she wasn't taking it well.

"Apologies for Reli. She's a little stunned because she thought you were a man at the party."

"Oh... I see... I'm not really one for dresses. That's why I had the men's formal outfit prepared in secret. Though the old man certainly gave me an earful about it!"

The old man? Oh, she probably means Zerorick. I think he looks after her affairs.

"You prepared this dress for me, didn't you? I don't really understand why women want to wear such fluffy, unwieldy things... It's more practical to wear something you can actually move around in, no?"

I'd called up her father beforehand to ensure she'd be wearing something girly for this meeting. I wanted her to be recognizable as a girl even at a glance, to prevent any misunderstandings. Now that that goal had been achieved, I was fine if she wanted to change.

"It looks good on you, though. It's rather pretty."

141

"Really? I wasn't so sure about it," Listis mumbled as she played with the hem of her dress, replying to Yumina.

It didn't exactly look easy to move in. We seated Listis upon one of the garden chairs, then waited for Princess Reliel to snap back out of the shock she was suffering from.

"I suppose I'll have to get used to dresses... My brother recently got engaged, so Father's been insisting I find a partner before long."

That explains it... Her dad was certainly eager about the masquerade, come to think of it. But she was dressed as a man! How was she supposed to find a partner like that? Wait, no... technically, she did?

"Uh... Princess Listis, are there any men you're affectionate toward?" Linze asked her a question that was phrased just vaguely enough to not be intrusive.

"Mmm... I've lived as a man for most of my life, so I'm not entirely familiar with those sorts of pursuits. Men are kind of a pain to deal with, too. They're prideful, stubborn, often arrogant... More trouble than they're worth in many cases."

The princess cast a brief glance toward me. It was unavoidable... I was the only man at the table!

"That's why I couldn't stand by when I saw Princess Reliel in trouble at the party. The man she was with was your typical brute."

"You're not wrong, Princess Listis. I'm sure many men walked by the scene thinking nothing was wrong. I think your conduct was incredibly noble that night. That's why you were invited here, to show our appreciation," Yumina responded as she smiled gently. Reliel, on the other hand, was pale as a ghost. It looked as though her soul had crawled out of her body. Was the situation really that shocking?

Chapter III: Great Expectations

"I suppose I shouldn't be too surprised... Even now, I'm still mistaken for a man fairly often. I'm a bit like Shannon from Lilydef in that regard."

Listis' words prompted Reliel to twitch slightly. Yumina and Linze also seemed surprised.

Lilydef? Shannon? What's that mean?

"Wait, Princess Listis... you know about Lilydef?!"

"Of course! It was one of the books gifted to us by Brunhild. I read it in one sitting because of how enthralling I found it. There aren't many books like that in Triharan," Princess Listis said, then chuckled gently in response to Yumina's question.

Oh, right... We did do a book exchange with Triharan and Primula at one point, didn't we? Pretty sure I didn't oversee what titles we sent out, though. I think I just put Fam from the library in charge of that... Her and...

I mouthed "Oh," as my eyes met with Linze's.

"...So, what's Lilydef? The book title or something?"

"Hm? You don't know, Grand Duke? It's a nickname for a book series, the full title is Defenders of the Lily."

"...Oh!" I suddenly glared daggers at Linze, prompting her to stare down at the floor. She was sweating.

I know I left it to you, but why'd you include Reliel's books in our cultural exchange?! I know you're a fan, but show some restraint!

"Shannon's the main character. She comes from the countryside and ends up in a spot of trouble at first, but she's rescued by a handsome knight. Then she goes to train as a knight herself, only to find out that her savior is her senior instructor at the academy, and a girl to boot! Hoho, I suppose the situation mirrors Princess Reliel's a little, doesn't it?"

"Uh, kinda... I... I guess..."

Oh man, she wrote that story. To have it turn out like this...

Yumina and Linze were barely able to contain their laughter.

"You must've really enjoyed it... It's a genre that isn't super common even over here."

"I care little about genres. Interesting is interesting. As for romance, gender's pretty trivial. So long as the love's pure and simple, I think I can appreciate it no matter who's pining for whom."

"That's exactly it!"

Out of nowhere, Reliel suddenly scrambled up and yelled. She knocked her chair over in the process, even.

Calm down, lady! You scared the crap outta me!

"That's precisely what I wanted to portray in the book! Gender, age, race, social status... Love knows no bounds if it's true love! You actually get it!"

Yumina and I sort of stared quietly, while Linze nodded along with Reliel's rant.

"Oh my, Princess Reliel. You're a fan of Lilydef as well? Isn't it a nice series?"

"Of course it is! I wrote it."

"...What?" Listis looked flabbergasted. And I felt a strange sense of déjà vu.

"Oh, yes... Princess Reliel here is actually the author of Defenders of the Lily... Though she uses an alias..."

For some reason, Linze almost sounded apologetic when introducing Reliel's secret... I briefly wondered if it was okay for her to say that, though Reliel herself had just confessed, so it was probably fine.

"Hm? Really?"

"Really."

Chapter III: Great Expectations

"But… why would the princess of a great nation do such a thing?"

"Because to write is to scratch the itch of creativity!"

In a flash, Reliel had righted her fallen chair… only to stand on it and strike a flashy pose. She was getting way too amped up. It was hard to believe she was the same dead-eyed person as before. I was glad she felt better, but she needed to sit like a normal person.

Princess Listis looked a little confused, so Linze tried to veer the subject back to something more normal.

"Who's your favorite character, princess?"

"Hm? Oh, well… I think Crystelle is a fascinating character, but Freesia really has a cool, mysterious charm."

"That's true! I should add more scenes with her! In truth, she's— Oh wait, spoilers!"

"Wait, I want to know! Is it related to the hooded figure in volume four?"

"Oh, right! That person was obviously up to something."

"Hehehehe… It's a secret!"

The three girls were passionately chattering about the series, its lore, and its characters. Yumina and I were completely lost. Though Yumina knew bits and pieces, she was more interested in it casually and wasn't a hardcore fan.

"Uhhh… all's well that ends well, I guess?"

"I suppose so… Seems our worries weren't necessary."

The three girls were gossiping with each other like old friends. They just seemed happy to have another person to share their interests with. That was probably good?

I shrugged my shoulders casually, glad to be done with the whole situation. At that exact moment, my phone began to ring. I pulled it out of my pocket and saw the caller… It was Karen.

Tsk... Showing up when things are finally good and done? Some use you are... Wait, did she not show up this whole time because it had nothing to do with love? Gimme a break!

"Hey Karen, 'sup?"

"Your big sis is in a teeeeeeny spot of trouble, Touya... Please help me..."

Wait, what?!

Chapter IV: The World of Tomorrow

I arrived at the Pantheon Temple. It was a holy place that existed beyond the heavens; a gathering point for the gods of the Divine Realm. Essentially, it was an area for all the divine to have some downtime and hang out.

I wasn't a fully-fledged god yet, but my connection to God Almighty let me bypass any restrictions and I was generally allowed to come and go from the pantheon as I pleased.

I had mixed feelings about that, to be honest... It was kind of like nepotism, in a way. I hadn't gotten in on my own merit, after all. I didn't feel super comfortable there, either... The air was tense, and kind of intimidating... but what else would you expect from a place full of literal gods?

Heading through the pantheon gates, I found myself in a large courtyard. The pantheon was made up of several rooms and spaces, and there were no fixed routes to get to any of them. If you were used to that kind of disorderly structure it was fine, but if you weren't, then it was easy to get lost.

The courtyard was a central hub of sorts, and I wasn't entirely sure how to reach Karen from there. As I pondered the matter, a sparrow fluttered by and landed on my shoulder. However, it was no ordinary sparrow.

"Oh, the newcomer. Long time no see, child."

"Ah, hey. Nice to see you. You're the uh... god of flight, right?"

"Indubitably."

This little bird was a fully-fledged god. I'd met him the last time I came to the temple with Karen... Since he was the god of flight, I wondered if his domain included other flying things like planes or bees.

"What brings you here today?"

"Oh, well... I'm here to meet Kare—er, the goddess of love. I'm not entirely sure how to get to her from here, though..."

"Ah... I see... Her..."

The sparrow sort of made a nervous motion and shook his head, inexplicably wiping his bird-brow with one wing.

Uh, what's with that response?

"Well, no matter... We might as well make a tour of it. Come."

The sparrow flapped his tiny wings and launched from my shoulder. I didn't understand, but I decided to follow him all the same. Not like I had any other options, really.

We headed through an archway in the courtyard and were greeted by another completely new sight as we exited the other side. This time it was a large room with a spiral staircase made of glass that trailed upward.

To be more precise, we were on the staircase and a glass, cylindrical wall surrounded us. On the other side of the glass was a beautiful gathering of marine life that was freely floating amidst the blue.

What, are we underwater now?

"This way. Don't get lost, or you might end up wandering forever."

*...R-Really? Like I can't even use **[Gate]** or my divinity warping here? That's a scary thought...*

Chapter IV: The World of Tomorrow

I quickly followed the god of flight up the staircase. And as I did, I looked a little closer out at what I was assuming to be seawater and noticed people there too. Some looked like regular two-legged folks, while others were mermaids. They were probably gods and those with their blessings.

Upon even closer inspection, I realized the fish were probably members of the extended divine family as well... It was unlikely that anything mortal existed here.

Another archway waited for us at the top of the staircase, and we passed through it. This time the entire room was pitch black, save for the glittering of numerous far-off stars above our heads. It was a corridor that seemed to stretch on forever. All I could do was keep my vision trained on the sparrow in front of me, lest I lose my way.

"Speed up a little. If you take too much time in here, they'll get you."

"They?!"

The god of flight's words instilled a primal fear within me, so I picked up the pace. From behind, I suddenly started to hear the sounds of clicking tongues and smacking lips... I heard the sound of something heavy dragging itself toward me in the pitch black... so I pretended not to hear any of that and pressed onward. It got to the point where I was charging through the darkness after the god of flight, and eventually, we made it to the next "room." The place was a terrifying labyrinth without end... Or at least, that was how it felt.

We carried on through several rooms, spaces, and realms after that. I greeted gods, fled from entities, and just tried my best to match pace with the sparrow. Eventually, we made it to wherever Karen was supposed to be.

"Huh...?"

149

We came out into a place filled with dense foliage and blooming flowers. A cool breeze blew through the area, and a beautiful stream ran along nearby. There were spirits gathered near the treetops, and in the distance, I spotted a dazzling white gazebo. There was a tunnel of flowers leading toward it. It was like we were in a fancy, expensive rose garden.

As I stood there stunned, the god of flight made straight for the gazebo. I followed him through the flower tunnel until we arrived at our destination. There was a table there, and a lone woman sitting at it. But she wasn't sitting, she was slumped over.

"Karen?!" I roared as I ran over to the table to try to support her. For some reason her face was pale and her eyes were unfocused. She looked weak.

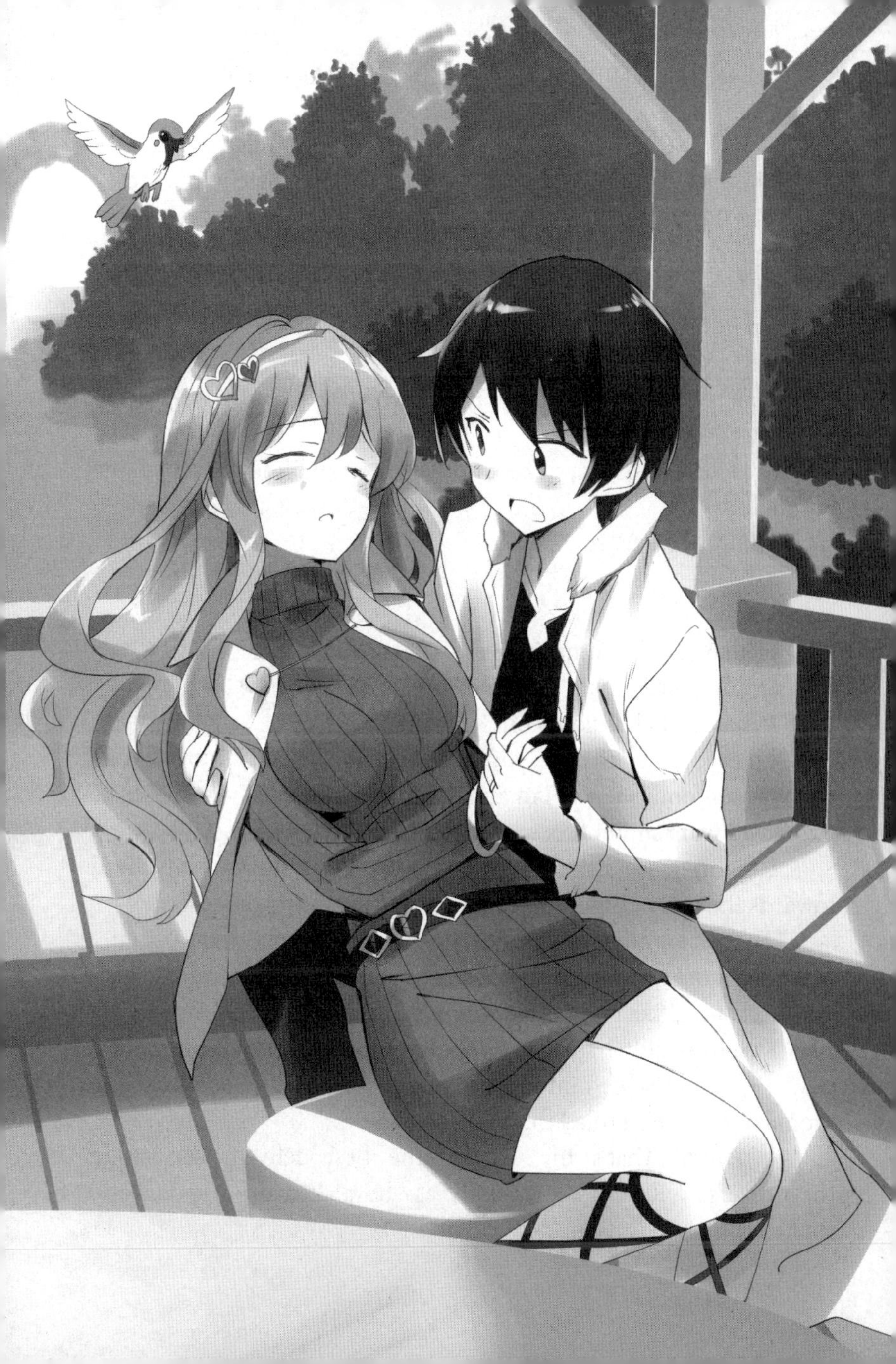

I quickly cast **[Cure Heal]** and **[Recovery]** on her, along with various other restoration spells, but she was completely unaffected by any of them.

Shit, does regular magic not work on gods?! But I'm a god, right? If it works on me, it should work on her... Don't tell me she's been attacked by that venom from last time?!

"Tou...ya..."

"Don't waste your energy, it's okay! I'll get God Almighty to help you!"

I reached into my pocket and began scrambling for my phone, but then...

"Hung...ry... Want... food..."

"..."

"...Ow!"

I let go of her, prompting her to fall and smack her head.

Hold on a goddamn minute. She was just hungry?!

"What the hell is going on, Karen?"

"I haven't eaten in days, you know?! I can't take it! I know I won't die without food because I'm a god, but I miss food! I've had a taste and now I want more! More, you know?!"

I ignored my sister's prattling and turned to bow my head towards the god of flight.

"Thanks for all your help. I'm heading home now, though."

"You can't go home, you know?! You can't abandon your sister!"

"Ack, geez! Let go of me, you idiot!"

Karen wouldn't stop crying and clinging to my coat, so I let out a sigh and reached into **[Storage]** for some of Lu's cooking. The aroma of tasty food filled the area.

"Woohoo! That's my Touya! The best delivery service in the universe!" Karen said merrily as she picked up a spoon and started eating.

Chapter IV: The World of Tomorrow

You sure turned those tears off fast, you little shit! You're the worst!

"I'm... sorry you have to deal with her, newcomer."

Please... Please don't look at me with such pity.

I sighed quietly, staring up through the gazebo's semi-transparent ceiling.

◇ ◇ ◇

"So, what are you doing out here?"

"I'm in the middle of my Ascension."

"Your what?"

Is that like a promotion?

"It's a test to raise her divinity. I'm sure you know that there are various rankings when it comes to us and our roles. There used to be a strict hierarchy of gods back in the day, but nowadays, things are a touch more progressive. We all stand on a roughly even keel, but the higher ranks generally get a little more admiration... What is this thing?! I can't stop pecking at it! It's so tasty!"

The god of flight couldn't keep himself from jabbing his beak into Lu's food over and over again. It was an omelet, by the way... One covered in ketchup, resulting in him looking more like a blood-splattered sparrow than anything else.

"So you take it to increase your rank?"

"I suppose. Not many have taken it over the last few tens of thousands of years, though. The promotion doesn't really do too much to affect your standing... Most of the exam stuff is more annoying than anything else."

Huh... I see... So wait, why's Karen going to all the trouble of doing something that doesn't seem all that important, then?

Karen stopped eating her omelet, then turned toward me as if to speak. Had she read my mind again, I wondered.

"Touya, you've been granted God Almighty's blessing, you know?"

"So?"

"You're going to be in charge of that world eventually. And managing a world is something tasked to a higher tier of god, you know? That means... if things carry on, you're gonna outclass your big sister!"

"...Huh?"

...What's her problem, exactly?

"You're my little brother! You can't be better than me! That's why I gotta study my butt off and get to the bottom of this! You can't— Oof!" Karen started getting heated, so I brought a swift karate chop down on her head.

"I haven't seen you in days! I was getting worried, you idiot! And this is your reason?! I'm gonna karate chop you again, dumbass!"

"Why twice?!"

Sure, God Almighty favored me, but in terms of divinity, I was still way lower than any of the gods I'd met. Hell, I knew it'd take roughly ten thousand years for me to be properly recognized as a god anyway. I'd be nothing but a rank novice until then, and that was that.

Any god worth his salt would know the stark difference between Karen and me. And so, even the god of flight looked utterly baffled by her reasoning.

"Owie... But my dignity..."

"You never had any dignity to begin with!"

"I absolutely did, you know?! At least a little!"

Chapter IV: The World of Tomorrow

Good grief, what a moron... Stop worrying me... Guh, Moroha was right, I should've just left you be.

Divinity was one thing, but your actual ranking was another. Though it was true that you generally took on more responsibilities if you had more divinity.

Still, now I knew why this moron was out here... The only thing left to figure out was what to do with her. I knew that Yumina and the others were worried about her well-being, so ideally, I'd want to take her back home...

"When's this exam over, exactly?" I quietly asked Karen, who responded with a nervous expression. Evidently, something was wrong, but what?

"I'd like it to be done, but... it won't end until I resolve the current situation..." Karen mumbled as she looked up at the sky, a tired sigh escaping her lips. She then mechanically brought the omelet to her lips. Her eyes were so lifeless that I wondered what had even happened. Karen was in no state to answer, so the ketchup-soaked god of flight spoke in her place.

Uh, lemme wipe you down a little first

"In order to progress, you need to show clear development in your area of expertise. You effectively need to show that your abilities are good enough to justify the upgrade to your station. So in the case of a god connected to love..."

"Uh...She has to show a mastery of love?"

"Indeed. A couple of gods are currently in a lover's quarrel. If she can resolve their differences and bring them back to a happy relationship, then she'll pass. If not... she fails."

That made sense. Helping resolve a lover's spat was certainly a good test for a god of love.

I nodded quietly, then suddenly heard bickering voices from a nearby rose bush. The voices were drawing closer... Could they have been the voices of the couple Karen was supposed to save?

"Crap... They're here!" Karen groaned quietly, dropping her spoon and staring down at her plate. She looked mortified.

"W-Well, that's my cue to leave. See you later, newcomer! I'd love to try your interesting food again next time!"

"W-Wait! You can't just leave, you know?!"

But leave he did. He flew away from the gazebo. His panic actually had me concerned... Could this squabbling couple be that bad? My question would soon be answered by a voice from the nearby cobblestone path.

"Hey, Love Goddess! Tell this stubborn bag already!"

"Love Goddess! Tell this shallow man what's what!"

The two gods scuttled over to the table and slammed their hands down on it.

So it's these two, huh? They're a little scary...

The man had dark, tanned skin and a muscular body overall. He came off as pretty athletic on a whole. He had sapphire-blue eyes, short blond hair, and wore what resembled a stereotypical Roman toga and golden sandals.

The woman had fair skin and long black hair. She was more of a slender beauty. Her eyes were hazel, and she wore what resembled a white kimono with a blue sash. She also donned black leather boots on her feet.

"Uhm... How about, for now, the two of you talk. It'd be good if we calmed down, you know?"

"I've been trying to get her to calm down for a while now, but she just won't listen!"

"Who's the one who isn't listening, hm?! It's you! You just close yourself off like a spoiled brat!"

Chapter IV: The World of Tomorrow

"What'd you say?!"

"You got ears, don't you?!"

The two of them glared at one another. The intensity was palpable. Frankly, I was a little frightened. My parents sometimes had spats like this, but they didn't usually last long. Either my mom would apologize, or my dad would immediately fold.

"So uh... Karen? Who are they?"

"The god of the seas and the goddess of the mountains..." Karen sighed quietly as she pointed to them both. I would've expected the guy to be the god of mountains, personally... but it still kind of made sense. After all, the Greek god Poseidon was famously associated with the seas and he was most certainly male.

It was true that mountains had more of a rugged, manly feel to them, but there was also the concept of "mother earth." It wasn't worth fretting about in either case.

"So they're a couple...? I wouldn't have expected them to pair up like that..."

"Usually they work well together, you know? They just happen to get stubborn when they disagree..."

Upon hearing that, the two turned to Karen and roared, "I'm not the stubborn one here!" in unison. Karen most definitely had her work cut out for her.

"You're way too hard-headed! You're like a mountain hermit, woman! Try being freer like the sea's currents!"

"Ha! You want me to think more like you, jellyfish for brains?!"

"What'd you say?!"

"You got ears, don't you?!"

This is non-stop, huh? They can't even pause to hear each other out...

The two of them turned to glare at Karen, their terrifying gazes fixed on her. Then, at the same time, they both roared, "Tell us your thoughts, goddess of love!"

It felt like I was seeing things, but I could almost visualize the blazing fire between the two... Like the wrath of the gods had been personified, or something. Slowly, Karen opened her mouth to talk.

"W-Well, um... Oh, Touya! You're a newlywed, yes? That means you can give them advice, you know?"

"What?!"

H-Hold the hell up, Karen. What are you volunteering me for?!

"Who is this?"

"He's my little brother in the mortal world. You know, the newbie around here."

"Oh! You mean God Almighty's newest muse? He's married. That might help things plenty."

No, no, no! Wait! I-It's true that I'm married, but I've never had this kind of fight before! I'm no help! If we ever disagree, they usually outnumber me, so I just give in!

"You're a guy, so you should get it! Wives need to know their husband's needs, yeah?"

"Huh?! How am I supposed to know what you mean when you say 'Can you pass me that thing?' Am I supposed to be a mind reader?! Just tell me what the thing is and I'll pass it!"

"Like I said, any good wife should know off the bat!"

"I'm your wife, not your mother! Why should I be running around after you, anyway? What do you think, newbie?!"

"Oh, well... I mean... He should at least say thanks if you do stuff for him..."

I didn't really know how to respond to the goddess of mountains... I always tried to thank my wives for the things they

Chapter IV: The World of Tomorrow

did for me, but there were times when I'd forget. In response, she gave a smug grin, prompting the god of the seas to click his tongue.

"You're always so damn nitpicky, though! How many times do you want me to say sorry for something that happened like ten thousand years ago…?! Haven't I made it up to you by now?!"

"That's a fair point… If he's already apologized about it, it's uh… not super fair to hold it over his head, right?"

"See?!"

"Hey! Whose side are you on here?!"

…I'm not on any side!

The two continued to argue wholeheartedly. If either asked me for my opinion, they got mad if I said the wrong thing. The whole thing was a major pain in the ass. Constantly having to ask them to calm down was wearing away at my sanity.

Why was I even handling this to begin with? I glanced back at Karen, only to find her finishing up her omelet without a care in the world.

This is your mess, so fix it already!

I groaned quietly as the goddess of mountains followed my line of sight. Her eyes fell upon the omelet.

"…What is that? It looks good."

"Hm? Is this food from the mortal world?"

The two of them seemed awfully curious about her food all of a sudden.

Huh, they seem pretty interested.

Gods didn't need food or drink to survive, but there was actual foodstuff in the divine realm. There was wine, known as the nectar of the gods. There were berries known as amrit. And there were also fruits, referred to as ambrosia. They were supposedly the most perfect foods in all creation, so maybe they viewed mortal food as novel or fascinating.

"All the gods of cookery holed themselves up in heaven's kitchen a long time ago... I haven't had mortal food in tens of thousands of years... Hey, you got any more of that?"

"Uh, sure but... Actually, yeah! Why not try some? You always feel better after a good meal!"

Upon hearing the god of the seas' words, I quickly opened up **[Storage]** and set out a few dishes on the table. This was a prime chance to distract them from their argument.

"Ooh!"

"Now that looks delish!"

I brought out all kinds of different foods, from light snacks to heavier platters. The two of them paused their fighting to admire the vast array of food before them.

Sweet... It's not exactly a solution, but if this stops them from fighting even a little bit, I'll take it.

I sighed in slight relief. However, I still had no idea how to help them out in the long run.

◇ ◇ ◇

"Here you are, dear. Say aaah!"

"Mmm! Yummy! Hehe... It's even better when you feed it to me."

"Geez, you'll embarrass me saying things like that..."

I took a sip from my coffee as the duo in front of me exchanged sugary words. My drink was supposed to be straight black, but something about it was sweet.

"Ohhh! This is amazing too! A bountiful harvest from the mountains! Ah, it's a subtle earthy flavor... but it's just as lovely as you..."

Chapter IV: The World of Tomorrow

"And this seafood. It's so rich and deep… Though the flavor's plain, it's accentuated by so much else… It's just as charming as you, dear."

I gulped down my coffee, hoping they'd stop fawning over one another before long. I wanted to barf, frankly.

Bitter… I need my coffee way more bitter…

"How'd it come to this…?"

As the two began to eat, they started sharing their thoughts. At first, they simply agreed that the food was good, but then they started suggesting dishes to each other. Before long, they were happily talking and even feeding one another…

"I thought for sure this would be another long quarrel, but they're calm as can be. Fine job, goddess of love…"

"It wasn't me, you know?"

The god of flight had returned without me even noticing. This time he was covered in marinara sauce. Was he into tomatoes or something? Karen was just sitting there, utterly stumped. She quietly sipped some fruity water through a straw. She was probably feeling utterly defeated… And why wouldn't she? The problem she'd been struggling with basically just resolved itself.

It would've been better just to leave them be, most likely. There was a saying about not getting involved in marital spats, and it was probably true here.

"You're so sweet, dear!"

"Geez, no! You are!"

I stared blankly at the scene unfolding before my eyes. How had it come to this? How could they be so openly affectionate? I felt bad for anyone who saw them in this state.

Karen quietly muttered something in my direction. Her expression was still one of utter defeat.

What's that?

"What are you thinking...? You're just like that with your wives, you know? How can you not know that?"

Wait... what?! Th-That's not true, is it? Sure, we've been greeting each other more often with hugs and kisses, but... it hasn't been bad enough to make people angry, right? R-Right...?! Hrmm... I mean... I only just got married, so it's natural to get closer like that.

"You're newlyweds, so I think it's only natural."

"R-Right! Exactly! It's normal!"

I'm a newlywed! It's totally normal! That's right, bird!

I downed the rest of my coffee in one big gulp to hide the nervous blush on my face.

◇ ◇ ◇

In the end, Karen failed her test. It was because she hadn't brought the couple back together... They'd done it of their own accord. She had the option of retaking the exam with a different subject, but she just accepted the rejection for now. I think she was tired. It was understandable, really.

Once she returned home, Karen was swarmed by my wives. They'd been concerned for her safety.

"Welcome home! We're happy to see you safe."

"Hey, you okay?! You don't look so good!"

"O-Oh, we've drawn a bath for you, if you'd like to come with us!"

"Waaaaaah! You're all so kind!" Karen bellowed. She was so moved by the kind words from Yumina, Sue, and Linze that she hugged them all. She'd really worried them.

Chapter IV: The World of Tomorrow

"Welcome back," Moroha chuckled as she spoke to me and Karen.

"It was tough…"

"I told you not to go after her, didn't I?"

You could've given me more details… If I'd known it was something so dumb, I'd have just stayed home. Then again, if I hadn't gone, Karen might still be there.

"Not interested in taking the exam, Moroha?"

"No need. I'm happy down here with my swordplay. If I went up in status, I'd have more responsibilities, which would leave less time for training. There's just about no benefit in it for me."

Guess that makes sense… The only really higher-up gods I know are God Almighty, Granny Tokie… and uh… Oh yeah, the god of destruction, too.

Granny Tokie was always knitting or having tea, so it seemed to me like she had a lot of spare time.

"She's an exception. This is her first vacation in tens of thousands of years. Though time doesn't exactly matter to someone with her powers."

Good point… She can control time and space, so I bet she could travel through time if she felt like it.

"…Felt like it? Don't you know? Old Tokie's been to the future a few times already. She's played with your kids once or twice, too."

"She's what?!"

She's playing with my kids before me?! That's not fair! You can't mix your work duties with your personal life! Maybe I can get her to bring back a photo or something…

Either way, that was that. I was pretty damn tired.

Karen and the others went to take a bath together, and Moroha joined them.

I wanted to take a bath as well, but I had some business to attend to before dinner. Kousaka would get mad at me if I put it off too long.

Oh yeah, gotta talk to Ende about his wedding, too. I'll have him meet me at the tavern tonight.

I pulled out my phone and gave Ende a call.

◇ ◇ ◇

"Why wasn't I here when something so interesting happened?! That's... no... fair! You know?!" Karen exclaimed as she slammed her hands down on the table, groaning all the while.

I'd told her about everything that happened with the black mask incident, and that was her reaction. I didn't personally think it was that interesting. It was more a hassle than anything else, honestly.

"Damn it all! Why'd my test date have to be now? If I were there, I could've helped Listis and Reliel get to know each other better!"

"Y-Your love powers aren't solely heterosexual?!" Linze's eyes just about lit up as she spoke.

"Why would that matter when it comes to love? Gender, race, status, all things matter little in the face of love, you know? Feelings are what count, and whether they can be nurtured. It has to go both ways, though. One-sided love is never pretty, you know?"

You sound kind of like Reliel right now... I know love is love and all, but don't go poking your nose into their business at this point...

I sipped my coffee quietly, rolling my eyes at Karen's behavior.

Oh, got a text. Looks like Ende's waiting on me. Time to head on out.

"I'll be back in a bit."

Chapter IV: The World of Tomorrow

"Huh, you're leaving?! It's fine to hang out with guys, but you can't leave your wives high and dry too often, Touya!"

"Okay, who's teaching Sue weird stuff again?"

Cesca, who was standing quietly in the corner of the room, whistled a bit as she swept the floor.

You goddamn perverted maid! That's it, I'm issuing a punishment when I get back. No lewd comments from you ever again!

I glared at Cesca, then used [**Gate**] to head to the tavern. Once there, I pulled up my hood and went inside, finding lively music and general hustle and bustle in my ears. This place was lively as ever...

Wait... who's on the piano over there? Is that... Sousuke? Why's the god of music here?

"Yo, Touya. Over here."

"Sorry to keep you-—Huh?"

I was surprised to see Ende was already seated with his companions. Lycee sat by Ende's side, while Ney and Melle sat opposite them. It was a rare sight.

"Good evening, Touya."

"Been a while."

"Evening."

The three of them were wearing their pendants, giving them the outward appearances of regular human girls. They didn't quite look as prim and proper as they had the last time, however. Oh, and their clothes were real, too. It looked to me like they were getting pretty used to the world in general.

"It's rare to see all of you out here at once," I said as I pulled up a chair and sat between Ende and Melle. The four of them had already ordered their food and drinks, so I ordered a fruit wine. I was at a bar, so having one drink was fine. Even if I was still technically underage on Earth... Hurray for other worlds!

"It's my wedding day too! It's only natural I'd be here."

"Leaving everything to Endymion would spell chaos for Lady Melle. It's only natural I'd be here."

"I want to make sure the food's good. It's only natural I'd be here."

...I guess so.

I offered Ende a forced smile, noting that he was downing his ale rather fast. The poor bastard.

"So the venue's fine, but how many guests do you want, exactly?"

I wasn't sure what kind of relationships they'd even established. I knew I'd be attending, but I didn't know who else.

"I'm a silver-ranked adventurer, Touya. I'm friends with a lot of other adventurers and guild officials. Melle and the others have casual friends in the town, too."

Damn... *Didn't expect that, honestly. I always took you guys to be kind of antisocial.*

"I was Sovereign once, so I am used to dealing with other people and their needs. It's a similar principle here. I simply listen to others and help solve their problems," Melle spoke very matter-of-factly. That made me wonder if there was some way we could make use of her skills.

Maybe she can work in a supporting role under Kousaka or something...? Eh, we'll save it for later. Their wedding's the focus today.

"That reminds me, you guys in contact with any other Dominant Constructs?" I asked.

Melle was the Sovereign Phrase, and her species had followed her here in search of her power. Some wanted to take it for themselves, while others wanted to bring her home. After the whole thing with Yula and the mutants, however, all the other Phrase sent to this world ended up being destroyed.

Chapter IV: The World of Tomorrow

"I know Lycee's fine here, but you originally wanted to bring Melle home, right? Have you given up on that?"

My question prompted Ney to turn to me and start talking.

"It's far too late for that now... I did want her to return to Phrasia with me, but I now realize that wasn't what I truly desired. I simply wanted to live by her side, as I do now. I was envious of Endymion, so I wanted to drag her back to Phrasia in order to keep her there with me. But now that I'm here, I've come to terms with my feelings. There's no need for me to take her away."

Melle smiled softly, giving a little nod at Ney's words.

"Hehe... Don't worry, Ney. I'm with you now."

"L-Lady Melle! P-Please don't say such things in public, a-ah..."

Ney's face turned red, which was quite the rare, adorable sight. Part of me wondered if I shouldn't record it for posterity, just to prove she was capable of such a thing.

Ultimately, this situation had turned into a harem based around Melle... But if they were happy, I wasn't going to judge.

Eventually, the food arrived, so I picked up one of the meat skewers and took a big bite. It was really good.

"Oh right. Your brother is the new Sovereign back on Phrasia, right?"

"That's correct. His power as Sovereign is less than mine, but he's ruling compassionately. I feel sorry for causing him such trouble, but I hope we may meet again under brighter circumstances..."

Personally, I felt she could've gone to see him if she wanted to, but it was probably more complicated than that. If the old Sovereign suddenly showed back up, it could be seen as trouble for the current one who was struggling to make the best of a bad situation. I'm sure Melle didn't want that for him.

I couldn't go back to my home properly, either, so I understood how she felt. We just had to make the best of things in our new homes.

I didn't want to take things off in a sad direction, so I steered us back toward the main topic.

"So, uh... you want the ceremony done at our church, right?"

"Right. It's less of swearing before any god and more like making a vow before the spirits, isn't it? I'm fine with that."

Ende himself was a recipient of a god's blessing... so technically, that put him above the spirits, but I neglected to mention that fact. After all, the spirits that presided over my wedding were my direct subordinates.

"And we'll host the wedding reception at the Silver Moon Inn, sound good?"

"Mmm. There's enough room, and the food is good there. Is the set menu I requested okay?"

"It's just fine. Then we're just about sorted. Oh, wait... There's the matter of the wedding cake. I have some samples. My friend Aer, who runs the Parent Cafe, baked us some—"

"Ah! That's the most important thing of all! Let's see!"

Upon Lycee's urging, I reached into [**Storage**] and produced printout photos of each different type of cake that we had available.

"Amazing! They look too good to eat!"

"Hmhm... I like this white one with the flowery icing... But this fruit-filled one looks superb as well... Oh, I can't decide..."

"There are four of us, so... could we not have a cake each?"

No, no! That is not happening. A wedding cake isn't meant to be eaten like that... You're not eating one cake apiece on your wedding day!

Chapter IV: The World of Tomorrow

Ende quietly stared at one particular photo. It was a two-meter-tall cake.

"That's so big, man... What would happen if it fell? That'd be terrible."

"Oh, the really big ones are more imitation than real. They prioritize appearance over actual taste. A lot of these are inedible, actually."

"..." Silence reigned until Melle and the others plucked every tall cake photo from their hands and cast them aside. Evidently, they weren't interested in anything they couldn't stuff their faces with.

While they went over their lists, I turned toward the waitress to confirm our order.

"Lessee... Bean salad with simmered yams, sausage platter... and salted wings. Is that everything, folks?"

The waitress was met with utter silence from my four companions. They had gone completely still, staring into space blankly.

Uh... You guys okay? Hello?

"I can hear..."

"Huh?"

I heard Melle mutter something, but I couldn't quite make it out.

"I can hear an echo... It's faint... but I hear it..."

"Uhhh... A what now? What's going on, exactly?"

I was clearly confused, so Ende moved in to explain.

"The echo is the resonant sound that Phrasian lifeforms emit. It's the noise you sealed, remember?"

I did remember that. But if Melle was picking something like that up, surely I'd have known. We installed those sensor boards at the guilds to pick up those exact signals, didn't we?

"Huh...? Wait, doesn't that mean—?"

"That a Phrasian lifeform walks among us, yes."

I was about to stand up, but Ney grabbed my arm.

"Calm down. It's only one lifeform. Though, the reading feels strange."

"It's like a dominant construct... but also different, somehow."

"What?!"

A Dominant Construct?! Another one of Yula's followers?! Different, like a mutant?!

Ney immediately moved to dispel my anxiety.

"It's a complete unknown to me. I've never sensed this specific echo in my life."

"So he's not with Yula? Couldn't he be one you never met? Or like... Yula's offspring, or something?!"

I'd heard that the phrase could self-replicate... so maybe Yula had done something like that before dying.

"No, it's not like that. Asexually produced Phrase share the same echo as their parent. It sounds absolutely nothing like Yula's did, so it can't be related to him. If anything, it feels more like..." Ende trailed off as he nervously glanced toward Melle.

"It feels just like yours, Lady Melle... Could it be the Sovereign?"

Wait, what?

Lycee's words freaked me out even more. The Sovereign was Melle's little brother, right? Had he been mutated without us knowing?

"It is similar to mine... but it can't be my brother. It doesn't feel the same as him. Though, perhaps if he mutated, it could be different?"

Melle's expression seemed very conflicted. Even if it was the Sovereign, it would be very difficult for him to break through to

Chapter IV: The World of Tomorrow

this world now that the barrier had been repaired... so what was going on?

"Touya. Pull up your map."

"Huh? Oh, sure."

I did as Ende instructed, prompting him to stare at it for a few moments. After a while, he zoomed in on it and pointed toward a certain area.

"Right here. This is the source of the echo. Can we warp there now?"

"It's the Lassei Military Kingdom... I've never visited the area, so using [**Teleport**] might be unreliable. But I could manage it if I mix in a little divinity. You wanna go now?"

The four of them nodded. I knew Ende could use some form of teleportation magic, but apparently, it wasn't so good with long distances. Still, the course was set. Everyone wanted to go.

I canceled my order and paid the small compensation fee. I was a little annoyed about the extra expenditure, but there was no point worrying. Sousuke was still playing the piano, so I made sure to tell him we'd be out for a little bit in case anyone got worried.

The five of us headed into a nearby alleyway, and I told everyone to hold tight to Ende. No way was I going to be caught dead with the three Phrase girls clinging to me.

I placed my hand on Ende's shoulder, mustered some divinity up, and cast [**Teleport**].

"Oof!"

We manifested atop a building's roof, then promptly stumbled. Thankfully, we weren't right next to the edge, so we managed to steady ourselves on the roof without falling. I was stupid and hadn't considered taking the differences in distance from the ground into account.

"Didn't think we'd pop out into a city... Where are we, Touya?"

"Uhhh... Amatsumi. Yeah. It's a town, not a city. It's not that large, either."

Though it wasn't large, it was certainly lively. It was night, but the street lamps and neon signs illuminated the area pretty well. The wide streets were packed with bustling Gollem carriages.

The architecture was definitely unlike anything you'd find elsewhere on the western continent. It kind of felt like a town from an old western flick. There weren't any outlaws or cowboys, though.

"The town hasn't been destroyed yet, then..." Ney muttered quietly, her cautious eyes scanning the streets. Personally, I didn't like the ominous phrasing she'd opted for.

She had a point, though. If there was a Dominant Construct here, why wasn't it trashing stuff?

We scurried down from the roof and kept an eye on the people walking along the streets.

"Is it in this town, or..."

"I hear it... We're definitely in the right place. This way," Melle said, pointing toward a crowd of people at the end of a street. There was some kind of commotion going on over there.

There were so many people around that you'd think a celebrity had shown up or something.

"Hey, someone get the peacekeepers! And the Gollems, too!"

"There! Get him!"

"Take him out!"

...Huh? A fight? The Sovereign isn't getting in some kind of scrap over here, is he?

"Don't be stupid. Even if he's weaker than Lady Melle, the Sovereign is still insanely powerful. Neither humans nor their mechanical puppets could stand against him," Ney had clearly heard me muttering, and she was quick to correct me.

She was right. If a Dominant Construct was running wild, I doubted that it'd be a fight. It'd be more of a massacre.

Either way, whatever we were looking for was right in the middle of the crowd. I couldn't see because of all the people.

"Welp. Let's get this over with. [**Prison**]."

"H-Huh?! What the hell?!"

I formed a rectangular [**Prison**] in the middle of the crowd, forcibly pushing it apart like Moses parting the Red Sea. The five of us walked through the middle, and finally… we found what we were looking for.

"You little brat!"

"Too slow, bub! You're not gonna catch me moving like that. You even moving at all, mister?!"

The boy was surrounded by three burly men, but he was talking as if they were no match for him. He looked even younger than Renne… Six or seven, maybe? And yet, he moved with a startling level of grace, like a cat.

Or… a kitten, maybe? I couldn't help but compare him with Ende, who was standing next to me with a puzzled expression on his face.

The boy had flowing silvery hair, a teasing smile on his face, and a long scarf around his neck. He looked startlingly similar to Ende… Maybe a little too similar.

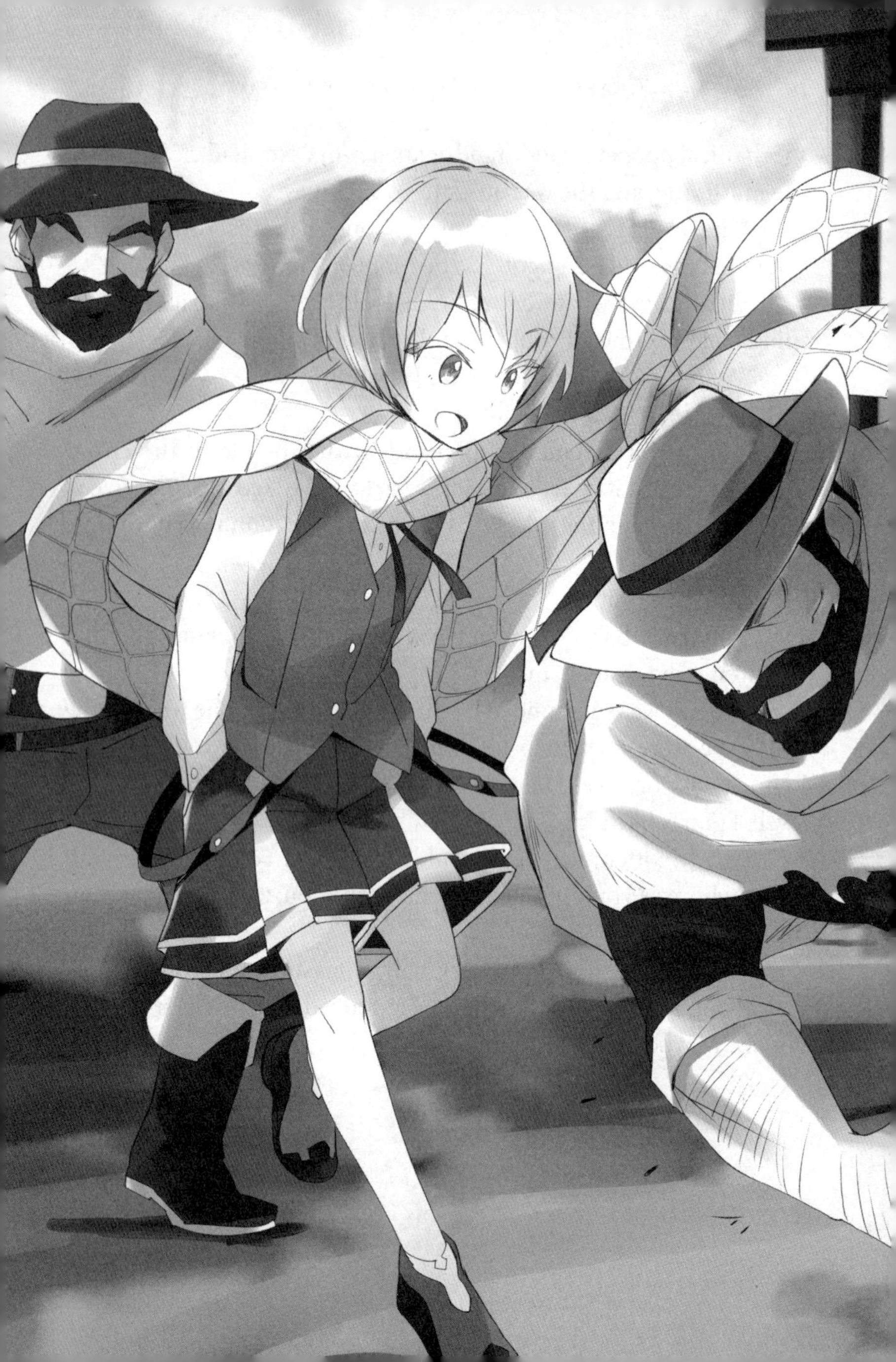

Chapter IV: The World of Tomorrow

"E-Endymion... You don't have a younger brother, do you?"

"Uh, no... And if he's the source of the echo, he can't be one of my species..."

Ney asked the same thing I was thinking, but was promptly shot down.

It's not his brother? But he looks just like him...

The boy turned to look at us. Hadn't taken him long to notice us, at least.

"Mmm? Oh, finally. Took you long enough. I ended up getting caught up with these weirdos!"

"Ghah?!"

"Hgagh?!"

"Bwagh?!"

The little boy casually struck all three men with incredible speed, knocking them to their knees.

What the hell is going on here? I could barely track those hits. He might be small, but he's seriously tough.

"Huh?!"

The boy ran right up to me with a huge smile on his face.

Do I know you, kid?

As the kid drew closer with that beaming grin, I realized I'd made a mistake. This wasn't a boy at all... It was a little girl!

Her icy blue eyes focused right on me.

"Wow, you guys don't look all that different! A little younger, I guess? Hey, can I get a photo?"

"Hold up... Who are you?" I asked, feeling exasperated. This kid was seriously full of energy.

The four behind me were so confused that I was the only one capable of interrogation at this point.

"Oh, riiight! You don't know me yet, huh? It's nice to meetcha, then! I'm Allistella! But my moms and dad just call me Allis. You can call me that, too!"

"W-W-W-W-Wait, hold on. You're Allis, and your... uh... Where are your parents?"

The girl, Allis, casually pointed toward Ende, then Melle, then Ney, then Lycee.

"That's my dad. And those are my moms."

Silence reigned for a good few moments. The blinking of the neon lights intensified as the world spun around me. I was taken aback, but not nearly as much as the four people behind me.

In unison, they all screamed into the night, their resounding, "WHAAAAAAAAAT?!" echoing through the streets of Amatsumi.

◇ ◇ ◇

"E-Er, so... this is Ende's daughter?"

"Apparently, yeah..."

I informed Yumina about the situation as I sat down on the sofa, glancing toward the little girl leaning against Melle's lap.

We'd returned to Brunhild in order to hear what Allis had to say, but... well...

"Sleepy... Naptime now..." she murmured, slumping down like her batteries were out of charge and rested her head against her mother's(?) lap. The girl sure marched to the beat of her own drum, that was for sure.

I turned to Ney, who was quietly thinking to herself.

"So uh, what's this all about, exactly? Do you think she could be your kid with Ende?"

"No. I don't think so. Not that way, at least. She has Phrasian characteristics, but her echo isn't similar to mine or Lycee's. She

Chapter IV: The World of Tomorrow

sounds more like something between Endymion and Lady Melle. That sound alone is proof of their relation."

Well, she does have Ende's hair color... And those icy eyes are just like Melle's too.

She probably called Ney and Lycee her moms because they were in a relationship with Melle as well. And in that case, Allis was Ende and Melle's biological child. But that meant...

"Are you guys doing a shotgun wedding because you knocked her up?!"

"...Touya, don't joke around like that ever again."

"I certainly don't remember giving birth."

Both of Allis' presumed parents glared at me.

I was just trying to lighten the mood!

"Well, my best guess is that she is their child. From the future."

"...From the future, Yumina? But... Wait... could Space-time magic be involved?!"

Yumina clapped her hands together. We didn't want to wake Allis from her sleep, so we spoke in hushed tones.

"Hey, *Dad*. How about you take her to bed?"

"Gah! I just told you not to mess with me!" Ende grumbled quietly as he picked Allis up and walked out of the room behind our head maid, Lapis. Ney, Melle, and Lycee followed after them. They seemed understandably on edge.

It was kind of nice seeing her get carried like that... My dad used to do that to me when I was little.

"Space-time magic... That makes sense. There's precedent for it, after all," Leen said as she leaned forward and nodded her head.

We knew about Alerius Palerius, the master of Space-time magic. We also knew that his son, Lerios Palerius, traveled to the Reverse World by mistake and founded the Primula Kingdom.

When he landed there, he was blasted back around two hundred years, but he hadn't noticed that at the time.

Though it wasn't a formal school of magic or anything, time travel had precedent under this world's magic system.

"So you're saying she might be a Space-time mage?"

"No, I think it might have been unintentional on her part. In the case of Lerios, it was an accident, remember?"

I didn't know about any spells that allowed for direct time travel, so she'd probably come back due to some kind of mistake. But that made me a little worried... Was something bad going to happen in the future?

Augh... This is stressing me out!

"What about Granny Tokie? Isn't she the goddess of Space-time?"

"Oh, right."

As I grumbled, Sue suddenly asked the right question.

Granny Tokie was the goddess of Space-time. If anyone could tell me what was going on here, she could. Hell, maybe she was the one who brought Allis back here? Moroha told me that Tokie had made visits to the future before, after all.

"Where is she?"

"Uhm... She was on the balcony earlier, but..." Linze trailed off before telling me Tokie's daily routine. In the mornings and afternoons, she sat on the balcony knitting away. She was actually repairing the shredded world barrier through her knitting. Around dinner time, she'd eat with the girls (and me if I was around) before chatting with Sue, Linze, and the others. Then, she went to bed fairly early.

It was already past ten at night, so she was probably asleep.

Chapter IV: The World of Tomorrow

Right when that discussion ended, I felt a presence behind me. I turned to find Tokie waving at me.

"Apologies for keeping you waiting, dear."

She'd received the blessing of God Almighty in the same way that I did, so we both had the ability to sense one another.

I opened my mouth to ask her a question, but she suddenly spoke up as if she knew what I was going to ask.

"I understand, dear. It's about little Allis, isn't it?"

"You know about what happened?"

"She was time-warped. I could hardly not notice, dear. I thought she'd appreciate it more if you all went to fetch her rather than me. I was certain she would be able to take care of herself in the interim," Granny Tokie said as she smiled gently. She seemed pretty familiar with Allis' mannerisms.

"So is she Ende and Melle's kid?"

"Indeed. She was born to the two of them in the future. Unlike Melle and her kind, she grows much like a human being. Though she has the traits of her mother's species as well."

So Ney was right. Allis was the biological daughter of Melle and Ende. But why had she come from the future? That part was still completely eluding me.

"Did you bring her here?"

"In a manner of speaking, but not directly. The girl was caught in a timequake. One of the fault lines between space and time had shifted, creating a ripple in time itself. The ripple soon became a wave, catching the girl and threatening to sweep her away. That was why I guided her here, lest she become trapped elsewhere."

So she might've been adrift in time and space without your intervention, huh? That's nuts.

Back on Earth, there were urban legends about people who'd been spirited away to times not their own. I didn't know if those stories were true or not before, but they seemed more likely than not at this point.

"I tried to explain what was going on as she was set adrift from her location, but she was somewhat restless and sped off. A bit of a tomboy, she is."

Tomboy's an understatement. She beat the crap out of those huge dudes.

"But wait, what's that timequake thing? Does that mean something bad's gonna happen in the future?"

I'd seen a lot of movies about people coming back from ruined futures, so the thought of this being a similar scenario was more than mildly concerning.

"No, nothing like that. The timequake is a simple distortion in the fabric of Space-time. When a water droplet impacts a still surface, ripples run out, but the surface soon goes still again. The girl just happened to be near the impact point at the time. The future itself is quite peaceful, I assure you."

"Won't Ende and Melle be worried in the future, though?"

"Why would they be? After all, would they not already know that their child visited them in the past?" Granny Tokie smiled at Linze as she answered her question.

Huh? But...

"If the future Ende, and the future all of us, knew about the timequake, why wouldn't we try to keep Allis away from it?"

"There's no need to prevent it. The children caught up in the timequake return after only a few minutes from the future's perspective. The past is predetermined, dear. What has happened has happened. You couldn't have prevented it even if you tried."

Chapter IV: The World of Tomorrow

So... the future can't be changed? I guess it's like one of those time travel stories where someone comes back and tries to change the future, only to find out they were part of the events that led to it to begin with.

"Allis' arrival didn't affect the future or anything, right?"

"Not on my watch, dear. I have a job, after all. There's nothing to worry about in that regard."

Oh, fair enough. Guess she is a high-ranking goddess, and one of God Almighty's beneficiaries to boot. That's a little reassuring.

I asked for a little more detail and she mentioned stuff about time spirits repairing anything out of order, but I didn't fully understand. Either way, Allis' presence and us knowing about her being from the future wasn't enough to change it. Apparently, Granny Tokie would ensure that nothing would stray from its course. She'd ensure the world would converge no matter what. Kind of an ominous power, all things considered...

"I suppose that means Allis' arrival in the past is already confirmation enough that she'll return safely to the future..." Leen quietly pondered to herself.

I remembered that Doc Babylon's artifact didn't let you gaze into fully established futures, however... It made sense that something traveling back would make things more concrete, though... Plus, well... we had a literal goddess working with us. Expecting complete sense out of something like that seemed unreasonable.

I wondered if Tokie considered this interference on her part, so she was committed to not have it change anything.

"Hey, Granny! How long are we gonna have Allis here?" Sue leaned back against the couch and raised a brow toward Granny Tokie as she asked that question.

Hm... It's true that she's supposedly gonna return safely. But even if she'll only be gone for a few minutes in the future, what if she ends up staying here for a year or longer? It'd be bad if she stayed long enough to see her own birth!

"Oh, well... I will need to wait for the timequake to subside, dears. It shouldn't be much longer than a few months though, I'm sure. I'll be sure to send her safely on her way once the time is right."

"Er... I've actually been wondering something..." Hilde tentatively raised her hand.

Hm? What's on her mind?

"Earlier you said... children? When you were talking about being caught in this timequake... could you perhaps have meant..."

"Oh, yes! Of course! Apologies, I didn't quite explain that. I can't believe I forgot something so important!" Granny Tokie clapped her hands together and gave a light chuckle after saying that.

Uh? What?

"Allis wasn't the only one caught in the timequake! All of your children were as well. I'm sure they'll pop up in this era sooner or later."

A resounding "What?" rang out through the room. I was in perfect synchronization with my wives on that front.

My mind went blank. I could barely even process what I'd just heard. It was probably the same for the others too. It was as if time itself had stood still. I couldn't move a muscle.

...She didn't freeze time, did she? No... I... I can still think.

Our confusion gradually reached a crescendo. Then, the screaming began.

"WHAAAAAAT?! G-GRANDMOTHER, WHAT DOES THIS MEAN?!"

"K-KIDS?! M-MINE, TOO?!"

Chapter IV: The World of Tomorrow

"A-AH! D-DON'T FAINT, SIS! H-HEY!"

"A CHILD OF MINE MIGHT BE HERE, THEY MIGHT?! WHATEVER COULD THIS MEAN?!"

"M-MINE AND TOUYA'S...?!"

"G-G-GRANNY, REALLY? IS THAT TRUE?"

"What an astonishing situation... But really... my child with my darling? Could they be here already?"

"I-I'm not ready to be a mother yet! I-I'm not!"

"Th-This is much too soon! Far too soon!"

Everyone was in a panic. I was too struck by shock to say a thing. I couldn't even get a word in edgewise.

"Er... When did this happen? Did they all come together?"

"When they'll appear depends on where they were in relation to the timequake's epicenter. Allis happened to be the closest, that's all. If your children were close to one another, they may appear as a group."

"Th-This could be a disaster, couldn't it?! What if the children end up somewhere dangerous?!"

Granny Tokie gently squeezed Lu's shoulder to ease her anxiety.

"Allis and most of your children are gold and silver-ranked adventurers. They've slain many Behemoths without any special equipment, even. I wouldn't worry."

A resounding "What?" rang out through the room. Once again, I was in perfect synchronization with my wives on that front.

Gold and silver-ranks, seriously? And they've killed Behemoths? I had to use a Frame Gear the first time I duked it out with one... My kids aren't gonna surpass me that much, are they?

"G-Grandmother Tokie! Is my child silver or gold?"

"U-Uhm, how old is mine?!"

"How's my child's swordsmanship?!"

"Now now, settle down. You don't want me spoiling the surprise, do you? I'm sure you can learn things from them yourselves when the time is right. I'll make sure Allis doesn't go running her mouth, either."

All of my wives let out small, sad sighs upon hearing that.

But seriously, what?! We're skipping pregnancies and childbirth and going straight to meeting them, huh?

"Sorry, Ende. But your problems seem pretty goddamn small right now! Oh man..." I quietly opened up a search engine and typed in "how to deal with children."

.ıll Chapter V: Another Visitor

The next morning...

I looked out from the kitchen window. There wasn't a cloud in the sky. Even though it was a clear and calm morning, there was a tense air over the dining hall. Seated at the table were me, my wives, the god of agriculture, Granny Tokie (all the other gods except her and Kousuke were still asleep), and my guests. Ende, Ney, Lycee... and Allis.

Despite the abundance of people, there wasn't much in the way of talking going on. The only sounds were the scraping of silverware against plates and Allis' merry cheering.

"Yummy! I love this! Mom, you have some too!"

"R-Right... I shall..."

Allis smiled over at Melle. The two were sat next to each other, tucking into a meal of bacon and eggs.

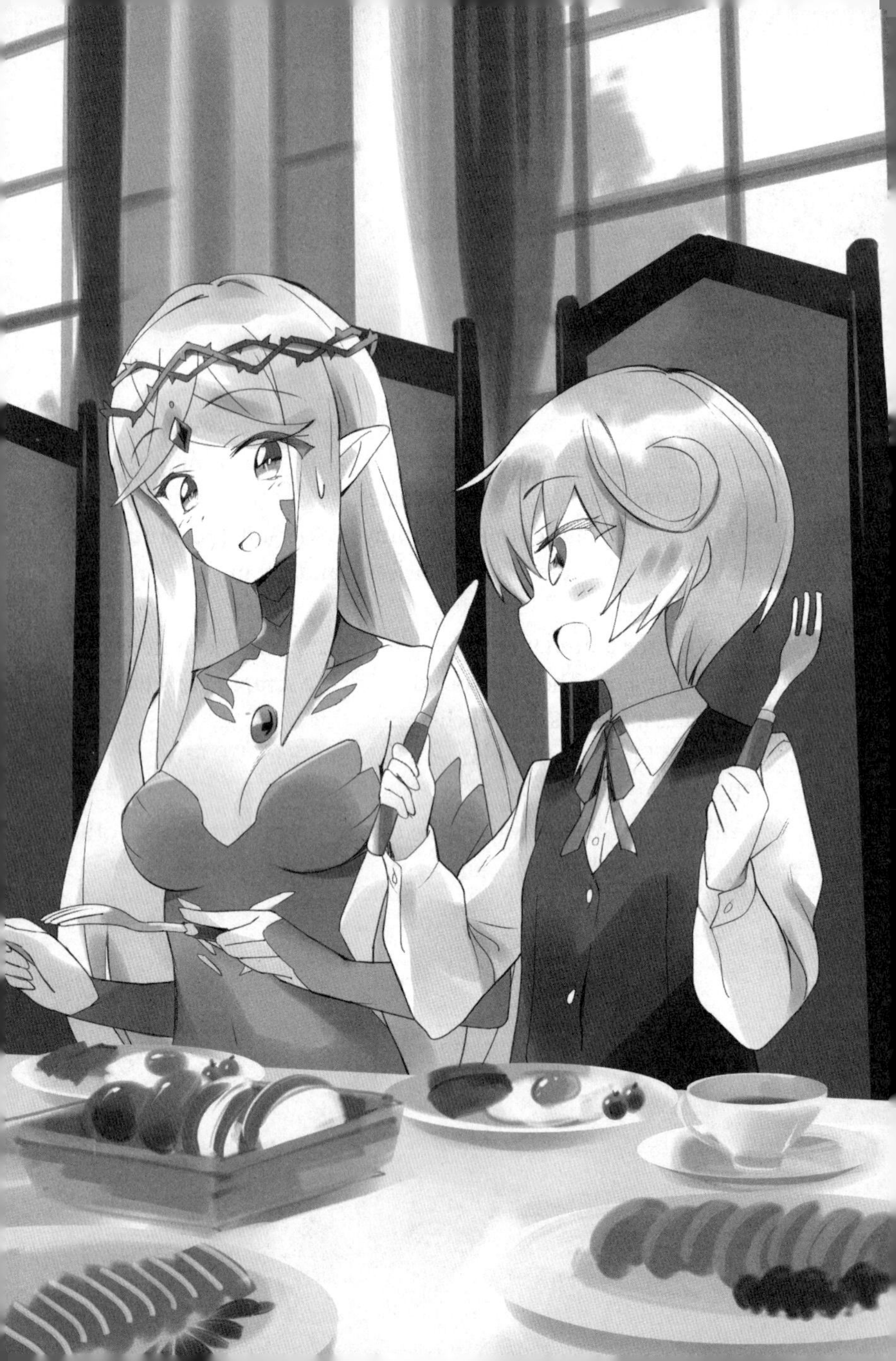

Chapter V: Another Visitor

We simply sat there staring, unsure of what to actually say. Granny Tokie had already told her not to tell us about the future, but obviously, we had burning questions.

"H-Hey, little Allis. How old are you?"

Looks like Elze is stepping up. I'm sure she's wondering about things as much as the rest of us are. She looks a little nervous though.

"Pfft!"

"Wh-What's wrong? Did I say something funny?"

Allis suddenly started laughing out loud, prompting Elze to grow flustered.

"You called me little Allis! That's so funny to hear from you, Master!"

"M-Master?!"

"Mhm. You're my martial arts teacher, duh! And I'm six."

"O-Oh, I see..."

Elze is teaching martial arts?! And Allis is her student...? I guess those punches from yesterday make a lot more sense now.

The little snippet of future information was certainly interesting. Her father, Ende, was a disciple of the god of combat alongside Elze. It kind of made sense that things would progress that way.

"...Hold on. If Elze is your master, then what about me? Don't I teach you?"

"You're not home very often, Daaad! And when you do come home, you're always too sleepy to play!"

"...He doesn't come home? What is the meaning of this, Endymion?!"

"Wh—?! How am I supposed to know?!"

Melle glared at Ende and gave a shake of her head. I didn't think that was fair, though. The future Ende was at fault, not this one!

"He's always busy with work. Or so he says..."

187

"So he says?! Wh-Why don't you believe him?!"

Ende was clearly getting no support from his daughter. His family dynamic certainly seemed colorful.

"Wait, he has a job?"

"D-Don't ask more, Touya..."

"Dad's a guildmaster! He works for the adventurer's guild. Not the one in Brunhild, though."

Oho. That's certainly interesting. I didn't think of that as a career path for him, but I guess it makes sense. He works for them as an adventurer right now, even.

"So that's why Elze is mentoring you. Wait, what about Uncle Takeru? Wasn't he available?"

"I wanted to learn from him, but Dad said no! He said it was waaay too early for me to experience that kind of pain!"

"Good job, me!" Ende said, suddenly looking very satisfied with himself. I could sympathize. I had a feeling that if she grew up with that guy as her main teacher, then she'd end up as some battle-centric maniac.

"S-So is my child training alongside you, perhaps?" Elze went on the offensive, asking for as much as she could now that she had an angle to work with. Nobody dared interrupt her. We all wanted to know as well.

"Umm... Elna doesn't like fighting very much. Linne and I fight lots, though! Actually, the other day..."

"Allis, dear."

"Huh? Um... Hehehe... That's a secret! If I tell you too much, it won't be as fun later. I don't wanna make anyone mad! Nope, nope!" Allis said that and giggled a bit as Granny Tokie looked her way. Seems like I couldn't learn too much about my own kids.

Still, we had learned something. We knew that Elze's kid was named Elna and that she didn't much like fistfighting. Hard to

Chapter V: Another Visitor

believe Elze's kid could be like that, though. Elna was probably a girl's name... But why wouldn't she be interested in fisticuffs like her mom? Based on the puzzled look on Elze's face, she felt the same way.

Allis had also mentioned someone named Linne. I wondered if that was another one of my kids.

I glanced over at Linze, who was making a perturbed expression of her own. She'd most likely been thinking the same thing as me. That Linne was her child. I was sure she had many questions, but she was clearly holding back on account of Granny Tokie.

If you got Allis in a one-on-one, you could probably squeeze answers out of her. She didn't exactly seem like the kind of girl who could keep secrets.

"Hey, Dad, if you're free today, we should spar!" Allis exclaimed as she tugged at Ende's arm.

"Huh? You want to fight me?"

...A daddy-daughter deathmatch?

Ende glanced at Melle, who just looked more bewildered than anything else.

"The training ground to the north should be free. If you're interested in using it, it could be fun to watch." Moroha casually mentioned a suitable fighting spot as she tucked into her salad. I hadn't even seen my sister appear at the table!

"Yay! Sounds good!" Allis certainly sounded happy about it. Still, the knights were trained by both her and Commander Lain, so they knew the schedule. If Moroha said the field was free, then it was free.

"I'd like to watch that fight too. It could be interesting."

"Y-Yes, I... I'd like to see it as well."

"I would be curious to observe, I would."

"M-Me too!"

Everyone gradually raised their hands and voices, asking to watch the bout. They were all clearly interested in what Allis could do... and I was no exception.

We all wanted to take the chance to learn more about what the kids from the future were capable of. We'd definitely find out sooner or later, but... it didn't hurt to know a little more in advance.

I saw a small bit of what Allis could do back in Amatsumi, but I had a feeling she was holding back. Besides, I was interested in seeing just how a gold or silver-ranked adventurer from the future would fare against Ende.

◇ ◇ ◇

"Hey, Touya. Should I go easy on her?" Ende quietly whispered to me as we walked along.

"That's a tough one, man..."

He was fighting his daughter from the future, after all.

"You should probably try to win, right? You've gotta keep your dignity as her dad. Plus, kids have to overcome the hurdles left behind by their folks! That's pretty basic, yeah?"

"I-I guess so?"

"But maybe that's better done against boys... You don't want your little girl to get all sulky and sad if you beat her up, right? She might yell about how she hates you or something."

"Wh—?! Why would you say that?! Now I don't know what to do!" Ende groaned. His eyes were pleading with me, but I didn't have a good answer for him. Frankly, I expected my own kids to want to fight me at some point, so I was going to use this battle as a frame of reference. He'd make a perfect test run.

Ende continued to worry until we made it to the northern field. It wasn't quite as intense as the main training field, but this area was

Chapter V: Another Visitor

protected by a divine barrier. In other words, you could go all-out without worrying too hard.

We mostly used this place for magic or tech experiments. Or for Moroha or Takeru to show off their stuff. Sometimes I'd bring monsters here for mock battles with the knights too. In one corner of the field stood a small elevated arena for one-on-one fights, which was the main stage.

Ende and Allis both equipped fingerless gloves made out of monster leather. I didn't want them smashing each other with heavy gauntlets, after all. None of our gear fit Allis, but Linze took her sewing kit out and almost immediately refitted those gloves to a child's size. It was kind of insane, actually.

Don't tell me that rapid sewing is her divine benefit manifesting...?

Allis clenched her fists as if to test the tension of the gloves she wore. Gloves were important in fistfights as they protected the fist, the wrist, and also reduced the damage you dealt to your foe. Though the hitting part was still real, so you could easily inflict pain. I wondered if that'd be okay.

Granny Tokie hadn't stopped anything though, so presumably, it was.

"Alright, let's begin."

On Moroha's call, Ende and Allis moved into the center of the ring.

"No magic allowed. If you fall from the area's edge, you're out. Time limit is five minutes. If I call the match, it's over. Got it?"

Both Ende and Allis nodded. When they stood by each other, their height difference was really accentuated. Ende was around a hundred and seventy centimeters, while Allis had to be only a hundred and twenty.

"Now... fight!"

"Here I gooo!" Allis roared as she rocketed forward with a boom. She swung out her fist with brutal force.

Ende swiftly caught it, but then the girl brought her left hand swooping up toward his chin.

"Oof!" Ende groaned as he kept on ducking and diving. However, Allis just kept the blows coming. It was a relentless assault against her dad.

"She moves precisely, she does."

"Mhm. She's maneuvering her body at just the right angle. But her moves seem a little too predictable, don't you think?"

Yae and Hilde discussed the battle off to the side. Was she using feints or was she actually trying? It was hard to tell. I turned to Elze to get her thoughts.

"What do you think? You're her future master, and all."

"It's hard to say right now. I might have only taught her the basics, from what I'm seeing now... Oh, wait."

"Haaah!"

I turned to look back at the fight and noticed that Allis had balled up spiritual energy, or chi, into her fists.

Wait, she can do that?!

"Ghaaah!"

Ende brought both arms up in a cross-block, but he was still pushed back by the impact. Allis seemed to have planned for this, as she thrust her arms out and unleashed a torrent of crystal thorns from her hands.

"Prisma Rose!"

"Huh?!"

Before Ende realized what was coming, his legs were tangled in the vines of a crystalline thornbush. He immediately swiped

Chapter V: Another Visitor

his hand at them to break them off, then jumped back to put some distance between him and his daughter.

"Lady Melle, that was..."

"Indeed. That was my Prisma Rose ability... How surprising."

"I suppose she really is your daughter..."

The Phrase moms seemed pretty impressed, but wasn't that a violation of the rules? Or did natural abilities using your body not count as magic? Moroha seemed to think it was fine, at any rate.

The crystal vines pulled back and wrapped themselves around Allis' elbow. They then pushed forward until they coalesced onto her hand and formed a huge fist-shaped object.

"Haaah!"

"What the—?!"

Allis pulled back, then punched forward, releasing the massive fist at Ende. The vines around it looked like a spring coil connecting to Allis' arm.

I was pretty sure I'd seen that in a cartoon before... Like a big red boxing glove that popped out and bashed someone's face.

"Oh, that seems like an alteration of my Prisma Guillotine. What a fine use."

I was dumbfounded, but Melle was simply nodding along with the fight. It seemed like Allis had incorporated a lot of her mother's biological traits into her fighting style.

"Gwugh!"

Ende dodged the crystal fist, but it was yanked back in an arc and biffed him hard in the head. Allis then followed up with a second crystal fist that was attached to her other hand.

You're done for, man!

"Divine Style... Echoing Thunder!" Ende screamed as he blasted a palm strike against the incoming fist.

A shattering sound rang out as it smashed into bits.

"I'm not done yet! Get pulverized!" Allis exclaimed as she charged forward and closed the distance, lunging right for Ende's midsection. It was kind of like watching a small version of Elze fight. That was no surprise though, given who'd trained her.

However, I had a feeling that mirroring Elze was a bad idea. After all, Ende trained with her just about every day. He knew all of her tricks, just like she knew his. When it came to fighting, the best thing you could do was outsmart your foe. And as Hilde had said earlier, her moves were predictable, since they were similar to Elze's and all.

Ende suddenly sidestepped the incoming strike. He then swept his leg out. Allis' legs were caught by the sweep, and she stumbled. This allowed Ende to close in and grab her.

"Huh?! Wha—?!"

The girl was flung high into the air, where she spun around before landing right on her back. Ende closed in and swung his fist right at her face... but obviously stopped right before hitting her.

"Game set. Ende wins," Moroha called the match, ending the bout.

Hm... So he won after all. Well, I figured he'd win. I'm just glad he didn't throw the match on purpose. I would've laughed if he'd gotten serious and still had his ass beat, though.

"Geez! I thought I could beat you when you were like this, Dad!"

"Hahaha... You're a bit too young for that. No way I was gonna lose to a kid," Ende chuckled quietly as he spoke to the girl. He then walked over toward me.

"...You're looking kinda sweaty, man."

"Gah! She nearly took me down, dude. What the hell's with this girl? She was full of tricks!" Ende muttered quietly as he passed me.

She's your daughter, man. You shouldn't be so surprised.

Chapter V: Another Visitor

Ney and Lycee suddenly grabbed Ende from either side, firmly restraining him.

"Agh?! What the heck?!"

"You could've stood to be gentler with your daughter."

"Indeed. Endymion... You're not acting fatherly enough."

With that, Ende was dragged off to a nearby corner.

Yikes.

Allis didn't seem to mind so much, and she promptly stood up.

"Hey, Duke! Lemme fight you next!"

"Huh?!"

I turned back to see Ende being chastised and realized the predicament I was in. If I wasn't careful, I'd end up in the same boat as him.

"Er, well... I appreciate the invite, but..."

"I'll fight you next. That fine, Touya?"

As I sputtered quietly, Elze came over with her own leather gloves on.

Thank goodness... Saved by the wife.

"Ooh! Yeah, I wanna fight a younger version of you! That sounds cool!" Allis said, sounding excited to face Elze. She was positively beaming, which highlighted how much of a kid she was.

"She is strong for a child, she is. We must be sure not to fall behind, Hilde-dono."

"Mhm. Let's do our best to at least increase our standing with the guild."

Yae and Hilde nodded to each other. They were all registered with the guild, but they didn't do many quests. And so, their ranks hadn't risen much. I was a gold-ranked adventurer, but Yae and Hilde only occasionally went to the dungeon islands to hunt monsters or patrol for lost adventurers. That was why the two of them were only red-ranked.

IN ANOTHER WORLD WITH MY SMARTPHONE

If Allis was truly a gold or silver-rank like Granny Tokie had said, that meant she'd outclassed Yae and Hilde in the eyes of the guild. Though, that was only talking from a future perspective. She wasn't even a guild member in this era. Still, that made me wonder just who had allowed a six-year-old child to register... I wondered if Relisha had some kind of hand in that move. I knew adventurers were accepted based on merit, but it was still a little much.

I wasn't really worried about Yae or Hilde beefing up their ranks, since they could easily get to silver if they just went hunting Dragons for a bit. After that, they'd just need to take out a Behemoth or two and they'd be set on the gold rank with me.

Man... I guess gold and silver's gonna get pretty busy soon. Most of them are gonna be my family members...

After the battle (Elze won, obviously), Allis wanted to walk around the castle town, so she charged off with her family. I was relieved, since it was hard just to keep up with her in conversation.

Elze, Yae, and Hilde went to the guild. They were keen to take on some quests. There were no big targets in Brunhild, but apparently, there was a Cyclops rampaging in the mountains of Roadmare. It wasn't as big a target as a Dragon, but it was still worthwhile. I sent the trio to Roadmare with a **[Gate]** and told them to call me when they were done.

In the meantime, I went to Babylon's library to look into Space-time magic. I ended up meeting Doc Babylon and Elluka there, along with Fam, the terminal gynoid in charge of the library.

"Magic that transcends space and time, you say... Most fascinating. Even a genius such as I can't say much about it for sure. Unless... If we have Allis return through a Space-time fissure, we could extrapolate point referential from that and..."

I left the muttering doctor to herself and turned toward Elluka.

Chapter V: Another Visitor

"Doesn't Noir, the black crown, use Space-time magic?"

"To an extent, but it's limited. It can accelerate time to a degree, and pull items from parallel timelines."

"Could it travel to the future or the past?"

"Hm... I'm not so sure on that front. It could hypothetically happen, but I think it would take a significant amount of compensation. Perhaps if you traveled in the right way that would become irrelevant, but who knows."

The price to pay for using Noir was having your own time rewound. Your body would be de-aged, effectively. It was a pretty cool power, but if you used it too much or misjudged how much it'd take, then you could become a child... Or even worse, back to how you were in the womb. That'd be too harsh a price to pay.

"Noir can feel things through time, right? Could it sense others coming back?"

"Well... perhaps? You might find out if you activate its active ability and share those senses for a time, but... you wouldn't want Norn to pay the price for that, would you?" Elluka asked as she glared at me from behind her glasses. I shook my head in response.

Norn was her sister, so she was obviously worried about me roping her into something dangerous. I had no such plans, though. I'd hoped that Noir might be able to figure out when my kids were coming back, or where they'd show up. But if we had to resort to Norn paying a price for that, it didn't matter.

If my kids were anything like Allis, they were crazy powerful. If they came up against monsters or beasts, they'd win. Though such things weren't the only threats in this world. Some evil people could trick kids into traps and slave traders, to name a few. I didn't want my kids getting mixed up with those people...

To be honest, Granny Tokie would probably let me know when my kids showed up, but I didn't want them getting into trouble like Allis had when she'd landed here. Or rather... I didn't want them causing trouble for innocent bystanders.

As I quietly pondered the matter to myself, Doc Babylon tapped me on the shoulder.

"What caused this timequake, anyway? Did you ask Allis?"

"Oh, uh, no I don't know. From what I understand, it's not like we can stop it, so I didn't really think to ask."

Allis had come here because of a timequake in the future. But presumably, there was something that had caused it. Much like how earthquakes beneath the ocean could cause tsunamis.

In the past, the white and black crowns went haywire and forced the invading Phrasian lifeforms back into the gap between worlds, as well as repairing the world barrier. Could the timequake be the result of Albus and Noir going haywire again? I certainly hoped not.

I looked over one of the old books left behind by Palerius, but it didn't result in me finding any new information. All in all, it seemed fruitless.

Part of me wished my kids could just call my phone when they arrived. That way, I'd be able to just pick them up... However, that was wishful thinking.

Nothing had happened yet, but I was still very worried. I wondered if this was something only a parent could feel.

A few days passed after that, and Allis had settled in.

"Kids are great, ain't they, Touya?" Ende smirked my way as he spoke an easily misunderstood line.

"...What happened to you, man?"

What's up with him? What's he smiling for?

Chapter V: Another Visitor

Ende was looking at a group of kids playing with the capsule machines outside the Strand store.

...Keep staring and you'll get arrested.

"I didn't really get the fuss when she first showed up, but since she's started living with us... I dunno, she has a real cute side to her. She looks just like Melle when she laughs. I think I finally understand how doting dads must feel."

"...Who are you, man? Did you get swapped with a fake Ende?"

"You'll see before long, my dude. It's only a matter of time. Once you're a dad, things just change."

"Keep this up and I'll barf."

His cheery face was really pissing me off. I felt like punching it, frankly. Maybe a firm smack would bring him back to sanity, even. It'd be a service!

"I didn't call you up to hear you talk about your kid, man. I wanna know if you learned anything."

"Oh, yep. We learned this and that."

I figured Allis would tell her parents more about the future than she'd shared at the breakfast table the other day. That was why I'd called Ende up to get that information from him.

"First up, you've got nine kids. One boy, the rest are girls."

"I know that already!"

"You do?!"

Oh wait, I guess I never explained that to Ende. Well, whatever. Just tell me more!

"Uhhh... As for the rest, lessee... Your oldest is eleven, I think? And your youngest is five. Your oldest kid is already a gold-rank."

Seriously? Nine kids born in the span of six years? Well, I guess it makes sense, since they're all from different women... Wait, eleven... That's how old Yumina was when I first met her. Don't tell me my oldest is already engaged. That can't be?! Oh geez... I haven't even met her, but I'm already fretting... Is this how a dad feels when he gives his daughter away on the big day?

"Your oldest isn't engaged. She says she'll only marry someone stronger than her. And nobody's really higher than gold, so there aren't any eligible suitors."

"Phew!"

I struck a victory pose, just for a moment.

I'm not sure that's the best dating policy, but sure! Works for me!

A royal family was important, even if it was a minor one. My daughter would be a princess, so a political marriage would obviously be something we'd have to consider.

Personally, I didn't want to force that on any of my kids, though. We could handle most of the things political marriages were made to cover by ourselves anyway. I wanted my kids to marry whoever they loved, and thankfully my wives agreed.

But, unfortunately, there were mandatory state socialization events we'd have to bring them to. That could cause issues down the line, which I was worried about as well. Then again, if any of my daughters met an overseas prince, fell in love, and built up a relationship... that might be okay?

Okay, I know... I'll just make sure my firstborn daughter knows how important she is! That she doesn't just have to go to any man! He's gotta be the cream of the crop!

Wait... what if I'm being influenced by the knowledge of the future. Won't that impact the future? Isn't that a paradox? I don't really know... Best not to think about it. I'll leave stuff like that to the gods.

I quietly directed all my problems toward Granny Tokie as Ende tapped my shoulder.

Chapter V: Another Visitor

"By the way... my daughter's apparently very fond of your son. You got any feelings on that?"

"Uh, what? M-My shoulder... Wh-Why are you squeezing so hard?"

"Yeah, Allis was saying she wants to be his wife. You know... **Any** thoughts on that, Touya?!"

Ack, E-Ende! Quit squeezing my shoulder! Ow! Owwww!

"My daughter's only six! Six! She's not getting married until she's older!"

"I-I don't know! Quit it, man! You're getting mad at a son who hasn't even been born!"

Before me stood a man who truly felt the pain of a father giving away his daughter on the big day.

Hm... I wonder how my son feels about Allis. Maybe they're childhood friends? It could be one-sided. Childhood friends don't usually win in stories like this... right?

I said as much to Ende and he damn near punched my head off.

Being a dad sure is rough!

◇ ◇ ◇

"Here we go!"

Allis was piloting a Chevalier unit, wielding a heavy mace in its hand. She charged it straight toward a Behemoth. It was a giant boar, mutated from the Tuskboar species. The great beast charged into the side of the metal soldier.

Just as those tusks were about to collide with the chevalier, it flew high into the air. It wasn't blown back, however. It had jumped. It rolled forward and landed perfectly behind the Tuskboar.

The Chevalier was a heavy Frame Gear, even among its peers. Most experienced pilots still found it quite sluggish. Making it move so gracefully was no small feat.

Evidently, Allis wasn't lying when she said she had a lot of experience riding Frame Gears.

"RAAARGH!"

The Tuskboar swiveled around and began charging toward the Chevalier. In response, Allis had the mech crouch and ready its mace.

"Take this!" Allis exclaimed as she suddenly lobbed the giant mace right at the Tuskboar's head.

You're throwing it?!

A dull crunch rang out as metal collided with bone. Blood was drawn, but the slaughter wasn't over.

"Crystal Armament!"

Crystal vines suddenly jutted out of the mech and wrapped around its arms, converging at the hands to form crystal gauntlets.

Hey, that's Melle's...

"Get pulverized!"

The Chevalier's fist slammed into the Tuskboar's snout. Its tusks were shattered to bits, and the beast was blasted back. Blood pooled down its mangled face... and it slumped down, life expiring from its body.

"Yay!"

"U-Uh... I don't know what to say..." I murmured. I could only laugh nervously as I watched the Chevalier strike a mighty victory pose.

Ney and Lycee narrowed their eyes at me.

"Whatever do you mean? Was that not a magnificent display on her part? What could our cute little daughter have done wrong, hm?"

Chapter V: Another Visitor

"Indeed. Allis happens to be a genius, and a charming young lady to boot."

...These guys are pretty hopeless.

I looked over at Ende, hoping to get some support.

"I think what Touya meant was that her method of killing it was bad. Allis fought excellently, obviously. She brutalized that thing perfectly, even! But her final strike there broke the tusks, which are really valuable materials. So it was a bit of a waste, even though she did so well."

Intact Tuskboar fangs were worth a ton of money, while broken ones were worth a lot less. You'd think someone silver-ranked or above would know that. She was probably trying to show off in front of her parents, which was why she was a little more reckless. That side of her definitely showed she was still a child.

"Hehehe... How was that?!" Allis asked as she rushed toward us with a huge smile on her face, her scarf fluttering behind her. She was brimming with energy. If she was a dog, she'd surely have a wagging tail.

Personally, I wasn't so sure about how she'd done... But it was true that she'd piloted the Frame Gear really well. Regardless, I wasn't going to say anything that'd take that smile off her face.

"Mhm! That's our girl! Great job, Allis!"

"You're really strong, Allis. Maybe even the strongest Phrasian princess who's ever existed."

Ney and Lycee took turns praising the girl... It was crazy how much they were doting on her.

Allis leaped up into Melle's arms and gave her a big hug.

"You okay, Allis? Not hurt anywhere, are you?"

"Nope, I'm okay! I'm really strong! But not as strong as my moms!" Allis exclaimed, purring like a kitten as Melle fawned over her. They'd gotten really close, it seemed.

The Behemoth we'd killed wasn't on the guild's hitlist. It was a creature native to Palerius Island. I wanted to test Allis' proficiency with a Frame Gear, so I figured that was the best opportunity to do so.

Usually, the Behemoths on Palerius Island dwelled away from civilization, much like Dragons. They'd hide up in the mountains or in the dense jungles, save for the odd straggler. But for whatever reason, that Tuskboar had come dangerously close to Palerius' central settlement, so I offered to take care of it for them. I even promised to sell the raw materials to the queen, but they were pretty banged up...

"Well, whatever. Ende, you can compensate them for the damage."

"What the heck, why?!"

Good luck, new dad. Go fight some big monsters to make up for your reckless daughter.

According to Allis, Behemoth attacks still happened in the future. In fact, they were even more common. That was because of all the pockets and wells of mana created by the fusion of the two worlds. Obviously, there'd be long-term effects on the wildlife.

Allis had also told me that my kids rode in Frame Gears to kill Behemoths alongside her. Just what was I letting them get away with?! Then again, if they were gold and silver adventurers, it was probably okay.

The Phrase threat was gone, but it seemed like retiring the Frame Gears was a foolish idea. Though we wouldn't be seeing any more large-scale battles with hundreds of them.

Chapter V: Another Visitor

I contacted Queen Palerius, opened up a [Gate] for her men, and then they started harvesting the Tuskboar's body. I decided to figure out compensation later on.

Just as I was about to open a [Gate] back to Brunhild, I heard a ringtone go off. It wasn't my phone, however, since that one was on silent in my pocket.

I turned to see if it was Ende or the Phrase girls, but it wasn't theirs either.

"Oh, that's mine," Allis spoke up, then took out a cutesy-looking phone from her pocket. It was white with a synthetic case on it. It had little kitty ears.

Huh…? We gonna make that stuff in the future? Doesn't look too different from the current ones, I guess.

"Oh! It's Yakumo."

"Uh?"

Yakumo? Who? What…?

"Heeeya! Mhm, I'm in Brunhild already! I'm with Mom and Dad. Uh-huh. Yep. Where are you? Uh-huh. Yeah? Okay! Gotcha! Oh, but… Oh, she cut the call."

Allis' conversation seemed to have been abruptly cut off by the other party. The dial tone let out a low, vacant hum. That wasn't important, however. What truly mattered was… who made that call?

"A-Allis? Who was that?"

"Huh? Yakumo! She's, uhm… Uh… Wait, should I tell you? But… Hrmm…"

"You can tell me. If you couldn't, Tokie would've showed up. It's okay."

I didn't want to seem too forceful, but I needed to know who was on the other end of that call… I needed to know if my hunch was right.

"Uhm… Yakumo's your oldest daughter! She's Yae's, too."

"I knew it!"

Yakumo. That name sounds so Eashenese that it had to be Yae's... And she's my eldest? So my first kid's with Yae?! N-No! I can't get caught up in these weird feelings!

"S-So, where is she?"

"Ummm... she was in Roadmare, but she said she's gonna go train a little. She'll head to Brunhild after."

"What?!"

Wait, huh? What do you mean she'll come after?!

"Yakumo reaaaaaally loves to fight and train. She says she wants to meet you when she's a bit stronger."

"No, no! Waiiit! I can't just let her wander on her own! I'm gonna get the doge of Roadmare to put out a search party right now!"

"I doubt that'll work. Yakumo can use a spell called **[Gate]**, so she's impossible to find."

"Wait, she has that spell?!"

What the hell?! She's stealing one of my cooler ones from me! Can she even use it to travel to places in the past? I guess so long as the place isn't too different, it might work... Guess that means she'll use it to come straight to Brunhild when she's ready?

I tried to use search magic to find her, but it was fruitless. I didn't know a thing about what she looked like. I thought about using **[Recall]** to peek into Allis' memories, but her parents seemed a touch reluctant. Plus, I didn't want to chance things with Granny Tokie.

Just a little peek can't be that bad, right? Gah... No, I can't... I shouldn't.

"C-Can't you call her back?!"

"I could... Oh, no... Sorry. Her phone's off.

"Gaaah!"

Chapter V: Another Visitor

What the heck's wrong with this girl?! She takes her training that seriously?! Ugh, whatever... Should I tell Yae? No, I should probably tell all the girls...

I opened up a [**Gate**] back to Brunhild, my head abuzz with questions.

◇ ◇ ◇

"M-M-My daughter is here, she is?!" Yae, who'd been in the middle of eating, stood up and almost sent her chair flying as she said that.

The other girls seemed surprised... and maybe a little disappointed.

I mean, she's here... but like... not actually right here.

I tried to explain the situation as slowly as I could. I knew Yae was concerned (so was I), so I wanted to be delicate and avoid potentially hurting her feelings. Also, I didn't want to agitate her too much.

"She is training, you say?! That is no good, it is not!"

"Gaaah! I'm sorry!"

There was nothing I could do other than apologize in this case. Yae had grabbed me by the scruff of my neck.

"Training, huh? That sounds like Yae's daughter alright..."

"Mhm. Can't say it doesn't make sense."

Linze and Elze quietly nodded toward each other.

"Hm? Wait, if Yakumo's the firstborn, then does that mean she's the gold-rank?" Sue asked, reminding me of what Ende had told me earlier. Yakumo had to be the girl who refused to get married to a man weaker than her.

If she was Yae's daughter, then she was probably trained by Moroha... She could even be more of a swordplay junkie than her mom... Hell, maybe she was even a beneficiary of Moroha's divinity... That was pure speculation on my part, though.

"Wh-Wh-What should I do?! My daughter is traversing the past all alone, she is!"

Yae was completely flustered. I could understand her feelings. She was flailing around a couple of chicken skewers without even eating them.

"Calm yourself. Nothing will be achieved through anxiety, Yae," Moroha called out to Yae, trying to settle her nerves. Yae rushed toward her, skewers in hand.

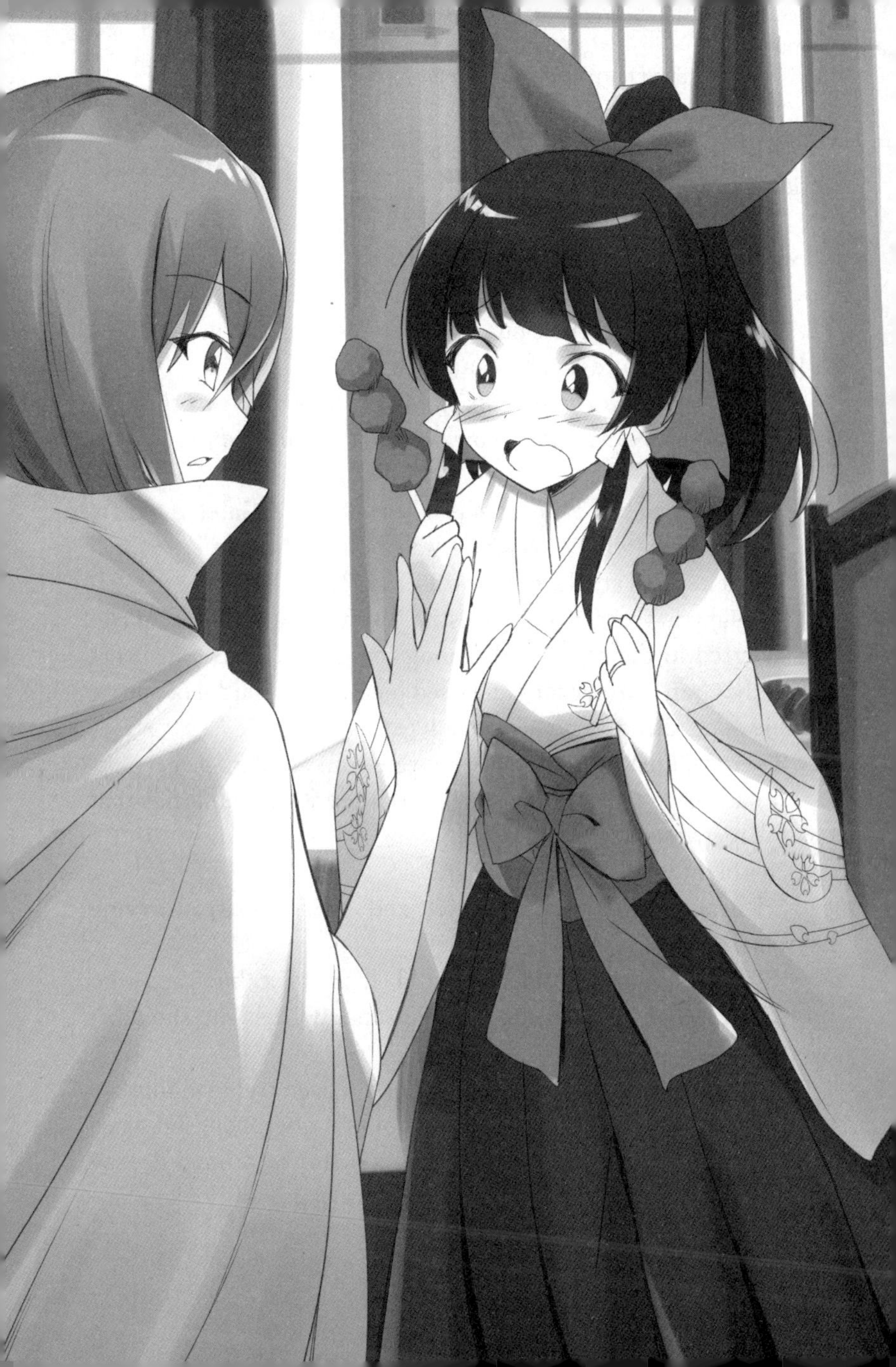

"I-Is it not dangerous to leave a child alone in a strange new world, is it not?!"

"Your kid's a gold-rank, right? She's gonna be okay. And how old were you when you first started traveling?"

"I-I was thirteen years and a half when I left Eashen, I was…"

"See? And you turned out fine. Parents should trust in their children. They're more capable than we know."

…Is that really a comparable situation? Sure, Yae was thirteen, but Yakumo's only eleven. Plus, how can you trust in a kid you haven't even met?!

"If something bad happens, she'll be able to use **[Gate]** to return. And Tokie's spirits will be keeping a watch out for her too."

"Tokie's spirits are the time spirits, right?"

I might have been the Celestial Spirit King, but the spirits still deferred to the gods. And among the gods, I was a small fry. Naturally, Granny Tokie far outclassed me in that regard. For spirits, the rule of obedience generally went like this:

Every god that isn't me > Me (newbie god) > Pillar Spirits.

I had yet to meet a time spirit… But there were all kinds that I hadn't met yet.

"It's okay, she'll come back soon."

"Hehehe… Not even born yet and she's already worrying her folks."

Moroha's light commentary did little to calm Yae, who was knitting her brow in thought. Personally, I felt she shouldn't overthink things.

It wasn't like I wasn't worried, either. I'd been trying to think of ways to use **[Search]** to track her most of that afternoon. But when I searched for "Yae's kid," I got a ton of hits, mostly around Eashen. Thus, it was way too broad. If we were just going off looks alone,

Chapter V: Another Visitor

clearly there were a lot of kids in the world that I could mistake for Yae's.

I asked Allis about using that kind of magic later on, and she said that all my kids (and her) had talisman-like enchantments on their smartphones that prevented them from being found by tracking spells. Just what was future me thinking?!

"But to think Touya's first child is with Yae... I can't help but be envious," Lu said as she let out a small, wistful sigh.

...C'mon, don't feel like that.

Usually, you adjusted to being a parent by going through pregnancy and slowly preparing for it, but we'd just skipped the whole thing and gone straight into knowing our kids were going to be born, then knowing they'd be hanging out with us soon. It all felt rather surreal.

"I-I see... So my child is to be your first, she is... S-Somehow, that is... v-very embarrassing, it is..." Yae's face turned bright red as she mumbled that and tried to hide her expression.

Man... my wife's way too cute, what the hell?!

"But geez... Yae's daughter's eleven?! That means she's not much younger than me..." Sue grumbled to herself. She was thirteen and had a bit of a complex about her relative youth. Hopefully, Yakumo didn't look too much older than her, that'd be unfortunate.

Hm... But that's right... Sue's close to her age and she's married to me... Does that mean Yakumo might get engaged soon?

I thought probably not, on account of the whole strength requirement thing. That was a little relieving.

I didn't know about the future, but in the present, the only gold-ranked people were me and Hilde's grandpa, Galen.

Galen was incredibly powerful, but Yae and Hilde definitely outclassed him at this point. I had a feeling that if Yakumo had Moroha's blessing, then she'd probably be stronger than him.

There are no men who have any beneficiary divinity, and there are none on the level of... Oh no. OH NO. There is one guy.

"What is wrong, Touya-dono?"

"Nothing, just... Yae. If our daughter ever takes an interest in Ende, let's kill him."

"I am confused, I am!"

I just need to cover all my bases, since you never know for sure. It probably won't happen, but I still have to be ready.

While I was thinking about stupid things, Sue seemed pretty fired up.

"Yae's daughter is our daughter too! I might only be two years older, but that's no excuse! I'm gonna act more mature!"

"She's from the future, you know? She probably already knows a more mature version of you, so you don't have to try so hard."

"That's even worse! It means I need to make sure she only knows the mature side of me! So I'll... Uhm... what should I do, Yumina?" Sue suddenly turned to ask Yumina a question. I personally didn't think there was much Sue could do. Hell, Sue wasn't super childish, even. She was more naive, which I thought was a charming aspect of her personality.

"Ways to appear more mature, eh? Hm... Leen, would you not know more about this?" Yumina wisely passed the buck.

"Hm?" Leen, the eldest of my wives, set down her tea and turned to Sue.

...You don't have to imitate her motions all the time, Paula!

"Clothing would be easiest, I suppose. And hair? Usually, maturity is first gleaned from outward appearance. Even just wearing something elegant can give you a different air."

"Ohhh, I see! That's pretty simple, yeah!"

Chapter V: Another Visitor

Leen had a point. Sue looked very different when she was wearing her fancy dresses to formal events. But even then, she looked more cute or innocent than particularly mature or glamorous.

Still, the type of dress was definitely something that mattered. Sue mostly liked to wear pinks, yellows, and more vibrant colors. She'd probably look mature in something more chic.

"Hey, Touya! Help me find some mature clothes!"

"Huh? I mean, sure... I guess?"

I wasn't the person to ask when it came to fashion, but at the very least, I could consult my smartphone.

The clothing I projected into the air caught not just the attention of Sue, but the other girls as well. I saved each image they were interested in, since we could take them to Fashion King Zanac later to have them made into real outfits.

Apparently, the girls had all taken Sue's words to heart, so they all wanted to look their best to meet their kids. That was certainly a parental thing to do.

As the girls looked through their favorite outfits, I started thinking about my own.

"..."

An imaginary voice floated into my head, saying, "Wow, Dad! You've been wearing that same coat your entire life?!" It might have been a product of my imagination, but it still stung!

There's nothing wrong with this coat! It's comfy! My clothes are enchanted so they don't wear out, too! They're practical! Ugh... Maybe I could stand to mix up my wardrobe a little...

Feeling some compelling force in the back of my mind, I grumbled my way through a men's fashion catalog.

◇ ◇ ◇

"Yae? Yae!"

"Ah?! Wh-What is it, Hilde-dono?!"

"Oh, it's just... Your fried egg appears to be mostly soy sauce now..."

"Hm? Ah!"

Yae was so distracted that she'd poured a mountain of sauce onto her egg... It was quite the sight.

She'd been like that all morning. In a half-daze, barely even paying attention to her food. Sometimes she'd even smile to herself. I had a feeling I knew what was going through her mind, though.

"Mm... Yae's a little dazed right now, isn't she?"

"A little? Can you blame her? If I were in her shoes, I'd be as well," Leen, who was sitting next to me, spoke matter-of-factly. She sounded a little envious, all things considered. I hoped she wasn't feeling too sore.

The feeling of my daughter being somewhere in the world was hard to describe. It was like a mixture of things, really. I wasn't quite upset... but I was worried. And at the same time, I was excited. It was... strange. And good. Probably.

It was like wanting to do something, but not knowing what to do.

"Is this gonna happen to me eight more times?"

I'm gonna die of a heart attack before this is through.

"Are all of them going to take detours? Shouldn't they come straight here?"

"Well, Leen... if you were in their shoes, would you come straight to Brunhild?"

Leen replied with a small grunt, jabbing her fork into a fried egg.

Chapter V: Another Visitor

"I wouldn't, no... It would be a rare opportunity to visit the past, and as such, I'd take a tour."

See? I bet my kid with Leen's gonna feel the same way. Kids take after their parents, and I've got a bit of wanderlust myself.

"Still, to think Yae's child would be able to cast **[Gate]**, of all things. I've heard of parents and children who share an aptitude for Null spells, but no such pairings that ever shared the exact same spells. I don't believe Null magic is something you inherit."

It could easily just have been a coincidence. I was capable of Null magic, and if my kid was capable of Null magic, then being able to cast **[Gate]** wasn't too unreasonable, was it?

"Fairies are highly attuned to Null spells, right?"

"That's right. To my knowledge, no fairy exists without one."

"So it stands to reason that our kid would have Null spell aptitude, right?"

Leen was a fairy, which meant that our child would also be born a fairy. The same went for Sakura. Our kid would no doubt come out the same species as the overlord's lineage, since those traits took biological priority.

Plus, about ninety percent of all fairies born were girls, so it was very likely that Leen and I were going to have a daughter.

"How long did it take for you to learn Null magic?"

"I can't say for sure, but I do remember using **[Discovery]** at around the age of five."

[Discovery] was a spell that worked much like my **[Search]** spell. It wasn't quite as efficient when it came to tracking, however.

I was amazed that Leen could cast something like that at the age of five. But if anything, that meant our daughter would be more than capable of doing it.

"Hrmmm..."

"W-Well, I think maybe some of them will come right here. I could see Linze's or Hilde's doing so."

Though actually, maybe not Linze's...? If I remember right, she's probably Linne. And according to Allis' story, she seems a little mischievous.

I could barely taste my breakfast because I was so preoccupied. I felt a little bit bad for Crea and Lu, since they'd put in so much work.

Yae, Hilde, and Elze headed off to the guild to do more quests. They'd already reached silver-rank... so it was only a matter of time before they struck gold. From an outside perspective, what they were doing might have seemed a little silly, but I could understand their reasoning.

After breakfast, I tussled with paperwork before heading to the castle town with Kohaku in tow. There wasn't much to do, really. If any of my more serious kids had arrived, they'd no doubt come to Brunhild right away... And nobody had shown up yet. Hell, if they were really good kids, they'd probably give me a call.

Still, the time travel stuff was largely unreliable. If Granny Tokie was to be believed, they could appear any time in the following months.

"Hm... It'll be weird to meet my kids."

"I look forward to it, my liege. Especially the young prince. I shall tend to him as a personal bodyguard, worry not."

"Huh? Wait, what?!"

Kohaku went on to insist that it was only natural.

Apparently, Allis had told Kohaku that in the future, the heavenly beasts acted as something like my son's personal entourage. That kind of felt like something she could've told me sooner!

"Miss Allis spoke so casually that I only assumed you knew..."

Chapter V: Another Visitor

Man, she really is Ende's kid. Blunder after blunder! Can't keep her mouth shut.

Wait, if my son had bodyguards, did that mean he was really young? Yae's daughter, Yakumo, was acting alone and it was clear that she was the oldest.

Some cultures consider it good luck to have a girl before a boy, but what if there's a first, second, and third princess before the prince? It's rough being the little bro...

We weren't blood-related, but I had two annoying older sisters. I couldn't help but feel sympathy for my yet-unborn boy.

A group of kids was playing outside Olba's store, fooling around with the capsule machines.

Wonder if my kids'll play like this too... I'm not sure I can picture them doing regular kid stuff... They might be more inclined to wiping out Goblins, Orcs, or... Hold on!

I narrowed my eyes when I recognized one of the children.

"Oh, hey, Duke!"

"Allis?!"

Allis was there, playing with a little toy she'd won from the machine.

"What're you doing here?! Where are Ende and the others?"

"I got my allowance, so I'm buying some stuff! Dad's doing guild work, and my moms are shopping right over there."

Allowance? Uh... Aren't you a silver or gold rank adventurer? You should have tons of cash to spare.

"All my money's in the future, and I can't join the guild now..."

"Oh... Have you heard anything from Yakumo?"

"Nope. When she gets focused on something, she doesn't stop focusing on it. Frei gets really annoyed when she's like that."

"Frei?"

"Oops."

217

Allis had let another secret slip... She really was bad at this. Frankly, I worried about her.

"Who's that? Is she one of my kids?"

"Hahaha... Yep, she is. Her name's Freigard, but everyone just calls her Frei for short. She's like a big sis to me!"

"Freigard..."

My immediate guess was that she'd be my child with Hilde. Since her full name was Hildegard and all. That made sense to me, at least. Allis said she was like a big sister, so that meant she had to be older than six, but how much older?

"Hey, can you—?"

Just as I was about to ask for more information, Allis received a phone call.

Oho! Is that Yakumo?!

"Hello? Oh, okay. Coming back."

Allis cut the call short. That was fast.

"It was mom. I gotta go back with her now, see ya!" Allis said as she trotted off, ever-merry.

"Away she goes, my liege."

"Mhm... Away she goes..."

I wondered if my kids from the future even had my phone number... I might have changed it. They'd probably call Allis first and foremost, though. Just to check on her.

I shrugged my shoulders, turned away from the Strand store, and carried on my way.

"Hm? Your Highness?"

"Oh, Lanz. What's up?"

I looked up toward the source of the voice and saw one of our knights. It was Lanz. He wasn't wearing his armor, which meant it was probably his day off. He held a bouquet in his hands for some reason or other, which piqued my interest.

Chapter V: Another Visitor

"Heh... Off to see Micah, are we?"

"Huh?! I-I'm... Ahem... Y-Yes," Lanz nodded as he said that, a faint flush forming on his cheeks. He and Micah, the owner of the Silver Moon Inn, had recently started dating.

Apparently, the catalyst had been the bouquet toss at my wedding. Karen had said that any single man who caught the bouquet should present it to the girl he liked... and Lanz happened to catch one. Surely by coincidence and not my sister's design.

Micah was so happy to receive the bouquet from him that they made things official shortly after. She was quite a popular girl, though, so the news broke many hearts among the knight order. But perhaps no man was more shaken by the event than Dolan, Micah's dad. He did sort of come around to the idea, though.

Lanz was from a good lineage. He was a noble knight and had a great personality. Also, he was fairly handsome. It was hard for Dolan to write him off entirely.

"Glad things are working out for you two. Wedding bells in the future, maybe?"

"Oh, not until I'm a fully-fledged knight at least. I want to work harder, enough to support Micah for the rest of her life..."

The man was crazy dedicated, you had to hand him that. A lot of Lestian men had those ideals. Hilde even had those ideals as a woman, and her brother, King Reinhard, was no different. Their grandfather Galen, on the other hand, was apparently not raised in Lestia to begin with, which explained a lot.

I believed everything Lanz had to say. He was dead serious about his intentions.

Since I was just walking with no real destination, I decided to tag along with Lanz for a bit. We entered the Silver Moon and were immediately greeted by Micah.

"Welcome! A-Ah, you're here!"

"Y-Yes. I'm free today, you see. S-So, uh... please take this! It might brighten up the room?"

"O-Oh! Thank you," Micah said that and smiled warmly as Lanz passed her the bouquet. The two of them were in their own little world.

...I'm here too, you know? I literally rule this country? Saved the world? Got some giant robots? No? Nothing?

"Oh, Touya. When did you get here?"

"Ghhh..."

The two of them had been close even before their relationship was official, so it was no surprise to see them acting this way. I wasn't exactly going to try and rain on their parade, either.

"Hm? Nothing to do? Well, you haven't been here much lately, so why not stick around?"

"Mmm... Guess I could."

I couldn't exactly say that I was aimlessly wandering, hoping to receive a phone call from my yet-unborn children, so I just gave a vague excuse.

The Silver Moon was technically owned by Brunhild's government, but Micah served as the manager. I used to visit often to eat at the place, but ever since I got married, Lu got way more into the home-cooking thing, so I hadn't actually stopped by in a while.

"It's almost lunch, so I can't do too much, but do you want anything to eat?"

"Nah, I'll just have lunch back at the castle. But could you get me and Kohaku some fruity water?"

"No prob!" Micah said that, then merrily hummed a tune to herself as she took her bouquet into the kitchen with her. She was head over heels in love, it seemed.

Chapter V: Another Visitor

Lanz had been pining for her ever since he came to Brunhild, and Micah just seemed completely oblivious. I was glad it had all worked out.

"Hmhm..."

It was early in the afternoon, but the cafeteria was bustling. That was good for business, but I wondered if Micah was okay serving so many people so often.

"After your wedding, we started getting a lot more international travel. Plus, the food here's great, so obviously people were gonna stop by! Micah's stuff is the best, right?"

"Uh-huh. I get it, you're in love," I quietly muttered as I sat in the corner with Lanz. I was wearing a hood to obscure my identity, and thankfully, it was also obscuring my annoyed expression. There were also plants in this corner of the room, so it was a little more secluded.

Merchants, travelers, and more roguish-looking individuals were spread out all across the cafeteria. There were a variety of races, too. Humans, beastmen, dwarves, elves, and even a few draconic folks as well.

A young waitress was nimbly making her way between tables. I'd never seen her before. She was presumably a new hire. Micah managed every aspect of the inn, so I didn't have any hand in the hiring process. I generally trusted her word as far as employees went, so there was nothing to worry about.

"Here's your fruity water! And one for you, Kohaku."

Micah smiled as she brought over a tray with a bowl, a glass, and a jug of fruit-filled water. It was ice-cold. I felt hydrated just looking at it.

"Who's the new girl?"

"Oh, her? I hired her a few days ago. She said she's on her way to see her family, but she doesn't have any money, so she's staying here temporarily and working to pay her board."

That sounded tough. I glanced over at the waitress, who was rushing all over the place. She seemed to be in her early twenties, which put her at a similar age to Micah.

"Have you decided what you want yet, Lanz? I'd suggest the teriyaki chicken set."

"S-Sounds good!"

"Okay! Thanks!"

Micah spun on her heel and headed off to the kitchen once more. She seemed really happy. Frankly, I thought Lanz could propose right that moment and she'd say yes. It wasn't my place to interfere, though.

"Hm?"

I felt a strange presence staring at me, so I turned around and... noticed the waitress from earlier.

Stare...

Staaaaaare...

Staaaaaaaaare...

Staaaaaaaaaaaare...

Something about the situation felt oddly familiar. What was she looking at me like that for? Was there something on my face? Could she even see my face? I was wearing the hood... but did she recognize me as the grand duke? Maybe Micah had told her? I tried looking away from her, but she trotted on over and got up in my face.

"You're Mochizuki Touya, right?"

"Uh, yeah...?"

She knows me, maybe? I sure don't recognize her.

Chapter V: Another Visitor

The waitress let out a little laugh when she noticed my visible confusion.

"Don't you know me?"

"Huh?"

Do I? Who is she? I don't know anyone like her... Uh... Maybe my memory's just acting up?"

《My liege, this girl's entire body is cloaked in strange magic.》

"Huh?!"

Kohaku's telepathic warning caused me to shoot up out of my seat. Upon closer inspection, I saw it too. A thin veil of magic coated her form. It was magic designed to conceal, like my [**Mirage**] spell!

"Who are you?"

"My name's Quun. This is not the first time I've met you, Father. But it's nice to meet you all the same."

"...Hwhuh?"

The magic around the girl's body began to waft away like cotton candy in the breeze on a hot summer's day.

*...I knew it... This IS [**Mirage**]!*

When the spell finally dissipated, the waitress was no more. What stood in her place was a young girl who looked to be around ten. She wore a white princess blouse and a black gothic lolita dress atop it. She had long silvery hair tied up in two tails, and her golden eyes flickered with a mischievous glint. However, the most eye-catching detail was her little semi-transparent wings that fluttered idly behind her.

A fairy... No way... Then she's...

"Pffft... Hahahaha!"

As I was trying to process what had just happened, the girl who called herself Quun began laughing uncontrollably.

"Your face, Father! Hahahaha! W-Worth every minute! Hahaha! Oh, I'm glad I came straight here! Hahahahahaa!"

"Er, what?"

She was hugging her stomach from laughing so hard.

"Um…?"

"Pffft… W-Wait a sec, lemme take a snapshot!" Quun said as she pulled a smartphone out from one of her sleeves and took a candid shot of my perplexed face.

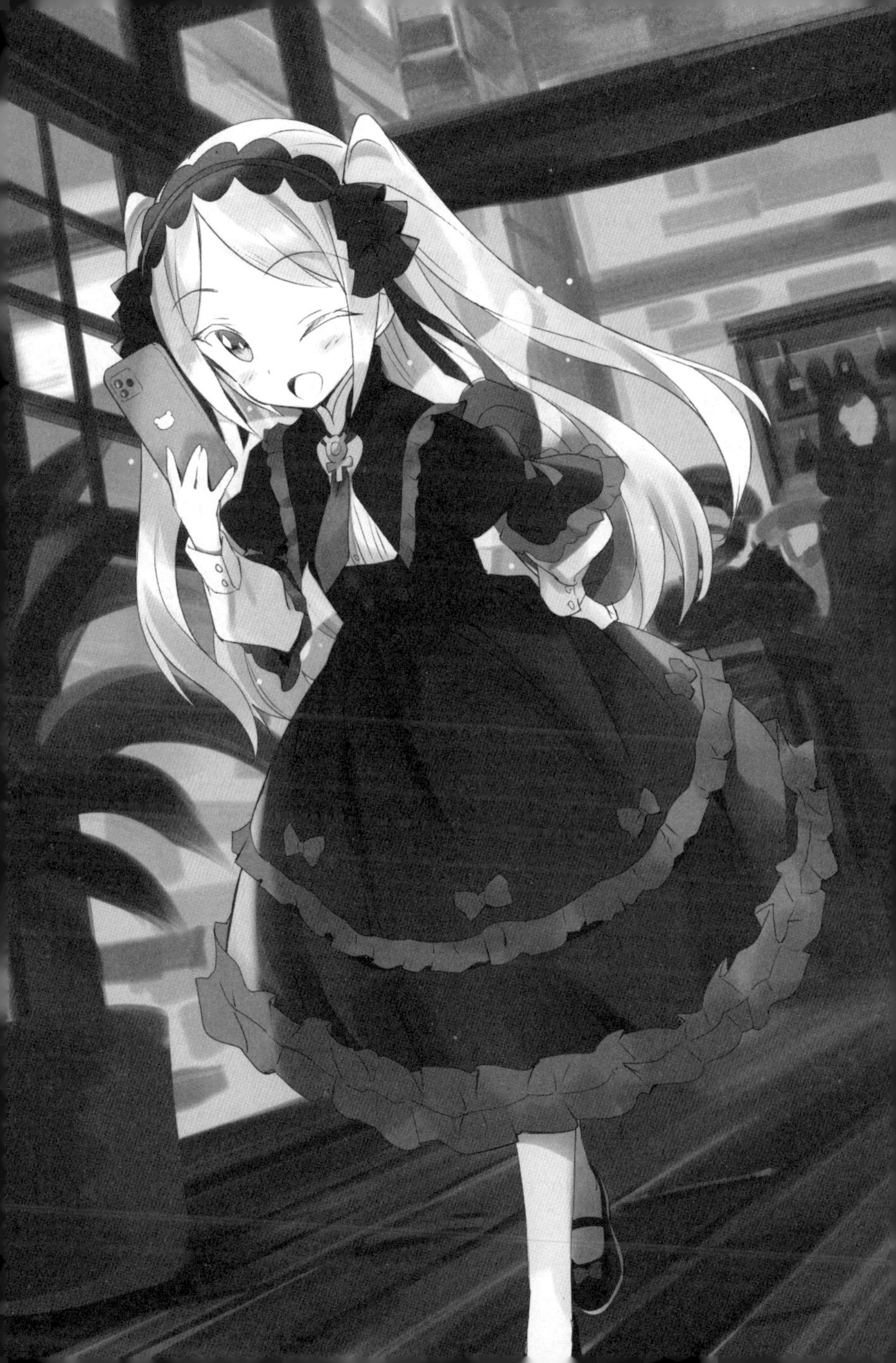

The hell?

"Hahaha! How comical! I'll have to show this to Mother when I get home. What a fine souvenir!"

"W-Wait a second! What'd you mean just now? You're... Are you, uh...?"

"Hm? Do I need to introduce myself again?" Quun asked as she stepped back, gently plucking at the hem of her skirt. She bowed her head then did a little curtsy.

"It's nice to meet you, Father. I am the daughter of Mochizuki Touya and his wife, Leen. My name is Quun, court mage of the Duchy of Brunhild. Let's work together well going forward, shall we?"

Her mischievous eyes stared right through me.

I knew it! She's Leen's kid! She's just like her, too! Right down to how much of a bully she can be...

"Er, Your Highness? What did she mean by father?" Lanz asked, looking absolutely stupefied.

"Oh... Crap."

"Hm? You must have misheard. I said big brother! We're distant relatives who knew each other as children! We had a familial relationship."

"Oh, really? That certainly makes sense! His Highness here is capable of transforming, much like you just did."

"Oh, is he now? Not causing too much mischief, I hope," Quun snickered quietly as she spoke.

I don't use my spells for pranks, dammit! Did she seriously use [Mirage] and come work here just so she could tease me?

My daughter laughed even harder when she saw how frustrated I seemed.

"We'll talk more after my shift. Later, Big Bro!"

Chapter V: Another Visitor

She clad herself in magic once more, taking the form of an unassuming waitress. Then, she vanished into the kitchen as if nothing had happened.

I was completely and utterly taken aback by what had just transpired. I never expected to be so thoroughly made a fool of by one of my kids.

◇ ◇ ◇

"I'm beyond words, really."

"Yes, that sounds about right. It's rather funny though, isn't it? I thought you might get a kick out of it, Mother."

"...I can't deny that."

Well... could you maybe deny it anyway?

Leen and Quun were talking. They looked like sisters no matter how you cut it. Paula was standing by their feet, spinning around in a circle and glancing at them both. She was definitely freaking out.

"I didn't think that Leen's child would be the first to show up..."

"They look quite similar."

"Oh... Where is my daughter, where is she...?"

Yumina and Lu talked amongst themselves as they watched the mother and daughter pair. Yae, on the other hand, simply despaired. I could get where she was coming from.

"I didn't think I'd be the first, though. Have the others not arrived yet?"

"Allis is here, as is Yakumo. But the latter went off on her own and hasn't shown her face in Brunhild yet..."

"That's very like my elder sister. I will have to speak with Allis soon."

Elder sister... Man, it's kinda weird hearing it like that. Leen and Yae's kids are sisters through me... Oh, right. I forgot to ask.

"How old are you, Quun?"

"I'm ten, Father. I am the thirdborn, at that."

"The thirdborn... So Yakumo's the oldest... Is my second child called Frei, perhaps?"

"Oh, so you already know of Frei? That must have been Allis' doing... She talks too much for her own good."

She's pretty careless, yeah. But that's good for us, since it means more info!

"Frei...? Who?" Sakura had been keenly following our conversation, and she finally spoke up. I wasn't sure if she meant who like "who was she" or "whose child was she."

"My sister Freigard is the secondborn of our family. Her birth mother is Hilde, of course."

"M-My daughter?!" Hilde's voice grew louder as she walked toward Quun.

That meant my eldest child was Yakumo, then came Frei, then came Quun.

"P-Please tell me, Quun. Is my daughter an admirable knight?!"

Quun seemed rather taken aback by Hilde's frantic questioning.

Calm down, or else we might get in trouble with Tokie...

"Er, well... It would be biased of me to make that kind of statement. But she's certainly a diligent knight! If not a touch... eccentric?"

"Huh? What does that mean?"

"Well, she's... No, I shouldn't. I think it'll be more interesting if you see for yourself."

...Damn it. Not this again. I don't want any more surprises!

That sly little grin on my daughter's face all but confirmed my hunch that she was just as much a sadist as her mother.

Chapter V: Another Visitor

"By the way, Quun. You can use **[Mirage]**, yes?"

"That's correct, Mother. I can use a total of four Null spells."

A whole four, huh? That's the same as Leen. Seems like fairies are just as compatible with Null spells as I figured.

"All of my siblings know at least one Null spell, of course."

"Wait, seriously?!"

*They've all got Null aptitude?! That's crazy! Guess it's not super surprising though, since Yakumo can use **[Gate]**.*

"As I'd thought. This must be the result of our darling's lineage..."

"Hrm... Maybe..."

According to God Almighty, my kids would be something like demi-gods. But they wouldn't be able to tap into divinity, and for all intents and purposes, they'd still be mortal. I never heard anything about them having special abilities, though... Just the potential of longer-than-average lifespans.

That said... if they were going to be raised in a place with so many literal gods hanging around, they were probably going to be on the receiving end of half a dozen different blends of divinity.

I wasn't sure if they'd awaken as full beneficiaries like Yumina and the rest, but it stood to reason that they'd be on the same level as them... Perhaps even surpassing them? As I pondered, Quun turned to me.

"Actually, Father. I need to ascend."

"You need to what now?"

"Ascend. To Babylon. I know I can access it from the warp room in the castle, but obviously, I need clearance."

Oh, she knows about Babylon? Wait, I mean... of course she does.

There was a room in the castle that allowed you to teleport right up to the floating isle, but you could only do so with the right clearance.

Thus, Quun, who had only just arrived here, needed me to grant it to her.

But what does she want in Babylon?

"I may look like this, but I'm quite dedicated to magical technology. Babylon's well equipped with that kind of tech, so I'd like to give it a look over and compare what we have in our respective eras."

"Huh?!"

That's shocking. I thought you'd be into magic like Leen, but you're into magic tech?

To someone fond of Gollems and artifacts, Babylon was probably like a treasure trove. That was probably why she came straight to Brunhild.

"My Null spells other than [**Mirage**] are [**Modeling**], [**Enchant**], and [**Program**]. They're well suited to magitech and engineering, are they not?"

That was certainly true. Those spells were just about the perfect kit for it, really. With those skills, you could probably craft just about anything.

"Oh, here. Let me show you some of my work," Quun said as she pulled a small card from her sleeve. It looked like a storage card from the Reverse World. She shook the card, and something large fell out of it.

"Awaken."

"What the—?!"

The small bipedal thing was about fifty centimeters tall. It was made of metal and stood tall upon Quun's order. It was some kind of Gollem, but it was the appearance that surprised me the most. A rounded face. Round ears. Stubby limbs, round eyes… and a little ribbon about its neck.

Chapter V: Another Visitor

I couldn't help but glance at the teddy bear by Leen's feet. She was frozen in shock at what she was staring at.

The metal Gollem in front of me was the spitting image of Paula. "M-Mechapaula…?"

"Its name is Parla. Give them a wave."

Parla, the robot that looked just like Paula, raised a hand into the air. Its movements were surprisingly fluid.

"Is this a Gollem?"

"Yes. The base is a broken legacy Gollem, along with a scavenged G-Cube and Q-Crystal. It has no functional Gollem skills, but it has some uses all the same."

Paula stood opposite Parla, and the two of them moved like mirror images. When Paula raised her left hand, Parla raised its right. When Paula jumped to the side, so too did Parla. When Paula began to moonwalk… Wait… when did Paula learn how to moonwalk?

"Well, Mother? What do you think?"

"I think it's incredible. It took me two hundred years to develop Paula… It may be a Gollem, but it's certainly impressive."

"…Hehe," Quun chuckled and smiled from ear to ear after hearing Leen's words of praise. Her smiling face was as cute as her mother's too. Leen smiled right back and gently stroked her daughter's hair. It was a heartwarming sight to be sure.

The weird little bears engaging in a dance-off at their feet kind of ruined the tender moment, though.

"Did Elluka teach you about Gollems?"

"That's right. And Doctor Babylon as well. I work with them as somewhat of a lab assistant. Though it's minor work at best, really."

Don't downplay yourself, kid. I can use all those spells you can, but I sure as hell couldn't create my own Gollem.

"So, is it fine, Father? Can I visit Babylon?" Quun grabbed my arm and practically pleaded.

"Hrm…"

Damn it… Why's she so cute?

I was mostly wondering if it would be okay sending my kid to those weirdos up there… I didn't want them teaching her anything weird. But if she was already studying under them in the future, then it was probably too late for that. Just what was future me thinking, honestly? He'd made some questionable decisions.

"Okay, sure. I'll take you."

"Thank you, Father!" Quun exclaimed. Then, she smiled and gave me a big hug.

…Th-This is dangerous. She's way too cute. Oh man, I'm not built for this.

In that moment, I understood Ende's feelings as a father, and I absolutely hated that I did. It felt as though I'd do just about anything for my daughter, that I couldn't resist.

I couldn't help but notice that grin on Quun's face, though… As she looked up, Leen cut in and just about yanked us apart.

Whoa!

"…That's quite enough, darling. You've places to be, no?"

"Aha, Mother… Are you jealous, perhaps?"

"…Don't be absurd. Or shall I ban you from visiting Babylon?"

"Nooo…" Quun bellowed. Then, she pouted slightly and stuck out her tongue. Their relationship certainly seemed like a fun one, at least.

It was weird, though. Even though Quun had only just arrived, she felt like family immediately. As if we'd known each other for a long time.

"What a nice family scene…"

Chapter V: Another Visitor

"Hrmph... Must be nice, being part of a family..."

I could feel Lu and Sue glaring daggers into my back.

Whoops... I better behave myself.

◇   ◇   ◇

"I see... So you're Touya and Leen's daughter. And a pupil of mine and Elluka's, hm?"

"Not formally, but I have been learning under you. I also maintain the Knight Gollems of Brunhild."

"Knight Gollems?" Leen asked, seeming curious. I was curious as well. I knew about Soldat Gollems, but I hadn't ever heard of Knight Gollems.

"They're a specialized type of Gollem deployed around Brunhild in the future. They're a subdivision of your knight order commanded by Yumina's Albus."

Albus? So the white crown? It's the captain of a knight order subdivision in the future?

"Hm... A peacekeeping force of Gollems, you say? I'd be lying if I said I hadn't thought about it. In fact, Regina and I had been discussing that very idea recently."

"Seems to me like we were on the right track, then. Let's move forward with the plan. We can start with what we discussed the last time."

"Hm... But if we replicated G-Cubes in that manner, then..."

The two girls started discussing a bunch of scientific crap that I had no interest in. I didn't like the grins on either of their faces, though. They didn't look anything other than evil when they got like that.

"Seems they're the same as ever even in the past."

"So they didn't change at all?"

I kind of knew these two were incapable of improving, unfortunately. Hopefully, they didn't cause any more trouble in the future at least. That was the best I case scenario, it seemed.

"Ahhh! M-Master! Master! C-Can I hug that little girl, please?!"

"Denied. No."

"I will end you."

Leen and I both replied at the same time, in our own ways.

We were in the research laboratory, which meant we had to deal with Atlantica and her heavy breathing.

Please keep away from my child. I feel like your obedience protocol's the only thing stopping you from molesting her. You're not getting your hands on my daughter!

Quun didn't seem all that disturbed. She simply let out a small sigh and shook her head.

"She's the same too, I see…"

"Ugh… So you've met her, then?"

It would seem that Quun had met Tica before, which made sense if she visited Babylon every now and then. As a parent, I had obvious concerns about that.

I furrowed my brow slightly, only to be distracted by my daughter tugging at my coat sleeve.

"Father, I'd like to visit the hangar. That's where your Frame Gears are, yes?"

"Hm? Yeah, why?"

The mischief in Quun's eyes had been pushed aside by bristling curiosity. It was almost cruel how cute she could be.

I didn't know she'd be interested in our Frame Gears as well. But all of those were kept in the hangar, since Monica and Rosetta were in charge of maintaining them there.

Chapter V: Another Visitor

Leen and I shrugged and headed over to the hangar with Quun, who seemed just about ready to sprint there. She was very excited for some reason.

We crossed the research laboratory, the storehouse, and finally made it to the hangar. Quun was so cheerful the whole way, which definitely hammered her age in.

"Woooooow!"

Her eyes were positively sparkling as she looked over the hangar's interior. Like I said… way too cute.

She toddled down the halls, looking at each and every Frame Gear. The unique ones were included in that, like Valkyries and my Reginleif. Leen's Grimgerde was there, too.

"Oh, it's Ms. Leen and Master, sir! Oh, is that one of your future children?"

"Wow, she like… totally looks just like Leen. Most interesting."

Rosetta and Monica descended from a nearby crane platform.

The Babylon gynoids were capable of sharing information wirelessly. It was a sort of hivemind. They probably learned about Quun from Tica.

"We've met in the future, but nice to meet you in the past! I'm Quun."

My daughter smiled as she greeted the two gynoids. I felt a little proud as a father. She was a very polite girl. Leen smiled and nodded by my side, so she probably felt the same way.

"It's amazing seeing so many Frame Gears. I'm so excited, really."

"Hm? Are there no Frame Gears in the future, ma'am? Nossir, that can't be the case. Did you just never see them?" Monica questioned Quun's excitation. It was a fair question. If the girl had been in and out of Babylon before, surely this couldn't have been her first time seeing our mechs.

"Many of these Frame Gears have been reconstructed and refurbished in my era. I never thought I'd get to see the original forms of my mothers' Valkyrie Gears. It's fascinating."

"Oh, that makes sense. I completely understand, ma'am!"

You do? Because I don't really get it. Aren't the new robots better? What's so good about seeing the old models?

"It's okay not to understand, Father. But when you're passionate about something, you want to see all sides of it. Like the time you told me how excited mother got when she learned about the library for the very first time."

"...Darling... Just what are you telling our daughter?"

"Gwuh?! N-Nothing! I haven't done anything yet! Owww!"

Leen made a frightening smile as she yanked my ear.

I know it was me, but it was future me! Don't blame me yet!

"My, you two certainly seem close. Would it be alright if I left you lovebirds be and went to speak with Monica and Rosetta? If that's fine with them, at least."

"We'd like... totally appreciate your company and stuff. It's not a problem at all."

Quun hopped onto the crane platform and ascended along with Parla.

Leen, my ear's starting to go numb. Please.

"Good grief... What kind of girl so readily mocks her parents?" Leen muttered quietly as she released my ear. I was simply glad to be free of the pain.

As for her complaints, we were the ones who raised that girl... I had no doubt we'd had a lot of influence on her. She was extremely similar to Leen in a lot of ways. She didn't compromise when it came to her interests, she was a risk-taker, and she clearly had no problem tormenting others. I wondered how she resembled me, though...

Chapter V: Another Visitor

"You're similar in that you both do as you please."

"That's a little rude!"

Don't say that...

I wondered if that meant she was the most headstrong and self-indulgent of all my kids... I looked up at Quun, who was merrily chatting about Frame Gears with the gynoids. She looked really happy.

"Hm... Come to think of it, she's ranked at gold or silver as well, no? I wonder if she joined the guild in order to obtain rare materials for her work."

Oh, good point. I'd forgotten about that.

I wondered if that meant Quun was especially strong, too... If she was, I wondered if her power came from technology or magic. Her spells certainly didn't seem suited for combat, at least.

We stood there for a time, quietly gazing up at our daughter.

"Never did I think I'd meet my child before even falling pregnant... But I suppose you can live six hundred years and still be surprised."

That was understating it. Leen and Sakura's kids would have longer lifespans than their siblings. If they weren't careful, they could be stuck serving Brunhild for a very long time indeed... Not that I was keen for them to die sooner or anything. I planned to go into hiding in Babylon at about the right time for me to die. That would hide the fact that I was basically immortal. Then, after that, I'd transition to the divine realm. Obviously, I'd take my wives with me. But my kids, I'd leave behind.

I don't want my kids to live as immortal beneficiaries. I want them to lead happy, mortal lives with families of their own. And when they eventually die, I can see them again in the world beyond... Heh... I might look younger than them, though... Geez...

"...Are you okay, darling?"

"...Yeah. Just thinking about how I want to stay close to you, Leen..."

"I'll be right here. Always. Whether you become a full god or not. I promise. I'll never leave you behind, okay?"

"...Thanks."

I gave Leen a big hug and a little smooch on the lips. At that exact moment, I heard the sound of a camera shutter go off. I glared upward at my wicked daughter.

"Oh my! It seems my mother's rather daring! What a happy couple you are... That's reassuring for me, all things considered!"

"...As a mother, I can't abide this. You've definitely raised her wrong, darling."

...On the contrary, I think we might have raised her right. She's more like you than you seem to realize.

I didn't say that, of course. Instead, I simply squeezed Leen's body against mine and chuckled.

Just what does the future have in store for me?

Afterword

Hello again, I hope you enjoyed reading Volume 22 of *In Another World With My Smartphone*.

This volume marks a new chapter in the tale, featuring a matchmaking party and mysterious visitors from elsewhere.

Things are going to get really exciting from here on out, so I hope you keep on reading.

I've entered a new chapter in my own life, too. I just finished moving. I'm not done organizing my stuff yet, unfortunately... When am I going to get rid of all these cardboard boxes, I wonder?

Anyway, here are my usual thanks.

Eiji Usatsuka, thank you. Some major characters are on their way, so I'm sure you'll have your hands full.

I'd also like to thank K and the Hobby Japan editorial department, along with everyone involved with the publication process.

And last, but definitely not least, I'd like to thank my readers, along with everyone who follows my work on Shousetsuka ni Narou.

Patora Fuyuhara

In Another World With My Smartphone

23
Patora Fuyuhara
illustration: Eiji Usatsuka

VOLUME 23
ON SALE
AUGUST 2022!

OMNIBI 1-5 ON SALE NOW!

Seirei Gensouki: Spirit Chronicles

My Friend's Little Sister Has It IN for Me!

vol. 4

Vol. 4 On Sale Now!

Author: mikawaghost
Illustration: tomari

HEY ///////
▶ HAVE YOU HEARD OF
J-Novel Club?

It's the digital publishing company that brings you the latest novels from Japan!

Subscribe today at

▶▶▶j-novel.club◀◀◀

and read the latest volumes as they're translated, or become a premium member to get a *FREE* ebook every month!

Check Out The Latest Volume Of

In Another World With My Smartphone

Plus Our Other Hit Series Like:

- ▶ Black Summoner
- ▶ Invaders of the Rokujouma!?
- ▶ The Sorcerer's Receptionist
- ▶ Her Majesty's Swarm
- ▶ The Apothecary Diaries
- ▶ The Magician Who Rose From Failure
- ▶ Seirei Gensouki: Spirit Chronicles

- ▶ Slayers
- ▶ Arifureta: From Commonplace to World's Strongest
- ▶ Der Werwolf: The Annals of Veight
- ▶ How a Realist Hero Rebuilt the Kingdom
- ▶ By the Grace of the Gods
- ▶ Lazy Dungeon Master
- ▶ Dungeon Busters
- ▶ An Archdemon's Dilemma: How to Love Your Elf Bride

...and many more!

In Another World With My Smartphone, Illustration © Eiji Usatsuka   *Arifureta: From Commonplace to World's Strongest*, Illustration © Takayaki

J-Novel Club Lineup

Latest Ebook Releases Series List

Altina the Sword Princess
Amagi Brilliant Park
Animeta!**
The Apothecary Diaries
An Archdemon's Dilemma: How to Love Your Elf Bride*
Are You Okay With a Slightly Older Girlfriend?
Arifureta: From Commonplace to World's Strongest
Arifureta Zero
Ascendance of a Bookworm*
Banner of the Stars
Bibliophile Princess*
Black Summoner*
The Bloodline
By the Grace of the Gods
Campfire Cooking in Another World with My Absurd Skill*
Can Someone Please Explain What's Going On?!
Chillin' in Another World with Level 2 Super Cheat Powers
The Combat Baker and Automaton Waitress
Cooking with Wild Game*
Culinary Chronicles of the Court Flower
Dahlia in Bloom: Crafting a Fresh Start with Magical Tools
Deathbound Duke's Daughter
Demon Lord, Retry!*
Der Werwolf: The Annals of Veight*
Dragon Daddy Diaries: A Girl Grows to Greatness
Dungeon Busters
The Emperor's Lady-in-Waiting Is Wanted as a Bride*
Endo and Kobayashi Live! The Latest on Tsundere Villainess Lieselotte
The Faraway Paladin*
Full Metal Panic!
Full Clearing Another World under a Goddess with Zero Believers*
Fushi no Kami: Rebuilding Civilization Starts With a Village
Goodbye Otherworld, See You Tomorrow
The Great Cleric
The Greatest Magicmaster's Retirement Plan

Girls Kingdom
Grimgar of Fantasy and Ash
Hell Mode
Her Majesty's Swarm
Holmes of Kyoto
How a Realist Hero Rebuilt the Kingdom*
How NOT to Summon a Demon Lord
I Shall Survive Using Potions!*
I'll Never Set Foot in That House Again!
The Ideal Sponger Life
If It's for My Daughter, I'd Even Defeat a Demon Lord
In Another World With My Smartphone
Infinite Dendrogram*
Invaders of the Rokujouma!?
Jessica Bannister
JK Haru is a Sex Worker in Another World
John Sinclair: Demon Hunter
A Late-Start Tamer's Laid-Back Life
Lazy Dungeon Master
A Lily Blooms in Another World
Maddrax
The Magic in this Other World is Too Far Behind!*
The Magician Who Rose From Failure
Mapping: The Trash-Tier Skill That Got Me Into a Top-Tier Party*
Marginal Operation**
The Master of Ragnarok & Blesser of Einherjar*
Min-Maxing My TRPG Build in Another World
Monster Tamer
My Daughter Left the Nest and Returned an S-Rank Adventurer
My Friend's Little Sister Has It In for Me!
My Instant Death Ability is So Overpowered, No One in This Other World Stands a Chance Against Me!*
My Next Life as a Villainess: All Routes Lead to Doom!
Otherside Picnic
Outbreak Company
Perry Rhodan NEO

Private Tutor to the Duke's Daughter
Reborn to Master the Blade: From Hero-King to Extraordinary Squire ♀*
Record of Wortenia War*
Reincarnated as the Piggy Duke: This Time I'm Gonna Tell Her How I Feel!
The Reincarnated Princess Spends Another Day Skipping Story Routes
Seirei Gensouki: Spirit Chronicles*
Sexiled: My Sexist Party Leader Kicked Me Out, So I Teamed Up With a Mythical Sorceress!
She's the Cutest... But We're Just Friends!
The Sidekick Never Gets the Girl, Let Alone the Protag's Sister!
Slayers
The Sorcerer's Receptionist
Sorcerous Stabber Orphen*
Sweet Reincarnation**
The Tales of Marielle Clarac*
Tearmoon Empire
Teogonia
The Underdog of the Eight Greater Tribes
The Unwanted Undead Adventurer*
Villainess: Reloaded! Blowing Away Bad Ends with Modern Weapons*
Welcome to Japan, Ms. Elf!*
The White Cat's Revenge as Plotted from the Dragon King's Lap
A Wild Last Boss Appeared!
The World's Least Interesting Master Swordsman

...and more!
* Novel and Manga Editions
** Manga Only
Keep an eye out at j-novel.club for further new title announcements!